A Sudden Interest in Shakespeare

Also by Paul Breen

Runner's Path

A Sudden Interest in Shakespeare

A Seamus O'Neill Mystery

Paul Breen

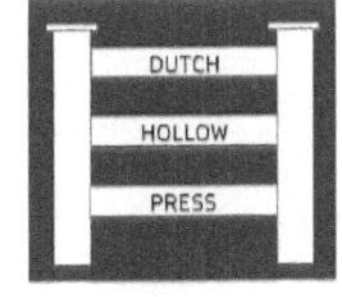

Dutch Hollow Press

Copyright © 2023 by Paul Breen

This is a work of fiction. Names, characters, organizations, places, events, and incidents are either the product of the author's imagination or are used fictitiously. Any resemblance to actual persons, living or dead, events, or locales is entirely coincidental.

ISBN 979-8-9862083-3-6 (paperback)

ISBN 979-8-9862083-2-9 (ebook)

ISBN 979-8-9862083-4-3 (hardcover)

Book Cover Design by ebooklaunch.com

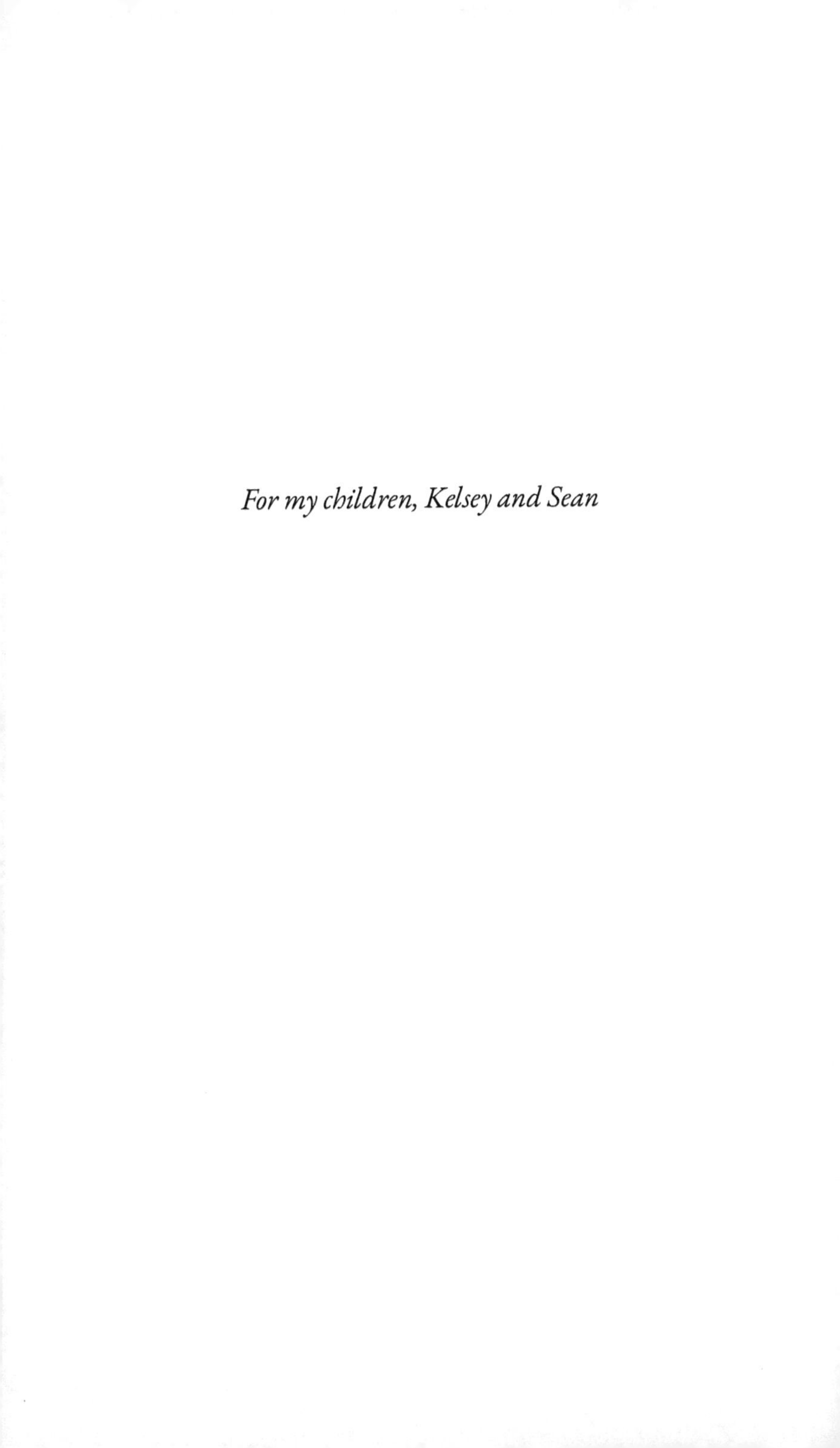

For my children, Kelsey and Sean

Chapter 1
May 2000

Seamus O'Neill awoke on a black foam couch in the Ryder Detective Agency's storage room. His eyes creaked open, and he licked his dry lips. The only light came from underneath the door and shined on the beige cabinets that lined the room. The sound of footsteps in the outer room came closer, and the door opened. O'Neill closed his eyes but did not move.

"Thanks for seeing me," a woman's voice said from outside the room.

"No problem," replied a man. O'Neill recognized it as the voice of his boss, John Ryder. "I wanted to open this back door. It helps the room circulate."

How does a room circulate? O'Neill wondered as he leaned against the cool metal of a filing cabinet.

"Please take a seat," Ryder said, presumably to the woman in the other room. "Tell me about your brother and explain why you are worried about him."

"Tom works in computers, creating and managing websites," she said. "Until last year, he worked on a bank's web team. He quit after deciding he was not the banker type and got another job with the State of Wisconsin Investment Board, or SWIB. That seemed an odd choice, since it doesn't pay as much, and he never expressed an interest in working for the government. Tommy's roommate told him about the opening, and they hired him. He views it as a short-term thing, though he's been there for a year."

O'Neill assumed the woman was a potential new client, yet her voice sounded familiar. He crawled off the sofa and inched toward the door.

"My brother has changed over the past year," the woman continued. "For instance, he's now into books and plays, which is surprising since Tommy had always been a gamer and a comic book guy. The deepest things he read until a few months ago were PlayStation game manuals." She laughed. "For movies, it used to be *Star Wars* or *Friday the 13th*, but now it is something serious. On his birthday, my daughter and I stopped by his apartment and he was watching *Hamlet*. Not the Mel Gibson one, but the one with the one English guy..." she snapped her fingers. "Kenneth... Kenneth..."

"Branagh," O'Neill whispered. "And he's Irish."

"Branagh," she said with a slight laugh. "Kenneth Branagh. Not only that, but two Shakespeare books were on the kitchen table. One of them looked like it was a thousand pages. While the whole thing seemed strange, my daughter and I laughed it off, and I assumed he met some woman who was into highbrow literature and the Toxic Avenger didn't compete. But now I'm not sure. Last week, he went on vacation for a couple of days and his roommate was also out of town, so he asked me to feed his fish. He lent me the key and—I should just say it—I snooped around his apartment and noticed a Reebok shoebox in his closet. Inside were a bunch of fake documents and other things that concern me."

O'Neill leaned into the doorway, trying to see the woman. Sunlight splashed across the white laminate flooring, and his eyes fluttered.

"How do you know these documents were fake?" Ryder asked.

"There was a passport and a Minnesota driver's license that had his picture, but neither were in his name. And his hair was blonde in the photos; Tommy hasn't had blonde hair since he was seven years old. There was also a library card, a video store rental card, and an odd list of names."

"What do you mean by *an odd list of names*?"

"Names of people, I think. A few had an equal sign next to them and initials or question marks. So, one might have said AB equals Smith, and another said CD equals a question mark. And there was money."

"How much money?"

"A roll of twenties. I'm unsure of how much. And there were three bank statements in the box. The last statement included a check he had written for twenty thousand dollars. He had circled the entry in red ink. The statement only gives the check number and amount, so I don't know who the payment was to."

"Do you know how he came up with that much cash?"

"Our parents are financially well off. He could have gotten it from my mom or dad or even from my sister, but I asked her and she knows nothing about it. Also, Tommy had a decent job at the bank and doesn't exactly live the highlife. He's only twenty-seven, but he doesn't have a serious girlfriend, a house, or even an expensive car. Maybe he has saved some money or maybe he borrowed it. But what, other than a car, would he spend twenty thousand dollars on? And why would he keep so much cash in his apartment?"

"Could he have bought a new car as you suggested, or a boat?" Ryder said, sounding disappointed. "That might cost twenty thousand."

"He drives a four or five-year-old Chevy Lumina, and I don't think either of us has boated before, so I can't see him buying a boat."

"Did you talk to him about what you found?"

"No, I thought about it but decided against it. I'm six years older than him, so he views me as his mom 2.0. He might close me off if I push, so I need more information, which made me think of hiring a detective. It sounded crazy at first, but I had to do *something*. I am afraid he's into something he shouldn't be. The money, the fake passport, the fake IDs, and the list makes me think he's doing something illegal. I'm scared for him."

"That was everything in the shoebox?"

"Oh, no. There were six or seven of these."

"What is it?" Ryder said.

"Yeah, what is it?" O'Neill whispered.

"I assume it is an access card which allows him to enter his office," she said. "Why would he need a half dozen of them?"

"Good question," Ryder said. "Can I hold on to this?"

"Yes, please. I hope he doesn't notice that one is missing."

"What do you think he is up to?"

There was a pause. "I'm worried he's messed up in a drug thing. That might be why he's got that list of contacts and why he keeps all that cash. It doesn't seem like him, but it happens. He has smoked marijuana, but he rips on his friends who tried cocaine or heroin, and he dumped one girlfriend because she was into ecstasy."

"What was her name?"

"No idea. It was maybe two years ago, and he's not dating her anymore. The other thing that worries me is gambling. I don't know if Tommy gambles, but I know people with gambling problems and it can really mess them up. Perhaps he got caught up and is doing something stupid because he owes money. Even that would not explain everything."

"What do you want me to do?" Ryder said.

"I'm not sure. If Tommy is in trouble, I want to help, but I don't want to get him into more trouble. I thought you might discreetly inquire and do whatever it is you do to find out what is going on. If he finds out I hired you, he will be angry and won't talk to me for a year. But I can't ignore it. I'm worried."

"There are a few things I would like from you," Ryder said. "First, I want a list of Tom's friends and acquaintances."

"Okay," the woman said. "I don't pretend to know his crowd, but I could give you a start."

"Second, I would love a copy of the fake identification. Do you still have his apartment key?"

"No."

"Could you get the key? Or could you visit him and borrow the documents for a few hours?"

There was another long pause. "That could be difficult since I have only been to his apartment three times in the last two years. If I show up and take them, I will need to return them before he notices they are gone. That many trips wouldn't seem right. If he is up to something, I don't want to make him suspicious."

"Could you take photos of the documents and the list? That would keep it to one trip. Do you own a digital camera?"

"Yes, I do. I could take photos, but it might take a few days to come up with some reason to visit him."

"It would help."

There was a rustling sound, as if they were getting out of their seats.

"What do you need now?" she asked.

"A deposit, and you have to sign a contract, which I can email you. I can take a check now, or you can send it after you've seen the contract."

"Now is fine."

There was silence, followed by mumbling. O'Neill leaned further into the doorway, finally seeing the woman's back. She was wearing tan shorts, a blue shirt, and white shoes and was of average height with a slight frame. She wore her blonde hair in a ponytail. O'Neill thought he had seen her before.

Ryder took the check and his enormous paw touched her back, as if he was pushing her out of the room. She glanced to her side, and O'Neill pulled back, sure he recognized the woman. A door closed and O'Neill crawled away from the storage room door, stopping at the mini refrigerator. He opened the door and took out a bottle of water. Less than a minute passed before Ryder was in the doorway.

"Seamus, get your drunken ass out here!"

O'Neill rolled his eyes and walked into the sunlight. "How'd you know I was here?"

"It smells like a distillery. And you left the outside door unlocked."

"Sorry about that."

"Give me the key."

"Oh, come on." O'Neill opened the bottle, and it made a crinkling sound as he gulped the water.

"Screw that. I gave you an office key, and you slipped in here at night like you promised you wouldn't, leaving the door unlocked. What if someone got in here?"

"I was tired, and it's, like, a mile walk home from here."

"You're tired every night. You're lucky you didn't puke in here. If you did, I would throw your ass out and leave you looking for a job. And don't think I will give you a pass because of prior success," Ryder said. "Any goodwill you earned from old cases has long expired. Give me the key."

O'Neill was relieved to find it in his pocket.

"Thanks." Ryder took the key. "Did you hear what the lady said?"

O'Neill nodded and sipped water as he followed Ryder. The sound of traffic entered through an open window, and sunlight shimmered on the floor in front of Ryder's desk. "What was her name? Thought I recognized her."

Ryder sat behind his desk. "The client's name is Mary Hoffman. She was here about her brother, Tom Hoffman."

"Yeah, I heard."

"What do you make of it?"

A smile slid onto O'Neill's face as he touched the building access card Mary Hoffman had left with them. "Something's up." O'Neill leaned on Ryder's desk, palming the access card. As he turned around, he slipped the card into his pocket. "Odds are drugs or something mundane, but even that doesn't add up. Then again, it might be nothing."

"That's what I thought, but she gave me a two hundred dollar deposit."

O'Neill turned back toward Ryder and leaned forward. "Is that enough to get me a twenty-five dollar advance? I'm broke."

"Tomorrow is payday."

"Doesn't do me much good today."

The big detective pulled out his wallet and threw a ten-dollar bill on the desk. "That will have to do. Go home and take a shower. You smell like you've been sweating and drinking."

"My shower doesn't work. Been broke for a few weeks."

Ryder's flat face seemed to widen. "You're shitting me?"

"No, a pipe's backed up or something. The mighty landlord is supposed to have someone there early next month. He's giving me half-price rent for the inconvenience, so I don't mind."

"You have not showered in weeks?" Ryder said. "No wonder you reek."

O'Neill ran a hand over his head. "That's why I shaved my head last week. I thought it would allow me to get by with limited showers for a month or more, though I have sponged a few off friends."

"Your sink works, I hope."

O'Neill nodded. "Can I use *your* shower?"

"No. Go to a friend's place."

O'Neill touched the access key in his pocket that Mary Hoffman had left with Ryder. He was sure that Tom Hoffman's employer was housed in the Wisconsin Administration Building, and he knew the structure had a locker room and showers. The access card was his ticket in.

"Sure," O'Neill said. "I'll do that."

Chapter 2

Menacing clouds punctuated the blue sky, forcing O'Neill to board a bus on Regent Street rather than walking to the building where Tom Hoffman worked. The other passenger stared as O'Neill walked down the aisle, searching unsuccessfully for an abandoned newspaper. He sat in the back, removed his earring, and stuck it into his jean pocket. The air smelled like rain, and he watched a pedestrian open her umbrella. Thunder clapped as he pulled the stop request cord, and he looked nervously out the window.

Once on the sidewalk, he hurried as raindrops slapped against the concrete and the sky darkened. He turned onto Wilson Street as the rain changed from a spattering of droplets to a deluge. At the Wisconsin Administration Building's side entrance, he stood under the awning and pulled out Tom Hoffman's access key card. He leaned the plastic against the reader, but the door did not unlock. A second attempt ended with the same result. A puzzled O'Neill considered waiting until an employee arrived or left the building, but the rainstorm brought foot traffic to a stop.

Deciding the key might open a different state office building, he contemplated his options. The rain made a long walk problematic, but several offices were nearby. He stared at the alley between the Administration Building and the adjacent Administration Annex, which was a separate structure but also contained state governmental offices. The rain had transformed the pavement into a large, flowing puddle, and water poured into the sewer grate and into the nearby manhole. He grew tired of waiting and made a run to the Annex, jogging toward the road to avoid the rushing water. If the card didn't get him into the Annex, he would wait for the storm to subside and go to the Department of Natural Resources building, which was a quarter mile away. He thought he could get inside without key card access.

O'Neill rushed to the Annex's front entrance and placed the access key against the reader. The locks thumped as the dead bolts retreated. Pleasantly surprised, he pulled the door open and stepped inside, brushing cold water off his arms.

The Department of Administration, known by its initials as the DOA, was centered in the Wisconsin Administration Building. But the office building didn't have enough space for their staff and other units such as the Investment Board, so they rented the adjacent Administration Annex. The directory in the hallway stated it housed staff from two DOA divisions and the Department of Tourism. Showers were typically in the basement, so O'Neill took the first staircase down and quickly discovered a locker room. There were a dozen small cubby holes and a half dozen full-length lockers which were next to showers and a bathroom. The entire area smelled like mold and dirty socks.

O'Neill undressed, stuffed his damp clothes into one of the small lockers, and checked the showers, where he found a piece of soap in the corner of one stall. He turned the water on and used the soap to wash himself. Once done, he shook himself off and took a handful of paper towels from the adjacent bathroom. An older man with a beard entered the locker area, giving O'Neill an inquisitive look. O'Neill needed more paper towels, but was afraid to return to the dispenser, so he stretched his damp clothes over his wet body. As he walked out, he glanced in the mirror and saw the man looking suspiciously at him.

O'Neill left the locker room and hurried up the stairs. The building had few staff, so it was hard to blend in. He would not use this shower room again.

He exited through a door by the loading dock and found that the worst of the rainstorm was past. Walking along the building's edge to avoid the remaining drizzle, he watched a pair of pedestrians close their umbrellas. After crossing the road, he cut through an alley and arrived at the Argus Food & Spirits restaurant. At the bar, he put his earring back on, pulled out his ten-dollar advance and ordered a Capital Blonde Doppelbock. He limited himself to one pint since he needed money for later in the day. Outside, the rain had stopped, and the pavement was drying.

O'Neill walked home, arriving at two o'clock. His efficiency apartment was on the second floor of a building that used to be a private residence. He changed clothes and crawled onto his mattress. An empty stomach prevented sleep, so he rummaged through his bare cupboard, finding three pieces of bread and an unopened bottle of Cheez Whiz. He took his only knife and made a sandwich. Carrying the meal to his mattress, he reached for his laptop and hit the power button. Within a few minutes, he started Internet Explorer.

Home internet access was new to him and paid for by the Ryder Detective Agency. It had a business use since he didn't own a phone, and it was the easiest way for Ryder to contact him.

O'Neill visited the State of Wisconsin government's portal, quickly finding SWIB's page. He clicked the "staff" button, but it only contained listings of directors and managers. He tried the state telephone directory next, and he found Tom Hoffman's name and work address on the sixth floor at the Wisconsin Administration Building. A white page search brought up Tom Hoffman's home address and phone number. O'Neill noted the information on a sheet of paper before running Hoffman's name through the State Circuit Court's website. The search came up empty, meaning Hoffman had no criminal record or activity in Wisconsin courts. Switching to Google, he tried a general search. Hoffman showed up on dozens of pages, most of them relating to his former position at Park Bank, others related to charities, including United Way. He also searched for Mary Hoffman in Madison, but found little beyond an address in a Madison suburb and membership at a local church.

By four, the rain was a distant memory. O'Neill caught a southwest bound Madison Metro bus. A *Wisconsin State Journal* sat on an empty seat, so he read the newspaper as the bus churned down Regent Street. Once on Monroe Street, O'Neill rang the stop request cord and exited.

Monroe Street was the heart of one of Madison's older, somewhat eclectic neighborhoods. O'Neill thought of the neighborhood as the connecting point between downtown Madison and its near west side. The area boasted a variety of shops and restaurants, but all he could afford was Pizza Extreme's Tuesday special of two slices for two dollars and ninety-nine cents. He walked a block with his meal and sat on the curb. The early June sun hid behind a bed of white clouds, but O'Neill left his sunglasses on. As he chewed the pepperoni pizza, he gazed across the road at the windows above Smoky Joe's Café. Tom Hoffman's address was 1880 Monroe Street. The two apartments were numbered 1880 and 1890. O'Neill figured the window on the left was Hoffman's.

O'Neill finished eating and threw the paper plate and napkin into a trashcan. Crossing Monroe Street could be hazardous, so he waited at the corner, hurrying across and passing a group of older women. With Camp Randall Stadium at his back, he grabbed the door to Smoky Joe's Café and stepped inside.

In his thirty-three years, O'Neill had never drunk coffee. He had never even tasted it, so the overwhelming smell did not interest or excite him. Instead, the sights, sounds, and smells felt foreign.

A café employee with a four-inch goatee waited behind the counter. O'Neill nodded, his gaze raising to the menu above the counter. Everything seemed to be coffee or food. O'Neill wanted neither.

"What do you have to drink other than coffee?"

"Do you mean like espresso?" the goateed barista asked.

"No, nothing made with a coffee bean."

The man laughed like a machine gun. "You don't want coffee?"

"You have beer?"

"Nope," the man said, laughing again. "This is a café, you know. We don't have a liquor license."

"What do you have to drink *besides* coffee?"

"We got tea, root beer, and bottled sparkling water."

"Okay, give me a root beer. Diet if you have it."

The man nodded, and his beard bounced against his chest. He reached into a silver cooler, pulled out a bottle of Sprecher Diet Root Beer, popped the top, and slid the bottle onto the counter. "Two-fifty, please."

O'Neill dug three dollar bills out of his pocket.

"Seamus?" a woman's voice said.

O'Neill turned toward the voice, recognizing Marlene Schultz. She dated someone from one of his bands back in the late eighties, though he couldn't remember the details. She stared at him for a moment, smiling.

"I hardly recognized you with the short hair," she said. "It looks different, but what a wonderful change." Marlene touched the silver cross that hung from his ear. "It makes your earring stand out. You gonna keep your hair short?"

"Na, the buzz is a onetime thing," O'Neill said, rubbing his head. "What's up?"

"Not much. I saw Benny Farina yesterday. Do you see him around anymore?"

O'Neill didn't know to whom she was referring. "No, it's been years."

"Benny got laid off at Cascade Technologies a few months ago. He got another job though, as a programmer at the University. Hey, Chuckie," Marlene said to the goateed man. "Ever heard of a band named Theoretically Trashed?"

"Don't think so," Chuckie responded.

"How about Fifty-Foot Drop? Or Sea City Chaos?"

"The Sea City one rings a bell," he said with little confidence.

Marlene rolled her eyes and turned to O'Neill. "What are you doing now, anyway? I have heard nothing since Sea City Chaos split. That has been, what, two years?"

"Almost two years. But I'm pulling a group together and doing computer stuff on the side," O'Neill said, purposely not mentioning that he was working for a detective agency. "Enough to pay the bills."

"The drink is on me." Marlene returned his three dollars. "Tell me about your band." She walked to the closest table, and O'Neill followed. "What kind of music do you play?"

"I'm not good at that question and I have trouble if I try to play to style. It ends up being a little rock, a little folk, a little Irish, and a little country. Maybe a few polkas, too."

Marlene laughed. "You have not changed, have you? I remember back when we'd go to Trashed shows and slam dance in the mosh pit. You would pull out your accordion and play 'A Town Called Malice,' pissing off the meatheads." Her head was shaking. "We have bands at our café, too, mostly folkie stuff or blues. My husband and I own this place, though I run it and manage any musical acts we bring in. There is a Celtic band we have named Reilly's Pub that you might like. Nothing like the old days, but we have fun."

"My new band is acoustic, at least for now," O'Neill said, even though he didn't have a band. "Maybe we could play here sometime?"

"How many you got in the group?" she asked, glancing across the room. "This place is small. We rarely have over four in a band."

"There are four of us. We got me, a guitar player, a banjo, and a whistler who plays a little fiddle."

"Do you play the guitar or something else?"

"Guitar, accordion, and a little whistle."

"Great," Marlene said. "I could see you playing traditional Irish music."

"I couldn't play traditional Irish music if I had to. Neither could Squeeker nor Ernie."

"They the guys in your group?"

"No, they're in Reilly's Pub."

"Oh," she said, blushing slightly. "You know them?"

"Sure. Squeeker's okay, but Ernie's a dipshit. Don't know the other guy. But, like I said, I'm pulling a band together, but I want to play places like this. I don't expect to play the sort of places we used to, like O'Cayz, Club de Wash, or the Rathskeller, and I'm too old to do frat parties and that shit. I want to do small clubs, festivals, and different venues."

Marlene stood and pulled out a notepad as a group came into the café. "I should get back to work. I'll contact you when a slot opens. How can I get hold of you?"

O'Neill gave her The Johnson's phone number. "That's our manager, Tim Johnson. He used to be in Shifts in Turmoil and Dead Folks Farming."

Marlene wrote the number on the back of a business card. "What do you guys call yourselves?"

He swallowed root beer and tried to think of a band name. "Schumacher's Flour Mill."

"That is *different*."

"My great granddad died in an explosion there."

"Then Schumacher's Flour Mill it is. It was nice to see you. Makes me think of old times."

"Hey, Marlene," O'Neill said before she turned away. "Are the apartments above this place available for rent?"

She glanced at the counter where the goateed one was taking customer orders. "I don't know. You looking for a place?"

"Kinda. They okay?"

"I hear they are decent. Hasdorff owns them. He's okay—for a landlord. There are only two or three apartments, but someone's always coming or going."

O'Neill nodded and headed for the door, carrying his diet root beer.

At half-past five, O'Neill returned to the Ryder Detective Agency, entering without knocking. Ryder was behind his desk, holding a pair of manila folders.

"Seamus, I'm surprised to see you. I thought you would be drinking my ten dollars."

"Ten dollars doesn't go far," O'Neill said as he sat in the chair in front of his boss. "I thought *you'd* be sleeping. What are you working on? Thinking about that woman?"

"What woman?" Ryder scratched his bald head.

"The one that was here this morning. The one whose brother has the phony passport and stuff."

"Oh, Mary Hoffman. No, I was working on Herbert Engineering. There is a potential buyout and they want me to review..." He stopped and pushed the folder away. "What am I telling you for? You don't give a rip."

"Course I don't."

"What do you want?"

"I was thinking about Mary Hoffman and I noticed her brother lives on Monroe Street above Smoky Joe's Café."

"Smoky Joe's? Never heard of it. Rib place?"

"No, a café. Not really your type of place. Not really my kind of place, either. They don't have a liquor license."

"You will never go there."

"Give me a minute." O'Neill got into his chair, booted up his computer, and searched through the Madison rentals, finding a vacancy at 1880 Monroe Street. The ad was for a two-bedroom apartment at $695 per month.

"What are you looking up?" Ryder finally asked.

"Information on Tom Hoffman's apartment." O'Neill printed the ad and handed it to Ryder. "It looks like Tom Hoffman's place is for rent at the end of the summer."

Ryder patted his fat belly and put the printout in a pile on his desk. "So he's moving. Is that supposed to mean something?"

"Wouldn't you like to know if he is moving somewhere in the city or whether he's leaving the area or the country?"

"He's got a phony passport. Odds are he's a drug courier, and he'll be back in Madison after a run."

"It doesn't feel right. Why would a courier bother with a fake passport? Wouldn't that increase the chances of him getting caught? Airport security is tough nowadays. At least that's what they say."

"Don't tell me he's a terrorist."

"Okay, I won't tell you he's a terrorist."

"Has he been busted for anything before?"

"Not in Wisconsin."

Ryder chewed on that thought before responding. "Maybe he isn't a courier. We just don't know what he's doing and neither does his sister. That's why she hired us."

"I would like to see that passport and the other stuff."

"So would I. His sister said she would get it after a few days. I don't think she wants to be too obvious. And don't suggest we sneak into his apartment. If we can't wait for her, we will need to go to Plan B."

"What's Plan B?"

Ryder sucked in his cheeks. "We do a background check on him. Maybe we shadow him for a day or two and see if it points us in a direction. It shouldn't take long to figure out if he's got a girlfriend who is making him act weird or if he's rolling in drug money. Mary Hoffman wants answers, but there is no deadline."

"Did you notice he works for the state investment board?"

"Yep, so what?"

"There's a lot of money to be had working for a business or the government. You can steal a few bucks here and there."

"Seamus, virtually everyone works for a business or for the government. Hell, even you are employed by a business."

"Yeah, but working for the investment board means the potential for lots of money. And you hear stories about people embezzling from the state. I knew a girl a few years ago who worked at Health & Social Services or something like that. She ripped off thousands. There was a company named RS Inc. that had contracts with the state. She started her own company called Reynold's Services Inc. She would have Reynold's Service invoice Health & Social Services. They set the government up to pay bills, so they paid the invoices thinking they were paying RS Inc. When they cut a check to RS, she would pocket the check and deposit it into Reynold's Service Inc.'s account. She said she only took five or ten thousand, but she was into smack, so I bet she took more. She got fired when someone got suspicious, but she never got arrested. The government didn't want the case getting to the press."

"What's this got to do with Tom Hoffman? Or do you think all state employees are sending phony invoices to their employers?"

"Course not. But most employees don't make lists of names that have equal signs next to them and then initials. Like Fred is JZ and Ted is SB."

"Like aliases, you mean? Possible. But it could be anything. Maybe they are passwords for his computer at work."

"Little far-fetched," O'Neill said with a yawn.

"Like your idea isn't far-fetched?" Ryder replied. "Your logic is that Tom Hoffman works for the state and has a list of names, so naturally, he is embezzling money. My idea is better. I mean, he probably uses multiple passwords for systems at SWIB? Suppose he writes the initials of each program and uses names as the password. Think about how people remember passwords. At one time I, for instance, used 'Packers' for one program, 'Nitschke' for another program, and 'Favre' for my email."

"I'm not surprised."

Ryder shook his head. "I'm just saying it could be anything, including a list of passwords. We need to see the sheet to make a reasonable guess."

O'Neill leaned forward. "My point is we have someone working at the State Investment Board for no good reason. This person has a cryptic list, fake identification documents, a load of cash, and a half dozen building access keys. He's also recently got interested in literature. It adds up to something."

"What about the courier idea? That could explain the aliases, the money, and the documents. That's a big deal, I guess, but not that big of a deal."

"It doesn't tell us why Tom Hoffman wants to work at the State Investment Board, why he has a half dozen access keys to a building he doesn't work in, or why he's watching *Hamlet*. Something is going on."

"What do you mean that the access key is for another building? What does it open?"

"The Annex, which is next to the office building Tom Hoffman works in."

"How do you know this?"

O'Neill pulled the card out of his pocket. "I took the card downtown and it doesn't work in the Administration Building, but it works in the Annex. That might not be odd if he worked in the facilities area, but this is a web guy. Why does he have the key to an office he doesn't work in? Makes me wonder whether the other keys are for the same place or if they are for other state offices."

"What's in this Annex?"

"Offices for the Department of Administration and the Department of Tourism, and storage for administration and the Wisconsin Lottery."

"Lottery, huh?" Ryder said. There was a long silence that Ryder finally broke. "Years of smoking and drinking may have left you penniless, but you have a point." Ryder got out of his chair and tucked his shirt back into his pants. "What are you suggesting we do? Like I said before, we can tail him and do a background check."

"I want to see what's in that shoebox."

"We will not break into his apartment. I'm not Magnum P. I."

"You don't look like him, either. Is Tom Hoffman's sister married? She's using her maiden name, but that doesn't prove she's not married."

"I don't think she's married, but she mentioned a daughter." Ryder opened a file cabinet and pulled out a folder. "Mary Hoffman is divorced with two kids."

"Great. I have an idea. Suppose Mary Hoffman has a boyfriend, and she wants to introduce him to her brother. And suppose I'm Mary Hoffman's boyfriend. She could ask her brother to invite us to his apartment."

Ryder laughed and slapped his knee. "No one would buy her dating you. She's a good-looking, classy lady. For once, I'm not trying to be mean. Think about reality. I realize some women are interested in you, but not high-class ones like her. Respectable people avoid you on the street because they think you're on drugs or you're going to ask them for a quarter. Why would anyone believe she would date you? Why would anyone even consider it?"

"I don't do drugs anymore. You know that." O'Neill fidgeted in his chair. "Little weed here and there, but that's it."

"You still drink like a fish."

"And you eat like a platoon. What's your point?"

"You're skinny and smarmy looking; that is the point. Mary Hoffman is beyond you. She's beautiful and has an upper class feel to her. Her brother wouldn't believe that she would date you."

"Then you do it."

Ryder didn't answer.

"It has got to be you or me," O'Neill said, "and there is no way she would go for a fat, bald, ex-cop with barbecue sauce on his shirt and five o'clock shadow. Plus, you're too old for her. Gotta be me."

"I never said one of us had to do this; it was your stupid idea. Why do you think she would pretend to be dating you?"

"Because she's worried about her brother, and she thinks something is wrong. Rich women don't go to detectives unless they think something is wrong, and both of us suspect that something is going on. She's desperate, and I know she would date me."

"Why would you say that?"

"Because I used to live with her."

Ryder's face went blank. "You're shitting me?"

"Afraid not."

"You lived with Mary Hoffman," Ryder mumbled as his head swayed side to side.

O'Neill nodded.

"Shit. This proves women have no taste."

Chapter 3

P aul's Club was Madison's only bar with a tree inside, yet it smelled of smoke. O'Neill arrived after six, coughing as he meandered through the room. Branches spread throughout the establishment and a thick trunk shot up through the middle of the bar. Shag carpet covered the floor, which was packed with padded chairs and couches. Lamps dangled from the ceiling and Christmas lights peppered the branches. Two couples sat at the counter and a group of women lounged on sofas while the Goo Goo Dolls played on the jukebox.

"Hey, it's The Johnson," O'Neill said to the bartender as he sat in front of the taps. "What's up?"

"Not much, O'Neill," The Johnson replied.

"Anything fresh?"

"Newcastle came in today, along with Miller Lite."

"Don't want brown ale tonight, and I stay clear of light beer. Rather drink something with a bit more gravity if I'm gonna pay an import price."

"Get an Icehouse," The Johnson said, running a hand over his mustache. He was a large man with thick brown hair on his head and face. Wearing jeans, a red shirt, and a vest, he looked like he belonged on a motorcycle rather than behind a bar.

"Is the Capital Amber priced okay?"

The Johnson nodded, filled a pint, and set the glass in front of O'Neill.

"Got a gig coming up," O'Neill said. "Something related to my job. I gotta put a band together on the quick—one to play this coffee house on Monroe called Smoky Joe's."

"Smoky Joe's Café?" The Johnson puckered his lips in a sour expression. "I hate coffee houses. Women who hang at coffee houses have coffee breath."

"Like I said, this is for my job. I'm trying to become a regular at Smoky Joe's, which is tough since I don't drink coffee. But they have bands and Marlene Schultz is the manager. Do you remember her?"

"She used to go with Benny Farina, way back."

"Yeah, that's her, I think. I told her I started a band, and she wants us to play at her place. The group has gotta be acoustic, though. She didn't set a date, but knowing her, she will call when something opens."

"Don't tell me you want me to be in a folk band?"

"It will be acoustic, but it won't be folkish. Remember, I'm doing this for work, so I can't ask musicians or people that will take things seriously. I need someone who is in on it, ya know? And you will play the guitar, so it won't be a stretch. We'll do simple stuff you already know or tunes you can pick up. It's better than not being in a band. And you can do a Son House song or some blues. But just one or two songs."

"What you gonna play?"

"Accordion, I figure. And whistle, of course."

"You ain't gonna play that piece of shit accordion, are you? It sounds like crap."

"I'll come up with something better," O'Neill said.

"You gonna sing? I ain't singing 'This Land is Your Land.'"

"Sure, I'll sing. But you'll have to handle the Son House song. I don't got the blues."

The Johnson broke away to mix gin and tonics for a couple at the bar.

"Who else you gonna add to this pretend band?" The Johnson asked as he returned.

O'Neill finished his beer and slid it forward. "I thought I'd ask Topper. He can play and split the singing with me."

"Topper?" The Johnson said. "Topper can't keep rhythm with his toes, let alone with a guitar."

"That's why we'll put him on banjo."

"Brilliant."

"I want someone else, though. Do you know any fiddlers?"

"Who do you think I am?"

O'Neill looked at the six foot two rock & roll musician and smiled. "Sorry, I forgot."

"Nix Topper if you find someone better."

"I don't think we'll get anyone good on short notice," O'Neill said after considering the suggestion. "Besides, he might know a fiddler."

"Topper will bring in some nineteen-year-old junkie who played violin in ninth grade. We'd be better with no one. I have a serious girl now, so I want to stay away from junkies."

"We'll see. But remember, it doesn't really matter how bad we are. If we're bad, we just play one or two nights. And neither of us will know anyone in the audience, so no damage done."

"Why the rush if we don't have a gig?"

"We gotta be ready. Like I said, this relates to my detective job. We're investigating someone who frequents the place and lives nearby."

"You got a name for the band?"

O'Neill looked at the counter as he spoke. "Schumacher's Flour Mill."

"What the hell is that?"

"The name."

"Schumacher's Flour Mill?"

"Yeah, what's wrong with that?"

"A lot, O'Neill. You've named a dozen bands over the years. I usually like them. But Schumacher's Flour Mill is worse than Sea City Chaos."

"Okay, maybe we can change it, but I had to come up with something on the spot. I just thought of us playing early to mid-twentieth century music. I thought about my grandpa and I remembered how his old man died in an explosion at Schumacher's Flour Mill. It seemed like the name fit, ya know?"

The Johnson shook his head.

"Oh, and you're the manager," O'Neill said. "I gave Marlene your number."

"Thanks a lot," The Johnson said sarcastically. "You want another pint?"

O'Neill put three dollars and fifty cents on the counter. "Nah. I'm low on cash, so I should head out."

"I would buy you one, but the boss is getting on me. He thinks you never pay."

O'Neill pointed at his friend and stepped away from the bar. "I'll let you know how things shape up for the band. After the lineup solidifies, we can practice."

Once outside, O'Neill pulled out his wallet and checked his change. He was down to two dollars and twenty-six cents, enough for two cheap drinks. He touched the tin whistle in his back pocket and looked west along State Street. There would be buskers on the street who he could join. Or he could start something of his own. He fought off the urge and turned east, deciding he would buy two singles at the nearby liquor store, Reilly's Wines of the World.

Trudging under trees and streetlights, he stared at the ground as a city bus rolled past and diesel fumes dissipated over the sidewalk. As he waited for the light to change, a man with a white eye patch and a long coat stepped next to him. The man was smoking and chewing tobacco at the same time. They stood silently until the walk light changed. They crossed the road and a trio of beggars studied the pair before turning away.

O'Neill woke after ten. Rain pounded against his lone window and lightning sporadically lit the room. He crawled off his mattress, opened the refrigerator, and pulled out a Diet Mountain Dew. After going to the bathroom, he grabbed the Dew and headed to the bus stop.

Within five minutes, the Regent Street-bound bus arrived. The only other rider was an old man, hunched forward as if dead. O'Neill leaned against the window and watched cars roll past, their wipers flipping and their lights bright. The vehicle paused at a railroad crossing, waking the old man who looked around nervously, muttering a barrage of swear words. The bus turned onto Regent Street, and after a few blocks, he hit the bell and stepped out the back exit.

O'Neill jogged through the rain, not stopping until he was under the awning that stood in front of Sal's Sub Shop. He walked up the stairs and pushed open the big oak door that guarded the Ryder Detective Agency.

"Ten fifty-five," John Ryder said. He was sitting behind his desk, wearing his standard white shirt and tie. "You're early, even for a payday. That makes three times in more than two years that you've been to work on time. All three were Wednesdays. I wonder if it has something to do with Wednesday being payday?"

"Course it does." O'Neill sat behind his desk and started his computer. "Have you contacted Mary Hoffman yet?"

"I left a voicemail on her cell asking her to call. I'm guessing we'll hear from her soon. You hungry? I've got an extra sausage biscuit if you want it." Ryder took one sandwich from a McDonald's bag and handed it to O'Neill. "Are you sure Mary Hoffman is the same woman you dated?"

"I think she is, but no, I'm not positive. It was a long time ago, and I couldn't see her face when she was in the office. I only saw her from the back, but I'm sure it was her voice. She always had a sweet voice. And her name rang a bell. It took a while for me to put it together."

"But you lived with her," Ryder said, after taking a bite of his sandwich. "How could you not be sure?"

O'Neill rolled his eyes. "It was, like, fifteen years ago. I was eighteen or something."

"What was she like in bed?"

"Even if I remembered, I wouldn't tell you."

"Were you serious?"

"Shit no," O'Neill answered. "I was a horny, drunken teenager trying to score coke and get laid while playing in a rock & roll band, you know?"

"Let me guess: Theoretical Trash."

"Theoretically Trashed. But no, that was later. This was, like, '86. I suppose it was Passerby. Yeah, Passerby. We pretended to be a punk band. There were two guys from the UW and this girl from Shabazz, Viola. She played bass and this geography student sang. He wanted to be Henry Rollins, and it pissed him off when I threw in something different. We tried to play fast and loud to cover up that we sucked. We played a lot of college parties. By a lot, I mean ten or twelve times before we imploded. Anyway, at one show this blonde was eyeing me. I eyed her back, and we ended up at her place. I stayed there for a couple of days and she said I could stay a little longer if I taught her to play guitar."

"Did you teach her?"

"Tried, but she wasn't any good. She got okay, I guess. What was funny was that she decided to learn guitar, so she buys this five hundred dollar Gibson acoustic."

"Doesn't sound like too much for a guitar."

"You can spend a lot less even now. Here I was, playing in a band with a hundred dollar electric Gremlin. She takes up the guitar and spends five hundred bucks. The cool thing was that, when she dumped me, she let me keep the Gibson. It was supposedly a loan, but she never asked for it back. I had it for like five or six years until some dick ass copped it. Best instrument I ever had. Hardly ever had to tune it."

"How long did you live with her?"

"A month. She was a freshman at UW living off campus in an apartment with a roommate who got sick of me. See, I didn't have a place, and the roommate thought I was freeloading."

"Which you were."

"Course."

"That why she dumped you?"

"She didn't like the crowd I hung with, and her roomie was complaining about me, and Mary started acting distant. One day we were at a bar—the Church Key, I think. She was flirting with some guy on the football team, so I flirted with some girl. Ended up walking this girl back to her dorm. The girl left me outside her dorm room, and I didn't have a place to stay, so I snuck into the dorm's laundry room and slept. At least I think that was the night. In the morning, I went to Mary's place and the football player was there, so I got my stuff and left."

"With the guitar?" Ryder asked.

"No. Couple weeks later I saw her, and she told me she was sorry about how things turned out. She knew I loved the Gibson, and she told me to stop by the next day and pick it up. She said I could borrow it since she wasn't playing anymore. She called it a loan, but it was a going away sort of thing."

O'Neill hadn't taken a bite of his biscuit, but Ryder was getting close to finishing his McMuffin.

"Doesn't sound like much of a romance," Ryder said.

"I never said it was *Wuthering Heights*."

"What's that?" Ryder said between chews.

"What's what?"

"Whatever Heights."

"*Wuthering Heights* is a book by one of the Brontës. There was a movie too with Laurence Olivier, but I never saw it." O'Neill bit into the sausage biscuit. "Maybe you should try Mary again. Let's get this done."

Ryder let a breath out of his wide chest. "All right, but I'm not leaving another message." He took a last bite from his McMuffin and pulled out a notebook and his cell phone. "Hello, Mary Hoffman? This is John Ryder of the Ryder Detective Agency. Perhaps you got my message from this morning. I was discussing your case with my associate, and we have an idea we would like to run past you." He gave O'Neill a thumbs-up sign. "That is what I was going to suggest. Sure. If five works for you, it works for us. Thanks and goodbye."

"Are we a go?"

"We are a go," Ryder said. "She lives in Seminole Forest, which is a ritzy area in Fitchburg. We're looking at a fifteen-minute drive, so we'll leave at four forty. Is there anything else you're working on today?"

"You gave me some background check stuff last week. That's two hours of work, and I got to update us to Office 2000. But that will take time, and I can do it after this case wraps."

"Get the other stuff you're working on done now or come back later. Either way, we will leave for Mary Hoffman's place this afternoon at four forty. If you're not here, I'll go without you. And change your clothes before we go. An old gray sweatshirt and torn jeans won't impress a classy woman."

Chapter 4

The automatic teller machine on State Street was O'Neill's first stop. The payment advice showed net pay of two hundred and fifty dollars and twelve cents. One hundred and ten dollars would go to rent, so he took out a hundred and twenty. He continued east on State Street, stopping at B-Side Records. After thumbing through CDs, he left empty-handed and walked to the University of Wisconsin's Memorial Union.

Having a week's pay in one pocket made O'Neill nervous, so he entered a first floor bathroom and holed up in a stall. Pulling out his wallet, he transferred twenty dollars to a separate pocket and stuck another twenty inside his left sock. Eighty dollars in his wallet was risky, but he knew it would deplete quickly.

He walked through Der Rathskeller, which was populated by dozens of studying students, and grabbed a sunburst chair on the Memorial Union Terrace. The rain had passed and the clouds had thinned, so he relaxed under a sun umbrella and read a *New York Times* he had found near a trash barrel. Students strolled along the Terrace's lakefront path, and O'Neill glanced occasionally at the women tanning on the dock. After thirty minutes, his eyes grew heavy, but he had two hours of work to finish before the trip to Mary Hoffman's house, so he stuffed the paper into a trash bin and started back to the office.

The walk was relaxing, but he was surprised to see Ryder sitting on the steps outside the Ryder Detective Agency. The big detective got to his feet and entered ahead of O'Neill.

"Seamus," Ryder said as O'Neill closed the door. "Where the hell have you been?"

"You told me I could come back later. What did I do?"

Ryder walked to his desk and pointed at his computer screen. O'Neill followed, sitting behind Ryder on the warm, sun-drenched windowsill.

"I had the TV on, and the news had a bit about a man who disappeared yesterday," Ryder said. "Crime Stoppers has a video of a person of interest and are asking the public to help identify him."

"So what?"

"I recognized this person of interest, so I found the video on the MPD website. Watch the clip and tell me whether you recognize the subject."

Ryder clicked on the play button and they watched the grainy black-and-white video, which showed a skinny man with short hair and sunglasses opening a door and entering a building. The man was wearing jeans and a gray sweatshirt.

"Oh, shit," O'Neill said, recognizing himself. The footage was from the prior day when he entered the Annex for a shower.

"What do you got to say?"

"Yeah, it's me."

"This was when you used Tom Hoffman's access key, right? The one you took without permission?"

"Like I told you earlier, I was checking if it worked for the building."

"Is that all you did?"

"Remember, my shower broke and you wouldn't let me use yours? So I washed up while I was there."

Ryder jumped to his feet. His eyes were wide and his fists pumped in front of him. A blue vein near his left temple seemed to pulse. "You stole evidence from me so you could get a free shower?"

"I stunk, so I *borrowed* a key card."

"How stupid can you be? And how stupid can I be to employ you?"

"What do you want me to do?" O'Neill asked after a long pause. "Obviously, I don't know anything about this disappearing guy."

Ryder fell into his chair, shaking his head continually. "Tell me what happened."

"Not much to tell. I recognized it was the type of key card used at state office buildings. I assumed it would be for the main Administration Building on Wilson Street, since that's where Tom Hoffman works. When it didn't work, I tried the Annex since it was next door, and it worked. Once inside, I found showers in the basement, so I washed up."

"Did you see anyone in the building?"

"There were two guys near the loading docks, and there was one guy in the shower area. He came in when I was getting ready to leave."

Ryder brought up a picture on the screen of a middle-aged man wearing a business suit. "Did you see this man?"

"No. The man in the locker room was older and had a beard. The guys by the docks were more my age. Is this the guy who's missing?"

"Yeah, he's a division administrator for the Department of Administration named Bertram Newman."

"What should I do?" O'Neill asked. "Someone will recognize me, even with the short hair, and call the cops."

"You're telling me the truth, right?"

"Course."

"Then I'll call Garcia. I doubt if he's handling this for the Madison Police Department, but he knows you, and he knows you're an idiot but not a violent criminal. He'll believe you and we can back up your story about the card. I'll say I left the access card with you so you could verify which building it was for. Yet we need to find out why they view you as a person of interest. It seems odd, since you would think hundreds of people go in and out of a state office building. Why focus on you other than because you look like you?"

Ryder picked up the phone and dialed. The City of Madison Police Department transferred him a few times before Detective Phil Garcia was on the line. It sounded to O'Neill like Garcia was not familiar with the disappearance. Ryder read him the link to the video, and after a brief discussion, they decided that O'Neill would go to the Madison Police Department for an interview. The MPD assigned the case to another area, but Garcia would be at the meeting.

"Is it good that Garcia wants to be there?" O'Neill said after Ryder hung up the phone.

"Yeah, he said the case is in the MPD's Central District, so he's not involved. The disappearance could get handed to his unit if they find reason to believe there was a violent crime involved. They have classified it as a missing person case, so it is with the Central District."

"Why did this make the news already? Not every missing person makes the news. This guy just disappeared yesterday."

"There must be something other than the video that is making them think you were involved, so they want to interview you. Garcia isn't familiar with the case, but he'll hook us up with the central district detective who they assigned to the case. I told him we would be there at two o'clock, so wrap up whatever you're working on so we can head out at one forty."

"You'll come with me, right?"

"Yeah."

"Will we still meet with Mary Hoffman at five?"

"Yes, unless they arrest you."

As they drove to the Madison Police station in Ryder's Chevy S-10, the detective explained how he expected the interview to go, saying O'Neill should say what he knows and answer their questions. O'Neill didn't pay attention.

Ryder parked along Martin Luther King Jr Boulevard and announced he would deduct the parking from O'Neill's next paycheck. They entered the building, checked in at the front desk, and waited. O'Neill found the prior day's *Wisconsin State Journal* on a counter and started the crossword puzzle. Shortly after two fifteen, a uniformed officer brought them upstairs and into a meeting room. O'Neill finished the puzzle as Garcia arrived.

"Hello, gentlemen," Detective Phil Garcia said as he came into the interview room followed by a tall woman. Garcia reached over the table and shook Ryder's and O'Neill's hands. "This is Detective Meyer."

O'Neill thought of Garcia as a big man, but he looked short and squat next to Detective Meyer. She leaned down and shook their hands. She had long, black hair and was wearing black pants, a vest, and a loose red shirt that was buttoned to the collar.

"Thanks for coming in," Garcia said as the two Madison Police Department detectives sat opposite Ryder and O'Neill. A mustache hid his upper lip. "Detective Meyer, who is with our Central District, is assigned this case, so I asked her to join u s."

Ryder nodded, and O'Neill folded the newspaper, setting it flat on the table.

"Detective Garcia says that you, Mr. O'Neill, are the person in the video from yesterday morning," Meyer said. "Is that correct?"

O'Neill nodded.

"Can you give me details on when and why you were at the Administration Annex?" she asked.

"First off, I work for the Ryder Detective Agency, and we had this case where our client brought in a building access card. The state uses the cards for all its offices, and this client worked for DOA, so I told my boss I would verify the access card was for that building. I went there and tried the card, but it didn't work, so I tried the Annex and it worked. I expect you saw me on tape at the main DOA building maybe five minutes before I showed up at the Annex. It was pouring rain."

"What case are you talking about?" Meyer said.

"The case has nothing to do with this disappearance," Ryder said. "I can give you some details if you need to know, but we have client confidentiality issues to consider."

"I will follow up with you on that later if necessary," Meyer said before turning back to O'Neill. "What did you do once you entered the building?"

"My shower is on the blink. When I spotted showers in the basement, I figured I would kill two birds with one stone."

"I didn't expect him to use their shower," Ryder said sheepishly.

The MPD detectives exchanged glances.

"Did you see anyone while inside the building?" Meyer said.

"An older guy with a beard came into the locker room as I finished showering. I thought he made me out to be an interloper, so I hurried along and got out of there. There were also two guys I walked past near the loading dock."

"Was one of them this man?" she asked, sliding a photo in front of O'Neill.

"Don't think so. The guy in the locker room was an older gray-haired guy with a beard. The guys near the dock were younger. My age or younger."

"What were you doing in that area of the building? The lockers are on the other side." Meyer put the photo back in her folder and turned several pages.

"I knew there was an exit at the dock. When I came out of the locker room, I noticed a loading dock sign and thought it would be the easiest way to leave the building without running into too many people. I had seen the exit from outside, so I knew there was a regular door beside the garage door."

Detective Meyer turned a few pages and whispered into Garcia's ear. Then she turned to Ryder and O'Neill. "I'll be back in a moment." She picked up the folder and left the room.

"Anyone listening in on us?" Ryder asked Garcia after the door closed.

"Not that I know of," Garcia said as he rubbed his goatee. He raised his right hand and spun it in circles. "No. No one's listening."

"How tall is Detective Meyer?" Ryder asked.

"I don't know," Garcia said. "She's taller than Detective McMichael who says he's six two and a half."

"Holy cow."

"Is she new?" O'Neill asked.

"She was a patrol officer in one of the other districts and got promoted a few months back here in Central District."

"What do people think of her?" Ryder said.

"They think she's tall."

There was silence until the door opened and Meyer returned.

"Sorry about that." She sat and turned her attention to O'Neill. "How, again, did you leave the building?"

"There's a regular door next to the loading dock garage door. Once outside, I sauntered along the side of the building since it was still raining and the wind was blowing in the other direction. I assume you saw me walk out?"

"No, that is what I was checking on. The technician informed me that the loading dock's camera was set high." She glanced at Garcia. "They wanted the camera to pick up the driver of any truck that pulls up or someone leaving in a vehicle, but to do that, the camera aims high and doesn't pick up someone on foot who turns directly right or left as they exit the side door. In other words, there is a blind spot."

"So the video doesn't catch me exiting? That's what concerned you?"

Meyer mumbled something and gave Garcia a confused look.

"You didn't see Seamus leave the building, which was why he was a person of interest?" Garcia said to Meyer.

"We didn't see him *or* Bertram Newman leave the building," Meyer said. "*That* is why he was a person of interest."

"Bertram Newman is the missing guy," O'Neill said. "He's an administrator or something with the Department of Administration, right?"

Meyer nodded.

"Seems odd that a big shot administrator would leave through the docks," O'Neill said. "Is that something he regularly did?"

Meyer shifted in her chair. "We did not focus on which exit Mr. Newman typically used, since there were only three—four if you count the dock's garage door separately from the regular door. Mr. Newman entered through the front entrance when he arrived on Tuesday."

"Can you figure out which exit he used on other days based on the key cards?" Garcia asked. "Do the cards identify which door he came in and out of?"

"No," Meyer said. "You need the card to enter but not to exit. The system picks up key card usage when a person waves it next to the key reader. While the card doesn't tell the system who used it, we can collate usage with the video to determine who entered. Obviously, people only use the card when they enter, yet it is not complete since one employee sometimes lets another employee in. As to the video, the DOA keeps them for a week, so we can watch and see which of the exits he used. Reviewing will take work since they do not need cards to leave the office. But if he exited at the loading docks on other days, it would tell us whether that was his practice."

"You could ask the guys that work in the dock area," O'Neill said. "The guy's a big shot. They'll know if he ever leaves that way."

"We will look into it, gentlemen," Meyer said. She stuck her papers inside the folder and glanced at Garcia. "This gives us the information we needed from Mr. O'Neill. Our tech thinks the Administration Building's side camera would pick up someone walking along the side of the Annex toward Wilson Street. If we verify his story, it will end this line of inquiry. If not, we'll be in touch."

"So, you have no record of this Bertram guy leaving the office building?" O'Neill said. "I'm still puzzled why this went to the press or Crime Stoppers or whatever."

"Go ahead and tell him," Garcia said. "Mr. O'Neill always asks questions, but they're usually good ones."

"Mr. Newman's daughter has been leaning on us," Meyer said, "and the captain has gotten pushed by our legislators. Mr. Newman is a prominent member of Madison's business community. The daughter is convinced that Bertram was kidnapped, since she doesn't think her father would run away or just leave on his own. Those factors, along with you showing up mysteriously in the office building, led us to push this case more than we normally would. I suspected you since we had no record of you or Bertram leaving the building. It turns out I was wrong."

"We don't have the staff to follow up heavily or quickly on every missing person case," Garcia said. "My guess is we will find out he left town for a few days and forgot to phone." He looked toward Detective Meyer. "Will this new information cause a priority drop for the case?"

"I wish," Meyer said. "The daughter won't let that happen. She's relentless, and she's driving me and the captain crazy. And she's leaning on someone in the mayor's office as well, who is then leaning on the chief."

Ryder slid a business card in front of Meyer. "Have the daughter call me. I could give her attention and get her off your back. If she thinks someone kidnapped this guy, she can use some of that money to pay for attention."

Meyer glanced at Garcia.

"Mention it to her as an option," Garcia said.

"Seriously?" Meyer said. "Any concerns with referring her to an agency, particularly when one of their employees was a person of interest?"

"Not if you verify Seamus' exit and update his status so that he's no longer a person of interest. And document our conversation and the reasoning why we don't see it as an issue. Basically, you recognize we don't have the resources to address this case to the degree the evidence warrants or the daughter expects. Note that you made her aware of outside options, but did not recommend she hire someone, particularly a specific agency. Feel free, however, to tell her that the Ryder Detective Agency has moved at least one significant felony case forward resulting in a closed MPD file. She can read into that as much as she wants."

"Okay," Meyer said to Garcia. She thanked Ryder and O'Neill and left the room.

An officer escorted Ryder and O'Neill up the stairs and to the lobby. Ryder shook the officer's hand, and O'Neill pushed the door open and rushed outside.

"Yes!" O'Neill raised a hand in the air as they walked down the front staircase. "There's no better feeling than leaving a police station."

Chapter 5

O'Neill was relieved to exit the City of Madison Police station, but it was Ryder who acted excited about the meeting. Not only had they cleared O'Neill from involvement in Bertram Newman's disappearance, but a detective from the MPD Investigative Services Division pitched the Ryder Detective Agency to a detective from the MPD's Central District. As they turned onto Regent Street, Ryder glanced at his watch.

"It's almost four thirty," he said. "Let's drive to Mary Hoffman's place. We'll be early, but we can park nearby until five."

The trip took nearly a half hour since they drove in circles for fifteen minutes before finding Mary Hoffman's house. The residence was an enormous two-story Georgian with a three-car garage and a cement driveway. There were a dozen front windows and a second-story porch above the door. The grass was green, thick, and free of the flowered dandelions that peppered most area yards in late May.

"This is the life," Ryder said, waving toward the house as they pulled into the driveway. "And we're on time."

O'Neill scratched his scalp as he slid out of the truck.

"You look nervous." Ryder tucked his shirt in. "I don't think I've ever seen you nervous before. At least you are sober."

"Must be why I'm nervous."

Ryder nodded and pointed at O'Neill's earring. Once O'Neill had the cross stuck into a pocket, Ryder pushed the doorbell and the inner door soon swung open.

"Hello, Mr. Ryder," Mary Hoffman said as she opened the screen door. She was wearing white shorts and a baby blue tank top that brought out her tan skin. "Please come in."

Ryder and O'Neill wiped their shoes on the entry rug. A staircase, flanked by a living room and a hallway, dominated the foyer. Two pre-teen girls were in the living room staring at a big screen television. Mary pointed to the hallway. Ryder took a few tentative steps on the wood floor before Mary brushed past and led them into what appeared to be a study.

A patterned rug covered a swath of the study's wood flooring. A desk with a computer sat on one side of the room and a black Kawai studio piano graced the other. Framed photographs peppered one wall. Some included only Mary Hoffman and her two girls, but several older photos included a tall man with a mustache, and a few newer ones included a good-looking man with a square jaw. O'Neill sat on the piano bench as Mary shut the door behind them. She pulled out a chair for Ryder before sitting behind the desk.

"Thanks for taking us on such short notice," Ryder said, gesturing toward O'Neill. "I would like to introduce you to my associate. This is Seamus O'Neill. Seamus, Mary Hoffman. I believe you two already know each other."

Mary fixed her gaze on O'Neill, but her green eyes did not betray any hint of recognition.

"It was back when you were in school at the UW and lived on Broom Street," O'Neill said. "I taught you to play guitar."

Mary's jaw dropped. "Shay? Why, yes. Yes, I remember." She smiled widely and, for a moment, she looked like the girl he remembered. "It has been a long time, and your hair is so different."

"Do you still play the guitar?"

"Oh, no." She leaned back and covered her mouth. "I was never any good. I play a little piano, though I'm not good at that either." They both laughed for a moment before she continued. "You're a detective now? I never would have guessed."

O'Neill was not a detective; he just worked for a detective agency. But he didn't tell her that.

"I thought you were still playing music," she said. "One intern at work was a fan of your band, Sea something, I think. But that was a few years ago."

"We broke up in '98. Or rather, they kicked me out."

"Oh, and now you're a detective."

O'Neill nodded again.

"As I told you on the phone, we have an idea," Ryder said. "My sense is you are worried about your brother, but you're not sure if you should be. We think you should be concerned, since everything you described implies that your brother is involved in something. We are thinking you want to keep him out of trouble."

She nodded her agreement.

"We want to see what is inside the box with the fake passport and the list of names," Ryder continued. "We think it is key."

"Why?"

Ryder's lips moved a few times, but nothing came out.

"We're viewing the shoebox as Tom's secret spot," O'Neill said. "Seeing what's in it could tell us what's going on. The things you detailed imply he's into something, yet we don't know if it means he's in trouble or doing something illegal. We need to hear enough of the notes to figure out the song."

"You want me to steal the shoebox?" Mary said after a long pause.

"We will settle for pictures of them."

"How do I get to the shoebox?" Mary asked. "As I told you this morning, it would be unusual for me to visit him again. Usually, we just see each other out or at our parents' house, so I don't go to his place."

"We have an idea," Ryder said with a bit of hesitation. "We thought Seamus could, umm..."

"Maybe you could introduce me to your brother," O'Neill interrupted. "Your brother's apartment is up for lease, so either him or his roommate must be moving. Tell him you knew me a long while back and we ran into each other. I mentioned I was looking for an apartment in the Monroe Street area. My interest made you think of your brother, since he lives on Monroe Street. And then, we ask if he could show us the apartment. When all three of us are in the bedroom—that's where the shoebox is, right? In the bedroom closet?"

"Right," Mary said.

"When the three of us are in the bedroom, Ryder rings the doorbell. You and I will wait in the bedroom. If you show me the box, I'll take the photos in ten or fifteen seconds. Then we put things away in twenty seconds, tops. Your brother won't suspect anything."

"Will it be safe? Will Mr. Ryder be able to keep Tom's attention for that long? And is it okay if Tom sees Mr. Ryder?"

"Did you ever hear stories about kids setting dog poop on fire on a porch and ringing the doorbell?" O'Neill said. "The person comes out and stamps it out or kicks it and shit splats all over."

"Yes," she said hesitantly.

"We could do that. It will keep him busy for twenty seconds—at the least. And he'd never see Mr. Ryder."

"Sounds crazy." Mary's gaze jumped between O'Neill and Ryder. "It sounds totally crazy."

"I understand that," Ryder said, glaring at O'Neill. "It sounds crazy to me too, but we need to see that list, and there is not much of a chance of you getting caught. We won't actually use dog poop; we'll just start a smoldering fire in a paper bag. It will force him to put it out and give Seamus enough time to take photos. It is unorthodox, but your brother may be in trouble and, other than confronting him, accessing his shoebox is the quickest way to figure out what's going on."

"Couldn't you sneak in and steal it?" Mary asked. "It seems foolish to go to such lengths."

"Your brother might suspect something if there was a break-in," Ryder said, "even if we didn't take the box. And besides, we don't break the law."

"Isn't that what you're suggesting we do?"

O'Neill answered before Ryder could. "There's a fine line between robbery and snooping. There's nothing illegal about taking pictures of an apartment when someone's invited you into it."

The room was quiet until the hallway's grandfather clock chimed.

"I'm willing to do it," Mary finally said. "You're just talking about me introducing Shay to my brother and us going into his apartment, right? What about David? He's my brother's roommate."

"If he's there," O'Neill said, "one roommate will answer the door and the other will go to the door when one gets excited and sees the bag on fire. If not, we leave without photos and come up with an alternate plan."

"Okay. When would you need me?"

O'Neill and Ryder looked at each other. "The earlier, the better," Ryder said. "Would tomorrow work?"

"Afternoon or evening," O'Neill added.

"As long as it works with Tommy, it works for me," Mary said. "I'll call him and explain about Shay wanting to see his apartment. I'll get back to you after we set things. By the way, Tommy sent me an email today, which is unusual. It is probably nothing, but I thought I'd tell you in case it matters."

"What was it about?" Ryder asked.

"Someone Tommy works with disappeared. He forwarded me a link to a Crime Stoppers video. Apparently, they suspect some homeless guy. As I mentioned, it is likely unrelated, but no one he knows has disappeared before, so I thought I should mention it."

Ryder gave O'Neill a piercing stare. Then he turned back to Mary. "Forward me the link." He got to his feet.

O'Neill stared at the Kawai piano. Stepping closer, he ran his left hand along the piano's fallboard. He hadn't played piano in months and was about to ask Mary if he could try it out when he noticed Ryder's glare.

There would be no piano playing today.

"There's a fine line between snooping and robbery?" Ryder said as they got into his Chevy S-10. "Where did that come from? And what happened to the boyfriend thing you wanted to do? That all goes out the window and instead I'm setting something on fire in the hallway! This is bullshit."

"It will work," O'Neill said, "and he won't see you."

"Sure, it will work. If it doesn't, I'll fire your ass and you'll be living on the street playing your tin whistle and begging for dimes."

"It will work."

"Enough already." Ryder started the car and backed out of the driveway. "But next time, tell me when you're going to go one hundred and eighty degrees on a plan. I had to sit there, smile, and pretend I had a clue."

"Figured you would be used to that."

"Screw you."

"This plan is better than the original one."

"They are both stupid," Ryder said. "I went along with the first one because I thought you had the hots for her. I was doing you a favor, but it's not that, is it?"

"Might have crossed my mind until I saw her. She's got, like, teenage kids, almost."

"She's your age."

"Yeah. But she's just, whatever. She's like you said, not someone who would see anything in me. You were right. Besides, she's not my type anymore."

"She's an attractive woman. She's everyone's type. But *I'm* not used to sleeping with twenty-something women who settle for failed rock & roll musicians."

"You're not used to sleeping with any women."

Ryder gave him the finger.

"What do you think about Tom sending her the Crime Stopper's video?" O'Neill asked.

"They have probably taken the clip down. If not, and she recognizes you, you'll have to explain why you borrowed Tom's keycard to get a free shower."

"You think this Bertram guy's disappearance somehow relates to Tom Hoffman?"

"Most likely not," Ryder said. "But who knows? Ask Tom about it if you have a chance."

They turned off McKee and headed north on Fish Hatchery Road. The sky was darkening and the incoming clouds smelled of yet another rainstorm.

"When do I ring the doorbell at Tom Hoffman's apartment?" Ryder asked. "You'll want to be in the bedroom when I do it."

"Don't you have some sort of beeper or something I could hit? Or you could bug me."

Ryder rolled his eyes. "Recording someone without their knowledge raises ethical questions. Besides, I don't have a beeper for you to hit. I could buy something and take it out of your salary."

"You do, and I'll unionize."

"That would just be like you. Most employers wouldn't put up with a drunk like you. Most businesses expect people to come to work on time. And if they come in drunk, they get their ass kicked out the door. Do you know how many employers would put up with your shit?"

"No, but I'm guessing you'll tell me."

"None."

"You're a prince among men—a not too svelte one, but a prince nonetheless."

They drove over the West Beltline Highway and turned onto Park Street. Only a hint of daylight remained.

"Maybe there isn't an option. Maybe I should wire you but not record it. You could mention that you're going into the bedroom, and I'll know when to start."

"Would you be waiting in the truck?" O'Neill asked.

Ryder nodded.

"I can imagine you jumping out of the truck when I say 'bedroom,'" O'Neill said. "Then you run up the stairs, start the bag on fire, and run back down and to the truck. There are screeching tires and three or four people in the café note your license plate."

"Hey, it was your idea."

"I have bad ideas, too. Maybe we have Mary say she's going to check her messages as we walk into the bedroom. She could dial your phone, which would tell you when to torch the bag."

Ryder's head was shaking. "I didn't imagine that running a detective agency would require me to set a bag of pretend dog poop on fire."

Chapter 6

Ryder dropped O'Neill outside Riley's Wines of the World. A gray-haired man at the counter waved and called O'Neill by name. O'Neill glanced at the liquor store's upper area, which housed expensive Scotch, and meandered past rows of wine. He didn't break stride as he grabbed a liter bottle of Old Crow Bourbon and turned toward the beer. After grabbing a six-pack of Berghoff Red Ale, he handed over a twenty-dollar bill and headed home.

The temperature was in the mid-seventies, but O'Neill was sweating as he entered his apartment. He locked the door before filling his two flasks with bourbon and opening a beer. The heat prompted him to change into a clean t-shirt. After finishing the beer, he stuck a black Sweetone tin whistle and flask of Old Crow into his pockets and walked toward State Street, stopping for a pint of Berghoff at the Red Shed. Then he tried the Piper. The store was dark, and a "Closed" sign hung in the front window. He knocked a few times and waited. After a few minutes, he continued down the street, stopping at the Flaming Lip bar.

Most student bars had a spattering of locals, but the Flaming Lip was an exception. It seemed to O'Neill that he was always the bar's oldest patron, which made him uncomfortable. But

Topper bought the bar six months earlier, and he often gave O'Neill free drinks.

The bar was dimly lit. O'Neill sat in front of the taps and slid his sunglasses up so they rested atop his head. The bartender did not recognize him, which was unusual.

"What's on special?" O'Neill asked.

"Lite bottles for a buck fifty," the bartender said.

"Not much of a deal. Give me a tap of Miller, I guess," O'Neill said as he viewed the taps. He put a five-dollar bill on the bar. "Is Topper in?"

The bartender glanced at O'Neill and filled the beer. "He's back in the office."

"When you get a minute, tell him Seamus O'Neill is here."

The bartender walked to the end of the bar and conferred with a female bartender. The woman waved to O'Neill and went to the kitchen area. After a few minutes, she returned, followed by Topper who was wearing a blue polo shirt and jeans. His hair was pulled into a ponytail and his mustache was trimmed thin.

"Seamus," Topper said as they patted shoulders. "What's the deal with the crew cut?"

"I got a buzz, not a crew cut. Just temporary. Grows back, ya know?"

Topper slipped around the counter and took a seat. He put his elbows on the bar and ordered a Glenfiddich. A song that O'Neill did not recognize played in the background.

"You want one?" Topper asked. "I'll buy."

"Course I want one."

Topper turned to the bartender. "You heard the man."

O'Neill gulped his Miller. "You up to playing banjo at a show? I'm putting an acoustic quartet together. It's something to do with my job."

"Your job with that fat ass ex-cop?"

"It's hard to explain," O'Neill said in a quiet voice. "There is this person I'm watching, and he lives above Smoky Joe's Café on Monroe Street. He's involved in something we are looking into. And, anyway, the lady who runs the place, Marlene Schultz, used to go to Trashed shows way back. I told her I had a sort of acoustic band and she wants us to play there."

Topper laughed as he lit a thick cigar. "Why did you tell her that?"

"Don't know. Just came out."

"Yeah, I know you." Topper puffed at his cigar. "Whatever comes to your mind comes out."

The female bartender slid the drinks in front of them. Even in the bar's darkness, O'Neill thought she was pretty with sandy blonde hair and a kink in her lip. Topper touched her hand lightly, and she smiled.

"Thanks, Angie," Topper said. He watched her as she walked to the far end of the bar. "She's got a boyfriend."

"Am I supposed to care?" O'Neill said.

"No, I'm the one who cares." Topper chuckled. "Though I'm settling in with another girl. Her name's Mandy."

"Is she a fine girl?"

"Mandy, not Brandy."

"Oh, sorry," O'Neill said. "Is this *The* Glenfiddich?"

Topper shook his head. "You're thinking of Glenlevit. I prefer Glenlevit, but this is a college bar. Glenfiddich is excellent too, and I can buy it for two bucks less per bottle and still sell it at four bucks a shot. Like I said, this is a college bar.

You get very little high-level business. Students see Jaeger as top shelf."

"Glenfiddich tastes good to me. I'm used to Old Smuggler or, when I'm flush, Grant's. But, shit, lately I've gone over to American whiskey, mostly bourbon. I buy a liter of something decent like Old Crow for less than I'd pay for Grant's or something along that line."

"Bourbon's cheaper, but it ain't Scotch. What's this again about me playing banjo?"

"I told Marlene there were four in the band. The Johnson's in, and I figured you'd be up to it. I'm looking for strumming the banjo rather than picking. If Shane MacGowan pulled it off on 'Johnny Come Lately,' you can pull it off in a coffee shop."

Topper shook his head. "I'd love to, but what sort of time commitment are you talking about? I've got this place and the pipe shop. Running a bar takes time and effort."

"Couple of shows at most. The band is for this one café and only a show or two. That's all, so it won't be long term. My guess is we'll practice twice and play twice. Thought you would like to be onstage again."

"If the band is temporary, that's cool. But why me? I ain't in the same league as you and The Johnson. And shit, banjo? I'm bad enough with guitar."

"You're better than you give yourself credit. I'd put you on the guitar, but if we need a second guitar, I can handle it. You can use my banjo."

Topper leaned back, blowing out a puff of smoke. "Who else you going to get?"

"Not sure. I think we want a folked-up music hall sort of thing with some rockabilly and Irish. But not boring folk, if you know what I mean. Kind of *The Sun Sessions* gets eclectic. The Johnson will play guitar and I'll play accordion, tin whistle, and guitar. I wouldn't mind adding a fiddler."

"Did you ask your sister?" Topper asked.

"She doesn't play anymore."

"And you want me to find one? Don't you know anyone else?"

"Sure," O'Neill said after finishing his Scotch. "There's that Maria girl that busks out here sometimes, but she's missing teeth and she's into smack. That may be okay here, but not in a café on Monroe Street. Worst case, we could add a bass. You could be on bass, but I don't think we have an instrument. But I would rather have a fiddler."

Topper waved over the bartender and ordered another Glenfiddich. "If you expect me to find some hot girl who can play like Kevin Burke, you're out of luck."

"Just looking for someone serviceable. Someone to play fiddle on a few songs, sing along on a few, and bang on a tambourine for one or two."

The bartender arrived again, smiling at Topper.

"Hey, Angie," Topper said. "Do you play a musical instrument?"

Her eyebrows pushed up, and she sucked in her cheeks. "I took piano lessons as a kid."

"Any good?"

"Not really."

Topper shrugged his shoulders. "Just curious." He turned back to O'Neill. "You say this is for work? You sure you just don't miss it a bit? Playing in a band, I mean."

"Course I do," O'Neill said. "Miss everything about it. But this is about work—at least somewhat."

"I can't think of anyone, but I'll get the word out. We'll find someone. Maybe we can check if a fiddler is busking tonight. You sure you can't get your sister? She's way better than anyone we'll come up with."

"She won't play. I'm sure of that."

The pair finished their drinks and made their way up State Street. There was a busker near Peace Park, but he was playing the saxophone, so they ignored him. A pair of teenage kids slapped hands with Topper and exchanged a quick conversation. O'Neill's days of knowing the regulars on State Street were long past, so he continued walking, stopping outside the Irish Pub. After a wait, Topper joined him, and they slipped inside and sat at the bar. Topper ordered two pints of Guinness and two shots of vodka.

"What do you know about the State Investment Board?" O'Neill asked.

Topper's pale face reddened as he grinned. "Why do you care about the State Investment Board? You thinking about getting a job with the state?"

"Course not. Just wondering. Something to do with my job." O'Neill paused as the bartender sat a Guinness in front of him.

Topper took the vodka and poured a shot into each of their drinks. "It's a Black Cossack."

O'Neill took his first drink of the fortified stout. "If you worked at the Investment Board, could you somehow rip money off?"

"Sure you could." Topper put out his cigar. "You can rip money off no matter where you work."

"How would you do it? I mean, if you worked for the State Investment Board and you needed money, how would you do it?"

"What are you asking me for? I don't work for the state."

"You've run a few businesses over the years. You know stuff, and you're smart." O'Neill raised his eyebrows. "And you get away with shit."

"I don't really know what the Investment Board does," Topper answered. "I assume they figure out what investments the state uses for its retirement funds and stuff. If that is the case, and I was desperate, I might buy, with my money, stock in a small company. Then I'd have the Investment Board buy a bunch of stock in the same company, boosting the price. Then I'd sell my personal stock off and make a little bundle. Kind of insider trading thing."

O'Neill did not look satisfied. "What if you were a computer guy? Or rather, a web guy?"

"I suppose there's inside information you could sell to people. I can't think of much else you could do by yourself."

"What if you were working with someone else?"

"Then it's easy," Topper said with a smile. "You could do a hundred things. Let's say, for example, you purchase software. You have a friend start his own company that sells software. You approve an invoice from your friend's company, and the state cuts your friend a check for software that you never get. It's almost like writing checks to yourself. That is true for any business or government, since most don't inventory software."

"That's what I heard from this one woman who worked for Health and Social Services," O'Neill said. "She was a regular girl, but she got caught up in something. I don't remember it all, but she ripped off some pretty good coin."

"There are a hundred ways to do it, so long as you have a partner or dupe someone into being your partner. A lot of it depends, of course, on the company and their controls. In the one I mentioned earlier, you might get caught if the company kept an inventory of computer software and did physical checks on it. It also wouldn't work if someone kept a close eye on software purchases or on the software budget. They would notice costs going up, and there wouldn't be a reason for it."

"The keys are collusion and lack of controls?"

"Yep. The same shit applies that we talked about with any business. And in government, no one loses money or makes money. If the state gets into trouble, like it is now, it just adds a few less jobs, buys a few less computers, and blames the school districts and local governments. Ripping off the government is easier since no one expects the government to make a profit. Yet controls are in place and they maintain separation of duties, which makes things more difficult. You often don't have strong controls in a small business if you don't have enough people for segregation of duties. That's why a small business is always at risk of someone stealing money. Stealing from a small business is even easier than ripping off money from the government."

"Any reason someone who was doing this would need a phony passport?"

"I can't think of any reason unless he feared someone had caught him and he wanted to run for it."

O'Neill shook his head. "I don't think that is what happened, which bothers me." He took a swig of stout before continuing. "It is one of those things that makes no sense. The whole thing doesn't. That's what's bothering me."

"Then forget about it," Topper said. "Think about girls. You got anything going on?"

"Unfortunately, no."

Topper laughed. "It ain't so easy anymore now that you're not in a rock & roll band. Is that why you wanna put a band together? You're looking to score chicks?"

"No, but it would be nice to have someone to think about. Know what I mean?"

Topper shrugged his shoulders. "I suppose so, but do you really think you'll meet someone playing at a coffee shop?"

"Oh, this isn't planned. The show came up and I miss being in a band. Women are part of that, of course, but if it doesn't turn out, so be it. That's not what this is about. It's this case. One of these things where Ryder could use help."

"This relates to the State Investment Board?"

"Not necessarily. At least one player in the case works there, though. Don't know if it's a big deal, but something is out of alignment. This stuff comes in waves to me, just like music comes to me. There are keys and chord progressions and, when something doesn't work, you sense it more than see it. You feel it in your body, in your mind, and in your soul, and you sense something's off. It's the same way with detective shit. Know what I mean?"

"No," Topper said. "But maybe it will if I drink another Black Cossack."

Chapter 7

O'Neill woke before ten in the morning and stumbled into the part of the apartment which he called *the kitchen*. He leaned his head into the sink and drank from the faucet. Water dripped from his chin as he pulled a bottle of Diet Mountain Dew from the knee-high refrigerator and returned to his mattress.

O'Neill had lived in the efficiency apartment for nine months, but a mattress and a folding chair were its lone furniture. A guitar stand holding two acoustic guitars and a banjo was the room's showcase and sat near his boombox CD player. The beige walls were empty except for a half-dozen nail holes and a University of Wisconsin calendar.

Light rushed in as he opened the window shade, and once he pulled up the window, he heard the rumbling of an idling vehicle. He looked onto the street and spotted The Johnson's green Chevy Impala.

There was a knock at the door. "O'Neill, it's me, Johnson."

O'Neill flipped the deadbolt and opened the door.

"I got a fiddler," The Johnson said.

"*You* got a fiddler?" O'Neill walked back to the folding chair, picking up his Diet Mountain Dew.

The Johnson laughed as he stepped inside and closed the door. He was wearing a black t-shirt and the shape of a pack of cigarettes showed against his left shoulder.

"Last night, my girl and I ate dinner at my sister's place. It turns out my brother-in-law has a niece. She's great, I guess. She came in second place in some old-time fiddler contest." The Johnson sat on the floor beside the guitars, leaning against the wall. "Her grandpa played, too. She says she's a country fiddler. I never thought Wisconsin had country fiddlers."

"What fiddlers did you think Wisconsin would have?"

"Never thought about it," The Johnson said, pulling the cigarette pack from his shirt.

"What is she like?"

"Cute as a button."

O'Neill gave his friend a puzzled look.

The Johnson kicked out a cigarette and lit it. He took a puff and blew out smoke. "She's young."

"How young?"

"Thirteen, I think."

O'Neill rolled his eyes. "Is anyone going to take us seriously with a thirteen-year-old fiddler?"

"I didn't think it mattered if people took us seriously. Isn't it a one-night show?"

"Oh, yeah. I forgot."

"If you don't want her, then fine. I thought you were desperate and, judging from what I was told, Mika is the best fiddler we'll find unless you get your sister."

"Mika? Interesting name."

"Jenna's husband's family is from Eastern Europe—Czechoslovakia or Poland, I think."

"Okay, she's in," O'Neill said. "Let's set up a practice. The place in the back of Topper's head shop works. Topper and I have jammed there a few times. It will fit all four of us. If this Mika is serviceable, why not?"

The Johnson nodded, and smoke twirled through the air. "Keep in mind that Jenna trusts me to monitor Mika. Jenna doesn't want drinking going on."

"It'll be a bourbon and Coke night."

The Johnson puffed out more smoke. "That is the other thing. Mika can't be out past nine on a school night. Her parents will make an exception for the show, but not for practice."

O'Neill chuckled lightly as he shook his head. "Okay, if she's good enough. If not, I'll start drinking Topper's Scotch, and you can take your cousin home."

"My brother-in-law's niece."

"Whatever."

"When do we practice?" The Johnson asked.

"Why not today?"

"Can't. I'm heading out of town this afternoon. My girlfriend Kate's little sister is getting married on Friday in Jefferson. I work on Friday, but I'm driving Kate there tonight so she can go to the rehearsal dinner. I'll stay overnight and will be back sometime around noon on Friday. I will pick Kate up on Saturday."

"Can't blow it off?"

"Kate is ticked about me missing the wedding and I will not piss her off so I can play folk music in a coffee shop."

"Then we'll practice tomorrow. Guess we'll have to."

"I'll set it up with Topper and will send you a note once we have the time and place set," The Johnson said. "After all, I'm the manager."

***

It was past noon on Thursday when O'Neill arrived at the office. Ryder was talking on the phone to a potential client, so O'Neill stumbled into the back room and crawled onto the foam couch. He was half asleep when Ryder came in.

"Did you get kicked out of your place?" Ryder asked.

"What you talking about?" O'Neill mumbled.

Ryder shook his head and walked back to the office area. O'Neill got off the sofa and followed.

"What are you talking about?" O'Neill repeated.

Ryder undid his tie and slid it off. "Today is Thursday, the day after payday, and you're in the office. It has been a month since you've been in the office on a Thursday. Either way, I'm glad you came in. The daughter of the guy who disappeared, Bertram Newman, will be here in about ten minutes. Her name is Kathy Siler. Brush your teeth and get the booze off your breath before she gets here. And take out your earring."

"At least I don't need to comb my hair." O'Neill walked into the bathroom and got ready. Once done, he sat in front of his computer. "Did Kathy Siler call you?"

"Yes. Turns out that woman detective is good at pushing clients to us," Ryder said. "We want to keep that relationship working."

"Glad I'll be at this meeting. I want to figure out how Tom Hoffman connects with the guy who disappeared."

"I want you to be there. The only reason I didn't mention it is that I assumed you would be sleeping."

"Has Mary Hoffman called?"

"Yes, about ten minutes ago." Ryder glanced at a yellow notepad. "You're meeting her and her brother at six tonight at Smoky Joe's Café."

"Both of them?"

"She called her brother, and he suggested they have something light to eat first. They will finish around six, so she wants you to meet them at the café after dinner."

"How will you get the poop?" O'Neill asked, as the Windows logo appeared on his computer screen.

"Like I told you earlier, I will not use poop," Ryder said. "I brought in a few old chocolate donuts. I wrapped them in paper, added a touch of accelerant and stuffed them into a paper bag."

"Why bother with the donuts? They won't burn, will they?"

"I want Tom Hoffman to assume that kids started the fire. Maybe he'll figure out it isn't dog poop, maybe he won't. But I want it to look like something kids would do."

"Okay, I'll trust you as the criminal genius."

Ryder fixed his tie in place. "Either way, let's not worry about Mary Hoffman right now. Let's focus on our other client, Kathy Siler, since she will be here any minute."

"What's the background on her and her father?"

"Kathy Siler is twenty-nine years old and works in IT at CUNA Mutual Insurance," Ryder said, reading from a notepad. "She's married with no kids. No record of any arrests. As for Bertram, he's a self-made man. He started in landscaping and got a college degree while running his own company. In '91, he sold the business and started a second business in automated car washes. He also owns real estate."

"Great, a landlord."

"The governor appointed him as a division administrator at the Wisconsin Department of Administration two years ago. He's well connected, but I see nothing implying criminal activity or scandal."

"What was your impression of Kathy?"

Ryder laughed. "I only talked to her on the phone, but let me put it this way: if she trips coming into our office, she'll sue me."

O'Neill chuckled, but stopped at the sound of footsteps. Ryder popped out of his chair and hurried to the entrance. There was a knock, and Ryder opened the door.

"Mrs. Siler," Ryder said as they shook hands. "Please come in, but watch your step. It is a rather awkward entryway, and we try to ensure that people don't trip on this step since it is easy to overlook."

"I understand why you are concerned," Kathy Siler said. She stepped in, letting Ryder guide her down the step. She was short and sturdy with blonde hair and blue eyes and wearing black pants and a striped shirt. Her purse was big enough to carry a laptop.

"This is my associate, Seamus O'Neill."

Kathy Siler nodded toward O'Neill. Ryder led her to a seat near his desk. O'Neill pulled his chair closer.

The conversation started with pleasantries that lasted longer than O'Neill expected. Finally, Ryder asked her to summarize what she was interested in from the Ryder Detective Agency.

"The Madison Police Department is apparently significantly under-funded," Kathy said. "My father disappeared, yet they don't do much more than put him on a list of missing people. He has been missing for forty-eight hours, and it's not like he just didn't come home. He disappeared from his office in the middle of the day. The dimwit rookie detective they assigned to the case says they are ramping up activity, but she can't explain what that activity is or what their strategy is."

"Are you working with Detective Meyer?" O'Neill asked.

Kathy nodded. "Yes, Detective Skyscraper. I told her to move the case to the investigation unit or at least to a more experienced detective, but she doesn't want to do that, or she doesn't know how to do it. Regardless, I have zero confidence in their approach. Initially, they thought my dad's disappearance related to some homeless guy who stole a building pass and snuck into his building on the day he disappeared. Now she says that was a dead end."

"Interesting," Ryder said, glancing toward O'Neill.

"I think she's in a cul-de-sac and doesn't know where to go." Kathy sat her bag on the floor. "While I think kidnapping is a distinct possibility, she's probably hoping my dad stumbles into the house this afternoon so she doesn't have to do anything."

"What do you know about the day your father disappeared?" Ryder asked.

"I don't live with my parents, so I only know what my stepmother told me and what I saw at my dad's home. That, along with what I heard from that detective." She shifted uncomfortably and licked her lips. "Do you have any bottled water?"

Ryder glanced at O'Neill, who walked to the storage room. Two water bottles were in the refrigerator, as was a bottle of Sprecher Maibock. The beer looked appealing, but O'Neill knew better than to open it. Instead, he took a nip from his flask before pulling out the water bottles. He closed the backroom door, handed a bottle to Kathy, and offered the second to Ryder.

"Kathy was just telling me that her parents divorced eighteen years ago," Ryder said to O'Neill, "and she doesn't have a strong relationship with her stepmother."

"That is an understatement," Kathy said, laughing. "My stepmother's name is Linda, and she's six years older than me. She's what you call a trophy wife. But a third place trophy wife at best."

Ryder opened the bottled water. "Do your parents get along?"

"They are civil with each other. My mom remarried and lives in Waukesha. She's moved on from him. I'm sure she has nothing to do with his disappearance."

"Do you have any idea what led to his disappearance?"

"No, though I know he was up to something recently. He told me he was looking into a new business, and he expected to transition from Clean Freak, which is his automated car wash company, to this new business."

"What is his new business?"

"No clue, as he was tight-lipped about it. But he told me it was in the art universe, whatever that means."

"Did that surprise you?" Ryder said.

"Yes, and no. Dad has always liked films, books, plays and music, though I never saw him as a museum person or as someone who would turn the arts into anything more than a hobby. He's gone to the theater for the past five or six years, but his attendance stepped up recently. Lately, he's especially into Shakespeare."

"Shakespeare?" O'Neill repeated.

Kathy nodded.

"How did your stepmother feel about this interest of his?" Ryder said.

"Linda doesn't mind going to plays and museums, but I think it has gotten to be too much. This year, my dad bought tickets for all the Shakespeare plays at the American Players Theatre out in Spring Green. She's okay with going to a few, but she's having me go with him on two of them. She says it is a father-daughter bonding thing, but I think she's had enough Shakespeare."

"Where did this Shakespeare interest come from?" O'Neill said.

"Probably from Rob Peacock. Rob's an old, retired guy who used to be my dad's business adviser. He managed Dad's personal finances and so forth along with Mike Gunderson. Rob retired when I was in college, perhaps ten years ago. Mike has handled Dad's finances ever since, but Rob and dad remained friends. Rob's wife Leona died last year, and Rob didn't want to go to the plays by himself, so he got Dad to join him for a few shows and it ballooned from there."

"Are there other Shakespeare things he's into besides going to his plays?"

"Linda said Daddy wants to visit England next year, including a stop at Shakespeare's birth city. She's okay with that, so long as she gets to go to London. He's also got a few books on Shakespeare."

"Does the name Tom Hoffman ring a bell?" O'Neill asked.

"No. Who's he?"

"Someone who works with your dad."

Ryder leaned forward, keeping his eyes on Kathy. "Anything else unusual about his activities over the last few months?"

"Not that I can think of. Linda says he's been busy the last several months, but happy."

"Is their relationship solid? Any chance one of them is seeing someone else or is interested in ending their relationship?"

"There is always that *hope*," Kathy said. "But nothing has changed much over the six years they've been married. Basically, he makes the money, and she spends it. She's not overboard or overly demanding. She is too lazy to be overly demanding."

"Do you have access to his business or financial accounts?"

"Both Linda and I have access to Clean Freak, though two signatures are required on everything, meaning neither of us could do something naughty on our own. I don't know about their personal banking and investments. Linda could answer questions, but I'd go to Mike Gunderson, Daddy's investment manager, who I already mentioned. I checked with Mike yesterday just to make sure they locked everything down. My worry was that someone had kidnapped my dad and would force him to give them access to his investments or his business accounts. Mike was not concerned, but he didn't explain why, other than saying nothing major could happen without his approval. Mike implied he couldn't tell me more than that. I don't know if that's true, but I trust him, as he's worked with Daddy for a while. I talked with Rob Peacock as well, and he was confident in things, too."

"How much do you think your father is worth?" O'Neill asked. "It might give us a sense of what his disappearance could be about."

"Do you really need to know?"

"You brought up kidnapping, which is about money, so it is relevant."

"Okay." Kathy took a large breath. "Clean Freak LLC owns a ton of assets, mostly real property and equipment, but has a ton of mortgages. The company's net assets at the end of the last fiscal year were about four hundred thousand dollars, including the real estate arm. I can only guess his personal net worth. The house is worth another four hundred thousand. Everything, including the house, his investments, and Clean Freak, would be worth between one and two million. I can't see it being over two million. Oh, wait. Add in another two hundred thousand for the condo, which would put things at or above the two million dollar range."

"That helps," O'Neill said. "If there were ransom requests, do you think the kidnappers would go to you, your stepmother, or someone else?"

"No idea, though no one has contacted me. Linda swears she has heard nothing, and the Madison police bugged her and my personal cell phones, or whatever the term is. That started this morning."

"We talked about your father's money and assets. But do you or your mother have access to Bertram's computer? It might be nice to determine who he's been in contact with and what searches he's been doing on his personal computer."

"Dad and Linda have a desktop and a laptop at home. Both of them use the desktop, but it is mostly Linda shopping and playing solitaire. Dad doesn't use it for business or finances. Instead, he uses the laptop for his business and for most work he does at home. He took the laptop to work with him on Tuesday."

"Did he routinely bring his personal laptop to work?"

"No, Linda said he brings it maybe once a month. She said he was in a rush because he didn't even unplug his Dictaphone from it."

"Anything else unusual about the day he disappeared?"

Kathy took a drink of her water before replying. "It may not relate to that day, but he owned a handgun." She opened her purse and pulled out a sheet of paper. "He and Linda own a Beretta M9. I only know the make because I found the registration in his safe. Linda noticed the gun was missing last night. After she mentioned it to me, I called Detective Skyscraper and told her about it."

"What did Detective Meyer say?"

"She was going to Dad's home today. She wants to figure out if someone stole the gun or whether he brought it with him to work or had sold it or lost it earlier or whatever. I have not heard from her yet."

"How comfortable was your dad with the gun?" Ryder said. "Would he bring it with him to work if he felt threatened?"

Kathy's lips crunched together, and she shook her head. "He would go to the State Capitol Police if he had concerns about his safety. I can't see him bringing a loaded gun to the office. It could get him fired."

"We didn't really talk about your dad's job," O'Neill said. "Is it a good job?"

"He's a division administrator, whatever that means. The division he manages doles out grants to cities and counties. The job is a sweet deal, in that he makes a solid salary and gets to travel the state, yet he is rarely stressed beyond a nine-to-five schedule. It gives him a steady income, but he has time to run Clean Freak."

"Does he work with SWIB at all?" O'Neill said. "That stands for the State of Wisconsin Investment Board."

"Never heard of it."

"Do you think Linda will be open to meeting with us and giving us access to the desktop that you mentioned?" Ryder said.

"I don't see why not. But if I hire you, how does it work? Do you have a daily fee or what?"

Ryder pulled a sheet from his desk drawer and handed it to her. "We charge hourly rates with a daily limit."

There was a pause as Kathy reviewed the sheet. "It says here that there is a per diem as well as actual expenses. That doesn't mean I would pay you to go out to lunch twice, does it? And why would I even pay for your lunch once?"

"If you look at the detail, the per diem only applies if we leave Dane County. Actual expenses don't refer to meals and incidentals, but to stuff like payments to the city or county for accessing property or vital records or for copies of police reports. I doubt we'll leave the city, so per diem and lodging likely should not be an issue in this case. Any mileage will be around town for meetings or surveillance."

"How about if you pay an informer or a source like on TV shows? That's not something I would pay for, right?"

"Correct. Besides, informers don't provide receipts, and we'll have receipts for anything we charge you other than mileage and per diem. There could be exceptions, but they would be rare, and we would ask you for permission ahead of time if possible."

"Okay, but before I decide, I want to understand how you would approach this case. I don't want to pay you two to sit around like the MPD and wait for something to happen, and you need to be ready if this is a kidnapping."

O'Neill leaned toward her. "There are a few angles we'll take. First, we want to figure out your dad's new business that involves the arts or whatever. Anything new is of interest, especially if it relates to money. Part of that might involve accessing his laptop or getting his internet service provider to provide activity history. The MPD should get that before us, so we'll work with them on the laptop. We'll talk to others about this new business, and I suspect we'll meet with the two financial managers you mentioned. Hopefully, they will have details on your father's finances and might know about his new business. They should also know whether anyone is attempting to access any of Bertram's money. Second, we will determine whether someone could have kidnapped him at hi s office building or whether he left the building on his own. If he left on his own, which is likely, where was he going and what happened? Third, we will figure out who he and Linda have been in contact with over the past few months. While it sounds unlikely, we will verify that neither of them is having an affair or has something going on. Finally, we will determine what happened to that Beretta. The gun didn't just disappear."

"That sounds reasonable. How do you go about it?"

"We'll talk to the MPD, to DOA building management, to people at his work, the financial managers, and others who interact with Clean Freak. We'll also talk to Linda, to you, and to others who know your father. Finally, we'll dig into the day he vanished and make sure we understand exactly what happened. How did he get to work? If he left the building, what exit did he take and where was he going? Also, accessing any internet activity could provide context for what he was doing. This new corporation is important. What is the business and who is involved? I'm hoping the financial managers help with that."

Ryder nodded. "There will be more, of course. Seamus is just providing a general outline for how we'll initially approach this. As things develop, we'll adjust."

"I think you're already ahead of that Madison detective," Kathy said.

"Don't be too rough on Detective Meyer," O'Neill said. "She's probably doing more than she's telling you. But you're right that she doesn't have enough time to spend on this. Could you give us contact information for your stepmother and these two financial managers?"

She nodded and searched through her purse. After a few moments, she pulled out a business card, wrote information on its backside, and handed the card to O'Neill. She turned back to Ryder. "Send me a contract, and I'll ask my lawyer to review it and get back to you this afternoon or tomorrow. You already have my email." Kathy zipped her enormous purse and got to her feet. "Does that work?"

"Yes," Ryder answered. "I'll email it to you within the hour. I do, however, want to point out that we will work on the case today and tomorrow. But I'll need a signed contract tomorrow to continue working."

"Yet if I don't sign, I better not get an invoice from you," she said as she shook Ryder's hand. She nodded to O'Neill and walked toward the door, her left side lower because of the weight of the purse.

Ryder followed her to the door, reminding her of the step. The detective closed the door and returned to his chair.

"What did you think of her?" O'Neill said to Ryder.

"I feel sorry for Mr. Siler."

Chapter 8

Internet searches related to Bertram Newman and arts-related organizations only uncovered him on a list of donors to American Players Theatre, a playhouse near Madison that often put on Shakespearean plays. The lack of information puzzled O'Neill, since people associated with the arts usually generated an Internet trail. Bertram Newman seemed to be an exception.

"Can we change gears and give one of those finance guys a call?" O'Neill said to Ryder. "Particularly Rob Peacock, since Kathy says he got Bertram interested in Shakespeare. Do we have time to drop in on one of them before meeting with Mary and Tom Hoffman?"

"Plenty of time." Ryder stretched his arms into the air. "I'm doubtful we'll catch the financial advisor with an open calendar; the retired one might be another matter. Toss me the business card Kathy gave you."

O'Neill handed the card to Ryder, pointing to the handwritten name and number. Ryder dialed and, after a few rings, they had an appointment with Rob Peacock.

"We're meeting at his home in Shorewood Hills. The house is two or three miles away."

O'Neill had not been to Shorewood Hills in years. The village sat along Lake Mendota, locked within the City of Madison, and included a country club and a slew of old, expensive houses. He slid on his sweatshirt and stuck a notebook in his back pocket.

"Seamus, don't you own anything other than t-shirts and sweatshirts?" Ryder said.

"Not for this time of year."

Ryder shook his head and pushed the door open. O'Neill stepped past, and Ryder flipped the sign to "Will Return" before locking the door.

"What is it you hope to get from this meeting?" Ryder asked.

O'Neill paused as his eyes adjusted to being outside. "I want to find out if Rob Peacock knows Tom Hoffman. I also want to verify how much money Bertram Newman has. If this case is about good old greed, I want to know the potential winners and the stakes. Also, it sounds like Peacock has known our missing man for a long time. He may be able to tell us about Bertram and his relationship with his wife and daughter. Since he's a Shakespeare guy and a close friend, he also may know about Bertram's new business. Anything you're interested in?"

Ryder opened the Chevy S-10's driver-side door and clicked the automatic door lock. "You covered it pretty well, though I want his impression of the current financial manager, Mike Gunderson."

O'Neill touched the black leather seat before slipping into the truck. He leaned his head against the window as the truck drove down University Avenue. The Thursday afternoon traffic was sparse, and they passed a group of bicyclists and a black hearse before turning into Shorewood. Ryder slowed

the truck, pulled to the curb, and took a City of Madison map from the glove compartment. A pair of joggers ran past as Ryder examined the map, muttering something to himself before putting the vehicle into gear. O'Neill yawned as he stared at the houses lining the road. Mature trees and bushes seemed to surround every home. Eventually, Ryder spotted Rob Peacock's house, a two-story red brick house with a wooden fence in its backyard. The house was at a higher elevation than the street, and a dozen steps led to the front doo
r.

Ryder parked in the driveway, putting on the emergency brake. "I'll take Mary Hoffman's house over this, but I'll take either over my place."

O'Neill stepped out and stretched his arms. A convertible drove past and its passengers looked nervously at him. He followed his boss up the steps and held the screen door open as Ryder reached for the knocker. The door opened after one knock.

"Mr. Ryder, I presume," a short, white-haired man said. "I am Rob Peacock."

"Yes, John Ryder. This is my associate, Seamus O'Neill."

A smile slid onto Peacock's face as he shook Ryder's and O'Neill's hands. "Come in, please. We'll go to the back porch."

Ryder and O'Neill followed Peacock down a hallway, past a staircase, and into the kitchen. There were a variety of photos on the wall, many of Peacock and a woman who O'Neill assumed was his wife. A table sat at the kitchen's edge, filled with books and newspapers. O'Neill paused and looked through the book titles but didn't note any on Shakespeare. Peacock opened a back door and walked onto a three-season porch. O'Neill followed Ryder into the room, leaving the door op en.

Stringed musical instruments were displayed in three corners of the room. Trees and bushes surrounded the porch, and it was dark and cool. Peacock sat at a table and extended his hands toward two empty chairs. Ryder sat next to the retired financial advisor.

O'Neill pointed at one of the instruments. "Is that a Moorish guitar?"

"My wife called it a *guitarra morisca*, but I think both terms are correct. Would either of you like coffee or tea?"

"Coffee would be great," Ryder said.

"Tea for me," O'Neill said while examining an instrument.

"The other two are lutes, which was my wife's favorite instrument," Peacock said. "I believe that the Moorish guitar is technically a lute as well." He leaned toward a side cart and poured coffee into one mug and tea into another, his hand shaking as he lifted each mug off the cart and onto the table.

"Did your wife play these instruments or were they for show?"

"Leona played everything she had. She believed instruments wanted to be played, and she loved music and loved to play. Before retiring, she was a professor in the University of Wisconsin's Musicology Department."

"We are sorry to hear of her passing," Ryder said.

Peacock nodded.

"Do you play?" O'Neill asked.

"No," Peacock said. "Leona tried to teach me, but she got fed up with my feeble efforts and gave up. I wish I did, but since Leona passed, they are here for decoration and memories."

"Would you mind if I played the Moorish guitar for a moment? While I have seen pictures of them, I have never played one. I can't tell if the lutes are old, but the Moorish guitar looks like a modern interpretation, so I'm assuming it would be safe to play a few notes."

"You play, I take it? If so, please do."

O'Neill picked up the guitar and gently plucked each of the four strings while his left hand tuned the instrument. After a few moments, he sat, lifting one knee higher to support the body of the guitar. After a few random notes, he slid into "Greensleeves."

"You play well," Peacock said. "You play *very* well."

"Can we get to business?" Ryder said, clearly not enjoying O'Neill's performance.

O'Neill stopped playing but kept the instrument on his lap. He always claimed he thought better when holding a drink, but the same was true for a guitar, whether it was an inexpensive electric or something exotic.

"Any news about Bertram?" Peacock asked.

"Not that we are aware of," Ryder said.

"That is puzzling."

"How well do you know Mr. Newman?" O'Neill played a few notes as he spoke.

Peacock's gaze moved from Ryder to O'Neill. "I have known Bertram for nearly thirty years. Bertram is a solid, hard-working man. We first met after he started his landscaping business and needed advice, which I was happy to give. He was one of many clients, but as years passed, we developed a friendship. Part of it was that, despite our age difference, we had similar interests and a similar temperament."

"What do you think happened to him?" O'Neill asked. "His daughter thinks someone kidnapped him."

"I wish I knew. If it was a kidnapping, it is odd that there has been no ransom letter."

"What would Bertram's wife do if she got a ransom letter? Would she go to the police with it, even if the kidnappers told her not to?"

"Good question," Peacock said. "I think she loves him, but Linda is a practical person who relies heavily on advice. The police would likely tell her that paying kidnappers would not increase Bertram's chances by much. She would only pay if they told her it was the right move."

"If kidnappers demanded money from Linda or Kathy, how would they go about obtaining it? Could Linda or Kathy transfer funds without involving Bertram's financial advisor, Mike Gunderson?"

"Linda could transfer money herself, but it would alert Mike. Yet I think she would go to him rather than managing things herself. While I never worked with her directly, my impression is that she is not financially savvy. Bertram's daughter, Kathy, would need permission from Linda to access money from anything besides the business. That would, however, still alert Mike. I'm sure he contacted applicable financial institutions so they are aware of the situation. If it were me, I would be concerned that, if it was a kidnapping, the perpetrators would force Bertram to log in to his bank account and transfer money electronically."

"Does Bertram have the amount of money that makes him a target for kidnappers?"

"I don't think so, though that is more in your department than mine. When I think of kidnapping targets, I think of people with tens of millions of dollars. Bertram is well off, but unless I'm missing something, his net worth doesn't approach that level."

"Bertram's daughter thinks he's worth roughly two million," Ryder said. "Does that sound right to you?"

"That is a reasonable guess, though I would say somewhere between two and three million, including the house, the business, investments, and the condominium."

"If this isn't a kidnapping, what is it?"

"I don't have the foggiest," Peacock said.

Ryder and O'Neill glanced at each other.

"If Bertram were to pass," O'Neill said, "who inherits his estate?"

"You would have to check with his lawyer on that. However, I expect his estate would go to both his wife and his daughter. A few years ago, Bertram told me Linda would receive enough so she could keep the house, and there was a modest life insurance policy that would go to her. I inferred Kathy would receive the bulk of the inheritance."

"Did Bertram have enemies?" Ryder asked.

"He is a small business owner, so there is always someone whose feathers get ruffled. But Bertram is not one to make enemies. He is not confrontational. In addition, Clean Freak is a passive operation running automated car washes. People don't associate him with the car washes and, even if they did, I can't imagine someone being irate over a dirty car. Clean Freak also has properties that are rented out, but a rental management firm handles those, so his involvement is minimal."

"I get your point," Ryder said. "What are your thoughts on Bertram's daughter, Kathy Siler?"

"Kathy is your client, isn't she?" A smile remained on Peacock's face.

"We're trying to gain an understanding of Bertram's home life."

"Kathy is a firecracker, but I can't imagine her doing anything to hurt her father. She loves and admires him."

O'Neill returned the Moorish guitar to its stand. As he sat, he took his first sip of tea.

"What do you think of the tea?" Peacock asked.

"Very good," O'Neill said, though he hadn't drunk tea for years. "One thing that Kathy mentioned was that Bertram recently started a business."

"Oh, yes," Peacock said. "It is something I am part of as well. Yet it is not something I can discuss at this point except with the police. I don't mean to be cryptic, but there are competition issues."

"That is puzzling." O'Neill sat his tea on the table. "What sort of business requires that level of secrecy?"

Peacock's head nodded slowly. "When I bought into the company, I signed an agreement that precludes me from discussing the business with third parties until certain events occur. The company does not want rivals to know what we are doing until we take certain steps. Bertram's wife doesn't even know details about the business, though I doubt she really cares about them. Let's hope Bertram surfaces today or tomorrow. Perhaps we will find out that he is on a trip and doesn't realize that people are worried about him."

"Could this new business tie in with Bertram's disappearance?"

"Doubtful," Peacock said. "This company has roughly one million dollars of capital, which is a considerable sum, but

Bertram is worth more than that. And it is a very low risk venture. Besides, we have already transferred most of the corporation's assets to a third party. There is no risk anymore."

"Is this business in the arts field?" O'Neill asked.

Peacock smiled. "Yes, it is. How did you know that?"

"Kathy."

"Oh. Linda and Kathy both know about it, but not the details."

"Would Mike Gunderson be a better contact?"

"No. I doubt he knows more than Linda or Kathy."

"That's odd," O'Neill said. "Why is Mike involved with Clean Freak, but not with this new company?"

"Bertram, Linda, and Kathy are the sole owners of Clean Freak, LLC. Of that, Bertram owns eighty percent while Linda and Kathy each own ten percent. This new business is a different animal, as Bertram owns less than twenty percent. Bertram completely controls Clean Freak, but he is only one of a half-dozen people involved in the new company."

"If not Mike, then are you managing the finances on this..."

"Corporation."

"Yes, are you managing the finances of this corporation?"

"No. I'm not a CPA and neither is Mike. We invest funds and help people and businesses manage their assets. This new business is an organization with multiple owners. One owner does not unequivocally give control of an organization's assets to another owner. Instead, the company needs an accountant to manage the books, pay vendors, and ensure the safety of assets. This accountant and other employees are accountable to all stockholders. This protects the owners from each other and from any employees. Internal controls are not my forte, nor are they Mike's. The business could very well go to Mike for advice on investing excess cash and tax issues, but that would likely be the limit of his involvement."

"Who else knows the details of the business? It seems too coincidental that this business came into play just as Bertram disappeared."

Peacock considered the question before responding. "Let me just say this. There are three groups of individuals, including our group, that are interested in investing in a certain arts-related joint venture. We don't want these rivals to know that we are about to become part of the joint venture. If these other groups knew about our plans, they could take actions to complicate things. The investors, as well as our joint venture partners, are the only ones who know details."

"Can you tell me who the investors are?" O'Neill asked.

"Talk to me tomorrow afternoon or on Saturday. The issues I'm talking about will be resolved by then, and I can answer your questions."

"We'll do that," Ryder said.

"Have you ever heard of a man named Tom Hoffman? He works for the Wisconsin..." O'Neill paused, glancing toward Ryder.

"The State of Wisconsin Investment Board," Ryder said.

"Yes, Bertram introduced him to me," Peacock said. "Tom is a pleasant young fellow."

"Is Tom Hoffman involved in this corporation?" O'Neill asked.

"I'll tell you tomorrow night or Saturday."

"One last question. Kathy mentioned Bertram had recently gotten into Shakespeare. She thought you might have been the source of this interest."

Peacock laughed. "Last year, Bertram and Linda joined me for a few Shakespeare plays. Bertram enjoyed them immensely and found himself interested in learning more about the bard and his works. Bertram has become a bit of a Shakespeare aficionado, but I don't think that is because of me. I think it is exposure to Shakespeare and his world and his works. That exposure can make a Shakespeare aficionado of almost anyone."

Ryder and O'Neill asked a few more questions and finished their drinks. Peacock led them out through the back so they could see his flowers. Then he took them to a gate in the fenced yard.

"It was good to meet you both." Peacock unlocked the gate's padlock.

They shook hands. O'Neill waved as Peacock closed the gate, and Ryder and O'Neill walked toward the truck.

"I thought I was going to die when you starting playing that old guitar," Ryder said as they got into the Chevy S-10.

"Hey, he liked it," O'Neill said. "Helped me connect with him."

"Either way, what do you think?"

"Bertram's disappearance has to relate to this new corporation," O'Neill said. "And Tom Hoffman is involved. Do you buy this secrecy bullshit?"

"No, but we don't have time to dwell on it. We've got to go back to the office so we can get ready to start our pretend poop on fire."

Chapter 9

At five o'clock, Ryder parked his Chevy S-10 a few blocks from Smoky Joe's Café. Traffic rolled past, and a pair of bicycles came within inches of Ryder's side mirror. O'Neill left his sunglasses on and put his earring back in as rush hour traffic passed by.

"This is a downer after meeting with the MPD." Ryder brushed the few hairs remaining atop his head. "Garcia would not suggest the Ryder Detective Agency to Meyer if he knew about this stunt. Oh, well. I'm gonna wait here. After a few minutes, I'll walk along Monroe Street, but I won't go near the apartment entrance until you and the Hoffmans leave the café. Remember, you are meeting Mary and Tom at the café, but you won't be eating with them. Go with them to Tom's room. Once you go inside the apartment, I will grab the outer door before it locks." He pointed to the brown paper bag on the truck's floor. "I'll bring that with me and will wait in the entryway or the hallway."

"Mary will signal you with her phone?" O'Neill asked.

"Yeah. Once you are in the bedroom, Mary will pull out her phone. If Tom asks, she'll say she's checking messages. She called me earlier so she'll just hit redial and let it ring three times and hang-up. Once she calls, I'll go up the stairs, set the dog poop bag on fire, and hightail it out of there. You'll have to walk back to the office."

"Sounds like a plan. Just don't run; it'll make you obvious. Not that you could run, anyway."

"Get your drunken ass in there. And remember, you don't need to make anything up. The only thing would be to not tell Tom Hoffman that you work for a detective agency." He handed O'Neill a small camera. "This is simple enough, even for you. Just push the button. The camera is digital, so you don't need to rewind for the next picture or anything. Take as many pictures as you need."

"I'll try it first." O'Neill aimed the camera at his boss.

"Not at me, dummy! What if you get caught? They would know I'm involved. Take a picture of the road." Ryder handed O'Neill a white handkerchief. "Also, don't touch anything in the shoebox with your bare fingers."

"Geez, you think *I'm* paranoid?" O'Neill stuffed the camera and the handkerchief into the front pocket of his jeans.

O'Neill stepped out of the truck and walked toward Ken Kopp's grocery store and onto Monroe Street. At a break in traffic, he jogged across the street and hurried into Smoky Joe's Café. Customers occupied most tables, and workers behind the counter were busy with a two-deep line. He didn't see Marlene Schultz or the guy with the long goatee, but Mary Hoffman waved to him and he meandered to her table.

"Shay!" Mary stood, and they hugged. "Great to see you. This is my brother, Tom."

Tom Hoffman got to his feet and extended a hand. The younger Hoffman had green eyes and dark features like his sister. He also shared her slender build. "This is an ex-boyfriend from Mary's youth? I bet there are stories you could tell. If you do, I won't tell Lily and Emmy—they are Mary's kids."

"They wouldn't believe them anyway," Mary said.

"You're right." O'Neill's shoes squeaked on the floor. "Her kids would not believe them."

"Oh, come on and take a seat. You can tell me."

"Leave him alone, Tom."

"You at least can tell me how you met?"

Mary kicked her brother's leg.

"What's that for?" Tom said.

"I don't need my little brother digging into my personal life," Mary said. "You don't want me digging into *your* personal life, do you?"

"Sure you can," Tom said. He turned to O'Neill who sat between the Hoffmans. "What's the deal? She says you were a musician."

"Yeah. My band was playing at a frat party, I think. Your sister was there and..." This time, O'Neill got kicked. He straightened up and looked her in the eye. "He's just curious, and then you can pump him on his personal life. Don't you want to know if he has a new girlfriend or if he's interested in someone?"

Mary's eyes softened. Then she leaned back in her chair.

"Like I said," O'Neill continued, "my band was playing a frat party, and I noticed your sister watching me, ya know?"

"I wasn't watching *you*. I was watching the band."

"Yeah, whatever. So, anyway, between songs, I asked her to grab me a beer. And then another. This is from a keg at the back of the room, so it was no big deal. When the show was over, she waited as we loaded our gear and next thing I know we're outside."

"Enough, Shay."

"No, it isn't," Tom said. "What happened between you two?"

"We were out walking near Camp Randall, and there was this old cannon. Like a civil war sort of thing…"

Mary interrupted him. "What cannon?"

O'Neill kept his gaze on Tom. "Camp Randall was a military base during the American Civil War. An old cannon is still there, kind of across the street from the Stadium Bar. We stopped there, and I was sure she was into me, ya know?"

"What are you saying?" Mary said.

Tom was laughing.

"She was leaning against the cannon and we were kind of getting into it, ya know?"

"We did not kiss or do… anything on or near that cannon," Mary insisted, her gaze bouncing between the men.

O'Neill ran a hand through his hair, which felt like it was finally growing. "I remember because…" O'Neill stopped, gasping in pain from another kick to the leg.

"Enough, Shay."

"This freaks me out," Tom said. "Miss perfect on a cannon!"

"I did not," Mary said in a hushed tone. "He's making this up. And if something happened, it wasn't what you're thinking."

Tears of laughter were dripping down Tom's cheeks. "Miss perfect? I didn't think you did anything wrong."

"I'm divorced. I can't be perfect."

"He was a jerk. That was his fault."

"Yeah, but I picked him."

Tom's laughing subsided.

"Let's talk about you now," Mary said to her brother.

Tom leaned back and crossed his arms.

"Gotta be fair." O'Neill rubbed his injured leg. "Your sister let you hear her dirty laundry. Now you gotta tell her yours. Just don't kick me."

"Yeah, let's hear about *your* love life," Mary said.

"There is not much to tell." Tom shrugged his shoulders. "I've had a few girlfriends here and there, but no one special."

"What about Angela?"

Tom took a deep breath. "Angela wanted me to go where I could be more successful. And once she started at Rayovac, she met guys that were successful." He glanced up at his sister. "It's not complicated."

Mary seemed to struggle to reply, but nothing came out.

"I dated Laura Williams for a bit."

"Laura?" Mary said. "Are you serious?"

"Yes, I'm serious. Do you remember Laura's sister's Christmas party?"

"I saw you two talking on the couch. Oh, that's wonderful. Laura would be an awesome match for you."

"She doesn't think so," Tom said.

"You and Laura didn't work out?"

Tom's head shook.

Mary turned toward O'Neill. "Laura's older sister, Macy, is my best friend."

"So, which one is the love of your life?" O'Neill asked.

"Laura. But I doubt she'd say the same. We only dated for a few months. All kinds of guys are after her, so I need to move on and find someone else."

"You're not seeing anyone now? Don't have your eye on anyone?"

"There are usually one or two I'm considering, but no one right now. No one special."

"Anyone at work?" O'Neill said.

"Hell, no," Tom replied. "IT is not a hotbed for women. There are only a few in my area, and none are close to my age. I'm working a side job as well, but there is only one woman in the entire business, and she's in her fifties."

There was a long silence.

"How about you?" Mary patted O'Neill's arm.

"How about me, what?"

"Come on. We put out our dirty laundry. You ever been married?"

"No," O'Neill replied. "No one has wanted to marry me."

"You can't be all that bad," Tom said.

"Didn't mean it to sound all that bad. I've dated a lot of women over the years. The good ones find someone else, but I suppose most of them were out of my league. That happens when you sing in a band, ya know? Being in a band gets you girls, but that doesn't mean you can hold on to them."

Mary glanced at her watch. "Oh, look at the time. I pick my daughter up from swimming lessons at seven fifteen. Shay, do you still want to see Tom's apartment?"

O'Neill nodded, got to his feet, and returned the chair to the table.

"Where are you living now?" Tom asked as he left a tip.

"In an efficiency apartment on Doty near Broom Street. The shower doesn't work, and my landlord's a jerk."

"Then this place would be an improvement."

They exited the café and Tom put his key in the door beside the café entrance. The lock clicked, and he opened the door. Mary and O'Neill went in first, and Tom followed. Rubber covered the steps, and the walls were gray. It was an early twentieth century building, but the hallway looked modern. At the top of the stairs, O'Neill glanced back, and he saw Ryder's hand holding the door.

Tom walked down a short hall, and Mary pointed at one of the two wooden doors.

"How's the neighborhood?"

"Nice, though different from where you're at in Fitchburg," Tom said to his sister as he unlocked the door. "There are younger and older people in the neighborhood, but not much variety in other ways. There are a few old hippies, but they're harmless. Things are crazy on football Saturdays, but you get used to it."

Tom pushed the door open, and Mary and O'Neill followed him in. The kitchen was to their left across from the bathroom. A man sat in the living room area with a laptop resting on his legs. A Brewers game played on the television.

"This is my roommate, David Leonard. David, you met Mary already, I think."

David Leonard was a heavily built man in his mid-thirties wearing dress pants and a white shirt. A tie sat loosely around his neck. He seemed transfixed by the Brewer game. "Yes, I met Mary," David said as he stood and shook Mary and O'Neill's hands.

"This is her old boyfriend, Shay. He's a musician, and he's looking for an apartment in this area. Mary knew we had a vacancy, so she asked if he could look around."

"Sure." David looked away from the game. "I'm moving out in August. Tom hasn't decided if he's staying."

"The next-door apartment is only a one-bedroom," Tom said. "I'll probably move to that one since David is leaving.

The woman currently there is ninety percent sure she'll give her notice. Then again, nothing's final." Tom glanced at the television and looked toward his roommate. "Are the Brewers still up?"

"Yep," Leonard answered. "Six to two in the bottom of the seventh. Looking good."

Tom nodded, then turned on the kitchen light and poked a finger against the fishbowl, leading a small blue fish to move toward him. He continued to play with the fish as he described the room and its appliances. O'Neill spotted a few books on the table, including *Shakespeare: A Life*, by Park Honan. The tour continued with a showing of two closets, a small pantry, and a bathroom.

"You will like the shower, since it works."

"That would be an improvement." O'Neill peered in. "This is a lot bigger than my current place. The shower is half the size of this one. I can barely turn around without rubbing against the curtain."

"That must suck."

"The only other place to see is the bedroom," Mary said, her voice cracking.

"Yeah," O'Neill said. "Where's the bedroom?"

Tom opened the door and flipped on the light. O'Neill tried not to watch, but he noticed Mary hit a button on her cell phone.

"It's not as exciting as a cannon," Tom said.

Mary rolled her eyes.

O'Neill pointed at a Rage Against the Machine poster that covered one wall and nodded approvingly.

Mary motioned toward the doorless closet, and O'Neill saw the stack of shoeboxes on the floor. The doorbell rang.

"I got it," David said from the living room.

"I wonder who that could be," Tom said.

"Shit!" David yelled from the hallway. The door slammed, and Tom muttered a few words as he rushed toward the door.

"Do you see it?" Mary whispered to O'Neill after the apartment door opened and closed.

The Union Jack design made the shoebox easy to spot. O'Neill took a handkerchief out of his pocket and pulled the box from the closet. He kneeled and opened the shoebox. A folded piece of notebook paper, a passport, a driver's license, other identification cards, building access cards, bank statements, and a roll of twenty-dollar bills filled the box. He unfolded the paper and set it on the light brown carpet. After taking one photo, he slid the identification cards along the floor so that virtually all were at least partially visible.

"Damn bastards!" said a voice from outside the apartment.

O'Neill took six more pictures, including two of the notebook paper and one of the cash. Then he slid the camera into his pocket and carefully placed the identification cards into the box. Re-folding the paper, he put the lid on the box and slid it in place. He stepped over to Mary, who was biting her lip, her green eyes wide open. In one movement, he took her by the waist and directed her out of the bedroom and into the hallway.

The door flew open, and Tom rushed into the apartment. "Some son of a…"

"Bitch?" O'Neill suggested.

"Yeah. Some son of a bitch torched a bag outside the door that was filled with dog shit." He was breathing heavily and pointing at his shoe. "David kicked it down the stairs and it finally burned out. Some of it got on his shoes. A little got on one of mine, but I rubbed it off on the hallway carpet."

"Must be kids," Mary said.

The door opened again, and David stepped inside, holding a shoe in his left hand. After entering the bathroom, he slammed the door closed.

"I have never heard of anything like that going on here," Tom said, looking out the window. "This would be something that might happen in Mary's neighborhood, but not mine. There aren't many kids around here, and I don't know how they got in here since the outer door locks."

"Should you douse it with water or something so it doesn't singe the carpet?" O'Neill said. "It might make a mess, but a carpet burn might give the landlord a reason to fine you."

Tom walked toward the door, and Mary and O'Neill followed. They watched Tom's foot push at the smoldering bag. "I think the fire is out. Later today, David or I will put it into a plastic bag and take it to the dumpster."

O'Neill and Mary nodded in agreement. The door opposite Tom's apartment opened and a skinny, dark-haired woman stepped out. She had obviously heard the commotion.

"Someone lit something on fire in the hallway," O'Neill said.

"What was it? Not a cigarette, I hope," she said.

"Dog poop in a paper bag," Tom said.

"How juvenile."

O'Neill and Mary nodded in agreement.

"It smells more like... burned chocolate than poop," Tom said as they returned to the apartment.

"It doesn't smell good, whatever it is," Mary said.

Tom spent the next few minutes assuring O'Neill that the apartment was in a safe neighborhood and that the dog poop was a onetime incident. David was still in the bathroom when they finished the tour. Tom gave O'Neill the landlord's phone number, and they shook hands.

"It was good to meet you," Tom said. "And I'm sorry about the dog poop or whatever it was."

"Not your fault. Oh, before I go," O'Neill said. "I was going to ask you about that guy that disappeared. Mary said he's a colleague. What happened? Have they found him?"

Tom nodded. "His name is Bertram Newman, and he's a division administrator at the DOA that I work with. I don't know him well, but he's a good guy. I can't believe he disappeared."

"What do you think happened?"

"Everyone at work is speculating about him running away with a woman or something. One guy told me that Bertram's wife is way younger than him, so people assume he's a womanizer. He doesn't seem that way to me."

O'Neill nodded, and Mary waved goodbye.

"Do you need a ride?" Mary asked O'Neill as they started down the stairs.

"That would be great. Dropping me at the office is fine."

Tom leaned out his door. "You two behave!"

"Shut up or I'll set the doo-doo back on fire." Mary walked back up the stairs toward her brother. "And don't say a word about this to Lily and Emmy or to Mom and Dad, okay?"

"A word about what?" Tom said.

"You know damn well what."

"About the cannon?"

She rushed at him, and he retreated into his apartment, shutting the door.

"I'm never going to live that down," Mary said.

"Sorry," O'Neill said.

Mary walked past him, stepping around the charred remains of the donuts. O'Neill followed as she walked down Monroe Street, eventually approaching a large black SUV. She unlocked the doors with a fob, and O'Neill climbed into the vehicle. The seats were black leather but cool to the touch.

"That Leonard guy thinks he's cleaning dog poop off his shoe, but it's actually charred donuts," O'Neill said. "I can't wait to tell Ryder about how well it worked. He's probably waiting in the office, and he'll want to develop the pictures or print them out or whatever. Do you wanna hang around and see them?"

"I would, but I got to pick up Lily and Emmy. Lily has swimming and Emmy is at a friend's house."

"Okay. We'll call and give you an update after we've reviewed the photos."

Mary slowed her SUV as they approached the corner of Monroe and Regent. The Field House and Camp Randall Stadium were directly in front of them. If they stayed on Monroe Street, they would drive past the cannon. Mary turned the vehicle onto Regent and they rode through an intersection before she pulled to the side of the road.

O'Neill said goodbye and slammed the door shut. The truck headed down Regent Street, turning south onto Park Street as he crossed the road. He patted the camera sitting in his pocket, eager to see the photographs.

Chapter 10

O'Neill hadn't eaten since morning, so Sal's Sub Shop beckoned. He stepped inside the shop and the young woman standing behind the counter wearing a Sal's hat looked past him. He could hear her chewing gum as he approached. Day-old bread was typically on the counter wrapped in cellophane, but the spot was empty.

"You out of day-old bread?"

"Yeah, some guy just bought the last two," the woman said. She chewed as she spoke. "We have fresh at regular price. We also sell sandwiches."

O'Neill had money in his wallet, his pocket, and his sock, but he would not splurge on bread and wasn't going to buy a sandwich. "Maybe I'll be back." He retreated from the sub shop and rushed up the stairs.

"What took so damn long?" Ryder said as O'Neill stepped into the office.

"I was just checking for day-old bread. They're out."

"I mean, what took so long at the café? Did you eat supper with them or something? You were in the coffee shop forever. I was standing on the sidewalk, leaning against the building, and holding a bag of combustible donuts for what seemed like fifteen minutes."

"Tom Hoffman wanted to talk, so I let him talk."

"Yippy, yeah." Ryder stuck a piece of Extra Cheesy Superoni Rocky Rococo pizza in his mouth. "Did you get the pictures?"

O'Neill took the camera from his pocket and tossed it to Ryder, who caught it with one hand, avoiding a pizza spill.

"There was a box of stuff," O'Neill said as he sat down. "I got a photo of the page of notebook paper with names on it. Then there was the passport, ten to fifteen credit cards, IDs, and cash. I spread those out like you suggested and took three pictures. There were a few bank statements, but I didn't take a picture of them because they were folded in envelopes and I didn't want to take the time."

"Was Mary Hoffman okay with how we handled things?"

"Think so. She gave me a ride home. So now what? You gonna develop those yourself?"

"It's a digital camera, you idiot."

"Oh yeah. How long till you have them ready?"

"Soon as I finish eating."

"Did you order a slice for me, too?"

"No. Like I said, I thought you ate at the café."

O'Neill bit at his lip and rubbed his head. "What would you say if I ran to Open Pantry for a six-pack? We can sip on a beer while we look the pictures over. They should still have maibock."

"Okay." Ryder handed him a ten-dollar bill. "But bring back the change *and the receipt.*"

After descending the stairs, O'Neill took a few steps along Regent Street before seeing a break in traffic, so he streaked across the road and was soon inside Open Pantry. He picked out a six-pack of Sprecher Maibock and added a single banana, which he ate in the Open Pantry parking lot. When he returned to the office, Ryder was at his desk, staring at his computer screen.

"They come out okay?" O'Neill asked as he handed Ryder a beer and opened one for himself.

"Just fine. But you didn't spread out the IDs and the credit cards too well." Ryder pointed at the screen. "The driver's license is on top, and most of the passport is visible underneath. Then there is a master card and a library card and three or four other cards. They look like credit cards, but they might be something else. Fake names are only on two driver's licenses and the passport. The counterfeit driver's licenses are expired. The name on the passport is William Stanley, while the name on the licenses is Derick Fondue. Doesn't make much sense."

O'Neill pointed at the screen. "Can you print that out? Just the photo of the notebook paper?"

Ryder zoomed in on the sheet, cropped the photo, and hit "print." O'Neill picked the sheet out of the printer and sat in front of Ryder's desk. The list was handwritten.

WS=BN
Bacon=?
Oxford=PC?
Marlowe=DL
Raleigh=?
Elizabeth=1 of 6
Stanley=TH

"They aren't all names, are they?" Ryder asked as he sipped his beer.

"Yeah, they are. WS is probably William Shakespeare, Bacon is Francis Bacon, Oxford is Edward de Vere, Raleigh is Sir Walter Raleigh, Marlowe is Christopher Marlowe, and Stanley is... someone. Wait, it's William Stanley, which is the name on Tom Hoffman's passport. Elizabeth is probably Queen Elizabeth."

Ryder looked puzzled. "Sir Walter Raleigh? The explorer? And Queen Elizabeth?"

"Sure. It's a Shakespeare thing. Do you remember Tom is all into Shakespeare lately, just like Bertram? The names on the list are players in the Shakespeare authorship controversy."

"What are you talking about?"

"They never reported it on ESPN, so you wouldn't have heard about it. There is controversy that has been going on for over a century about who wrote Shakespeare's plays and poems. My sister and I saw a PBS documentary about it when we were teenagers and it got me interested in the subject. The show focused on the Oxfordian theory."

"The only Shakespeare I ever read was in the Cliff Notes," Ryder responded. "I haven't even seen a movie of one of his books, unless you count *To Be or Not To Be.*"

"No, *To Be or Not To Be* doesn't count, especially the Mel Brooks one. But whoever made this list knew about the controversy. What are the odds of having Bacon, Raleigh, Marlowe, and Oxford? They could have used de Vere rather than Oxford, but the point gets across."

"Quit babbling and tell me what it means."

O'Neill stared at the list as he gulped beer. "They are aliases based on the Shakespeare authorship controversy. Tom has the code names of people in the gang and he's trying to figure out their real names. He knows some of them, but doesn't know others. Can't really say more than that."

"Why is he listing characters from Shakespeare novels?"

"Shakespeare wrote plays and poems, not novels. The names are different people who were alive in Shakespeare's time who someone proposed as the true author of Shakespeare's plays."

"Are you saying he didn't write them? Shakespeare, I mean?"

"He probably did. He certainly collaborated a lot and took ideas from other writers and from the rich folk he dealt with. And he may have changed his works to reflect feedback, so the versions we have reflect those impacts. But some people go further. Some people can't imagine a common dude like Shakespeare writing beautiful, complex plays and poems that reflect an understanding of law, medicine, and other things. They think it had to be a member of royalty or some upper crust type."

"You're saying that whoever made up this list was into this authorship thing?" Ryder said. "What does that tell us?"

"Maybe nothing, but if Tom's trying to figure out stuff about the authorship controversy, you'd think he would read books about the controversy rather than Shakespeare's actual plays and a biography. Though, I realize that evaluating the authorship controversy requires a thorough understanding of the Shakespearian canon."

"You sound like a professor in a Monty Python skit. I'll repeat my question," Ryder said. "What does it tell us?"

O'Neill pointed at the printout. "It says here that Stanley equals TH. TH is obviously Tom Hoffman, since it's William Stanley, the name on Tom's fake passport. And WS is BN. BN is possibly Bertram Newman."

"You are guessing."

"You can call it that, if you like."

"If you're right, these are not only code names, but the names the gang members use on fake passports?"

"I don't know about the names being used on their passports," O'Neill said. "Do you think Bertram Newman is traveling with a passport under the name of William Shakespeare?"

"Okay. That doesn't make sense."

"We're clear that Tom is associated with Bertram, maybe through this new business. What we don't know is whether Tom is involved in Bertram's disappearance. If he kidnapped Bertram, why bring it up with his sister? I asked him about it and my read was that he didn't know anything other than that Bertram had disappeared."

"He could be lying."

O'Neill nodded. "We'll have to figure out the other people. It says Marlow is DL and Oxford is probably PC."

"I'll have to get that list of Tom's close friends and associates from his sister," Ryder said. "Maybe we can identify DL, PC, and the ones with question marks on them."

"Tom's roommate's name is David something. I met him when Tom gave me a tour of his place. The roommate might work with him, since Mary said the roommate helped Tom get the job working for the investment board. I don't remember his last name, but Mary may know. Though it doesn't seem like she's close to her brother. She didn't even know that her best friend's sister was the love of Tom's life. She'll probably come back with a list of his friends from high school. At least ask Mary for the roommate's name."

Ryder leaned back, putting his feet on the desk. "There are seven aliases. What sort of plot would have seven people involved? If it were drug running, wouldn't there just be a contact at each end? Two at the most?"

"Suppose so. Maybe it relates to his work. I'll look at who he works with. It is odd, though, that Tom works with the SWIB while Bertram is with the DOA. Yet Tom said he works with Bertram. I wonder how their jobs intersect."

The two men sipped their beers.

"Where do we go from here?" Ryder asked. "We can follow Tom, but what if these initials don't lead anywhere? His sister is going to expect something out of this big production of yours."

"I'll try to figure out David's last name on the Internet. Maybe something unexpected will come through, or at least something related to Shakespeare or the Shakespeare authorship controversy."

"Or maybe not," Ryder suggested.

"Or maybe not. After all, Mary Hoffman was worried about her brother because of the fake passport, the fake IDs, the cash, and the access cards. The fake ID is long expired. My guess is he used the ID to sneak into bars before he turned twenty-one, but he kept it as a keepsake. The credit cards and video cards are also expired. The cash isn't all that much, four or five-hundred dollars. I'm thinking we need to determine Bertram and Tom's relationship and how it relates to them both getting into Shakespeare. The money, the passport, and the list will hopefully make sense when we understand Bertram and Tom's relationship. The list could be our Rosetta Stone for that. Then again, it could be some esoteric thing we can't imagine and has nothing to do with

Bertram's disappearance. Wouldn't it be funny if they were nicknames for playing Dungeons & Dragons or something?"

"Don't tell her that," Ryder said.

"Don't forget the key to the Annex building. Perhaps it means that Tom had routine meetings at the Annex or even with Bertram. There are only twenty or thirty people working in the building, including Bertram, so it makes you wonder. And what about Bertram's new arts-related *corporation*? The implication is that Tom is part of the business with Bertram and Rob Peacock."

"But there are no RP initials on the list." Ryder looked vacantly out the window. "Yet a plot doesn't make sense either. You certainly wouldn't need seven people in a plot to kidnap someone."

"I wouldn't involve more than two or three people to kidnap someone like Bertram. I realize he's a political player in Madison, but he doesn't have a security detail or a bodyguard. The guy bikes to work. I'll email Mary the picture of the sheet with the aliases. She can verify whether it's her brother's handwriting, and I'd like to find out the roommate's last name. Can you email the picture to me?"

Ryder nodded and turned his attention back to his computer. O'Neill spun in his office chair as he waited for the email to show in his inbox. Once it arrived, he emailed the photo to Mary and printed it before checking his voicemail. There was a double pulse on the phone, telling him there was a message. He typed in his access code S-E-A-M-U-S and a voice came on the line.

"*Detective* O'Neill," the voice said, "this is Johnson. Marlene Schultz, from Smoky Joe's Café, called. She said they have a cancelation for Friday night's show. She wants Schumacher's

Flour Mill to fill in. We haven't even practiced yet, so it would be a joke. She said the show is at eight. I was already figuring we would practice tomorrow afternoon. Well, anyway. It is a few minutes after twelve. She needs an answer by seven tonight or she'll pull in another band. Call me on my cell since I'm on the road."

"What was that about?" Ryder asked as O'Neill hung up.

"Got a gig playing at Smoky Joe's Café. That's the place I was in when I met with Mary and Tom Hoffman."

Ryder's eyebrows shot up. "Is that another coincidence?"

"No," O'Neill responded. "I know the coffee shop's manager, and we talked about it yesterday. They had a cancelation for Friday night, and she wants my band to play."

"*Your* band? You haven't had a band since you got kicked out of that last one. I remember because you were already working here. It was almost two years ago."

"Got a new one. Just a short-term thing. I thought it might be interesting to play at one of Tom's hangouts. Thought I might pick something up. I'm kind of going undercover."

"I'm not paying you to play your mind rot in a coffee shop."

"I'm not expecting you to pay for the show. Besides, the café will pay us for the gig."

"How much?"

"Don't know."

"You can bet it won't be much. Is it just you and The Johnson?"

"Me, The Johnson, Topper, and this girl fiddler."

"What are you doing still hanging out with Topper? He's a scumbag." Ryder paused and laughed. "Then again, I can understand why you hang around with him. I remember

Topper getting busted a few times. One time was just before I left the force. It must've been about, oh, '94."

"I don't wanna hear it," O'Neill said.

"Okay. All right. The Johnson is the big guy with the tattoos on his shoulders, right?"

O'Neill nodded and leaned back in his chair and dialed The Johnson's number. He remembered it for the second time in a row. The Johnson answered the phone with a grumble.

"Hear you got a call," O'Neill said.

"Yeah," The Johnson said. "Let me guess. You wanna take the job?"

"Course."

"Yeah, I figured you would."

"When on Friday is the gig?"

"Eight o'clock. My brother-in-law's niece will make practice since she's getting out of school for it. No idea if she can make the show. Yet we need to practice. Today still doesn't work since Kate and I are on the road. We just entered Cambridge. We'll be in Jefferson soon. Practice will have to be tomorrow."

"Let me know what time, and I'll fill Topper in."

"*I'll* call Topper since *I'm* the manager, and I won't have anything to do sitting in church while they go through the wedding rehearsal. Also, I'll talk to my sister and make sure the show works for our fiddler." He let out a loud sigh. "What we gonna play? You said I could pick two numbers. What else are we gonna do?"

"I'll figure out most of the set. Let your niece's cousin or whatever pick out two or three songs—up-tempo stuff. Country stuff is fine, but give her an idea of what songs Topper will know. He's the low bar, so it would be good if he was at least familiar with one of or both the numbers. We can probably play along with your songs. I'll come up with the rest, and I'll bring sheets if I think she'll need them. Should be simple stuff, though."

"You are coming up with most of the playlist yourself?"

"We gotta play stuff Topper can play, and I know what Topper knows and can handle."

"Got it."

"Send me an e-mail when things settle." O'Neill hung up. After opening a second beer, he called Mary Hoffman's cell phone and left a voicemail. She called back within minutes.

"Did the pictures come out?" Mary asked.

"Yeah. They're not perfect, but we got what we wanted. I want you to see them and to share our thoughts on what might be going on. I sent a photo of your brother's sheet with the names on it. Let me know if it's his handwriting."

"I'll try, but I'm not sure if I'll be able to tell, since Tom doesn't write letters." There was a long pause. "There might be a Christmas card. Yeah, I got a Christmas card from him last year, and I keep them for addresses and stuff."

"That should do. We don't need you to be one hundred percent certain. I'm just curious whether the list is in his handwriting or whether someone else gave it to him."

"I assumed it was his list. What makes you think it's someone else's?"

"It was just a thought." O'Neill rubbed his eyes. "Either way, I would like to show you the pictures and talk through them. Would tonight work, or would you prefer tomorrow?"

There was a pause. "Um, I'm checking my schedule. If we are going to meet tonight, it will have to be late."

"I've been in rock bands for most of my life. Staying out late isn't an issue for me."

"I'm at Emmy's soccer game. Once the game's over, I'll make them something to eat and settle them in with their homework. I could do it at nine. Tomorrow would be a possibility, though Lily has swimming. Let's do it tonight and get it done."

"Sure. Whatever you want."

"Do you know where Luigi's is?" she asked.

"King Street."

"Yeah. Let's meet there if it works for you. I forgot something at work, so that would give me the chance to pick it up. I'll see you at Luigi's at nine."

"Sounds good. I'll bring the pictures."

"I can't stay long, though. The girls need to go to bed since tonight's a school night."

"Okay," O'Neill said. "Wait, one more thing. Tom's roommate, David. What is his last name?"

"Leonard, I think."

"He works with Tom, right?"

"Yeah, he helped Tom get his job. Does it matter that they work together?"

"Maybe or maybe not," O'Neill said. "See you at Luigi's. Goodbye."

O'Neill hung up the phone, and Ryder's wide body rose from his chair.

"I found out the roommate's full name. It's David Leonard."

"That would work as our DL," Ryder said. "Interesting. Bring Bertram Newman up to Mary, but be careful. I don't want her to jump to the assumption that her brother is involved in a kidnapping plot. Explain to her that you don't need seven people to kidnap someone."

"Will do."

Chapter 11

O'Neill reviewed the Wisconsin Department of Administration's website, trying to find a work connection between Bertram Newman and Tom Hoffman. He also tried a variety of databases and general Internet searches through Yahoo!, Google, and AltaVista, expecting to find them both on a committee or to learn that the SWIB's web team also supported the DOA's web efforts. But twenty minutes of searching left him with nothing.

The focus of his searches shifted to Shakespeare. Earlier, O'Neill had found Bertram listed as a donor on American Players Theatre's most recent annual report. He pulled the list up again, but Tom Hoffman's name was absent from it. Two older American Players Theatre annual reports were available online, but neither listed Bertram nor Tom as donors.

While not Shakespeare related, O'Neill got general background information about Bertram on the Wisconsin Department of Administration's website, and found Bertram listed as Clean Freak LLC's registration agent. Finally, there were dozens of press releases from the Department of Administration which referenced grants provided to various counties and municipalities.

"What a waste of time," O'Neill said.

"I haven't found anything either, but the good news is we got a signed contract from Kathy Siler." Ryder buttoned the cuffs on his white shirt. "Yet she still worries me. My guess is she will nitpick us to death and expect us to explain every minute we put into the case. Getting money out of her won't be easy."

"Especially if we don't get results." O'Neill said, twisting his chair toward Ryder. "I don't understand why she is so impatient."

"She thinks someone kidnapped her father, and she knows that if he wasn't kidnapped, he might be dead. But *might* is the key word. All we can do is to try to make some sense of all this."

"I'm trying to verify a connection between Tom and Bertram either at work, with the new corporation, or through Shakespeare, but no luck. The two connect somehow, but I hope the connection doesn't imply that one of our clients is involved in the disappearance. Things could become uncomfortable. I mean, I don't think Tom kidnapped Bertram, but he may be intertwined with the disappearance."

"They know each other from work, but so what?" Ryder said, shaking his head. "Couldn't it be a coincidence that both Bertram and Tom are into Shakespeare?"

"Shakespeare hasn't come up in a single case we've worked on over two years, and suddenly he shows up in two. Can't be a coincidence. And remember that Rob Peacock, who also knows Tom, attended Shakespeare plays with Bertram and Linda Newman. Peacock mentioned they had shared interests. Odds are that all three of them are part of this corporation, and the business somehow relates to a dead playwright."

"Maybe Bertram is going to rebrand Clean Freak car washes as Shakespeare's car washes," Ryder said, laughing. "While you figure that out, we need to talk with Linda and Bertram's current financial advisor." Ryder went to his desk and paged through his notes. "Mike Gunderson is the financial guy. Kathy already gave us his contact information. We also need to talk with Detective Meyer."

"Can I meet with Meyer and go to the Annex again? I want to see Bertram's office, and I want to understand how he got out of the building without being seen."

"So do I," Ryder said, "but we need to split up. How about you meet with the wife and the finance guy while I meet with Detective Meyer and see if she can get me into the DOA building, though it may be a stretch to catch anyone this afternoon."

"Where does Linda Newman live?"

"Oh, shit. I forgot that my brilliant assistant doesn't have a driver's license." Ryder leaned back in his chair, stretching his arms in the air. "If I thought Kathy would pay for you to take a taxi to meet with her stepmother, I would send you. But there is no way, so we'll flip things. I will contact the wife and the finance guy while you touch base with Detective Meyer and go to the Annex. Maybe she'll take you through the building herself, but don't be surprised if she pushes you to DOA facilities management. You can take the bus to Wilson Street, right?"

"Course."

"Let me call Meyer." Ryder picked up the phone. "It's pushing seven thirty, but she may still be working. That's how shit goes when you're in charge of this type of investigation.

Would you want to meet with her tonight if she's got time? Or do you want to wait until tomorrow?"

"Tonight, if possible."

After a few minutes on hold, Meyer was on the line. Ryder nodded multiple times, asked questions, and finally agreed that O'Neill would check-in with Officer Jefferson at eight.

"Who is Officer Jefferson?" O'Neill asked after Ryder hung up the phone.

"She is assisting with the case and will meet with you tonight and take you to the Annex, which is only a three or four-minute walk from the MPD's Carroll Street office. Meyer is heading home. Does that work?"

"Would I be better off waiting until tomorrow so Meyer could walk me through the Annex?"

"Seamus, Meyer's working long days and she's busy as hell. Who knows her timeline for tomorrow? You're better off getting a walkthrough while you can. Besides, she is busy putting up with Kathy Siler's tantrums."

"Did Kathy's Detective Skyscraper line piss you off? She's not that tall."

"Detective Meyer?" Ryder asked. "She's got to be six four. She's a freaking giant."

"No way," O'Neill said. "I'd guess she's a hair over six two, which is the same as The Johnson. That is tall, but not *that* tall."

"Five bucks says she's at least six four."

"Sure, you're on." O'Neill shut down his computer for the night and checked his voicemail. There was a message from Mary Hoffman canceling their meeting at Luigi's. Mary claimed her daughter needed help to study for a test. She suggested they reschedule. After apologizing, she left a number for him to call. "Great." O'Neill hung up the phone. "Mary bailed on our meeting."

"Sorry."

"Nothing to be sorry about. I got more important things to deal with, like visiting a crime scene."

Chapter 12

O'Neill did not know when the bus was due, so he crossed the road and walked along Regent Street, passing the first bus stop. He glanced back every few minutes, and when he spotted a bus with "Capital Concourse" on its front display, he jogged to the next stop, arriving as the vehicle's doors flipped open. There were at least a dozen passengers, so he sat near the back, taking three nips of bourbon. A group of high school-aged boys sat nearby, and O'Neill did his best to ignore them as they punched each other's shoulders and talked about girls. He got off the bus at the Capitol Square and walked two blocks to the Madison Police Department's Central District office.

Police stations made O'Neill nervous. A day earlier, he and Ryder had met with Garcia and Meyer, but this time, he was alone. He took a gulp from his flask before scaling the concrete steps and entering the Madison Municipal Building. At the front desk, he asked for Officer Jefferson. The desk officer pointed to a chair. O'Neill sat, fidgeted, and looked vainly for something to read. Eventually, he leaned against a wall and perused press releases and announcements tacked to an MPD bulletin board.

"Mr. O'Neill," a woman's voice said.

He turned to his left and saw Detective Meyer approaching. *She is six four*, he thought, almost saying it aloud.

"Officer Jefferson wasn't feeling well and went home. I didn't realize she had left for the day when I told Mr. Ryder that she would meet with you." Her eyes darted about. "If you still want to tour the Administration Annex, I'll take you. The DOA gave us access and permission to enter. Can I assume Kathy Siler hired the Ryder Detective Agency to investigate her father's disappearance?"

"Yeah, she did. I want to look inside the building and talk about the case. Ryder said you were heading home, but if you can take me, that would be great."

"I am heading home, but I'll take you since it is on my way. We can talk as we walk."

"Are you sure?" O'Neill said. "You look burned out."

"I thought the same thing about you."

O'Neill chuckled and, as he looked up at her, he decided she was attractive. Her black hair was down, and she looked more relaxed than when she interviewed him. His gaze settled on her lips and stayed there too long.

"People say that about me," O'Neill said. "My boss tells people I either look drunk or hungover. I'm not drunk, so this must be my hungover look."

Meyer glanced backward. "Let me grab my bag so I can avoid stopping by the office again. If I come back, something will make me stay another hour. If you could wait two minutes, I'll be back."

"I'll be outside on the steps."

Meyer nodded, and he watched her walk away before trotting outside and sitting on the top step. The sun was setting behind his left shoulder, so he zipped his sweatshirt above his stomach and waited with his eyes closed. After a few minutes, Meyer touched his shoulder as she walked past. His eyes opened, and he popped up, catching her at the bottom of the steps.

"What do you want to know about this case?" she asked.

O'Neill picked up his pace, trying to stay even with the detective. "Anything you'll tell me. First off, what did you find out about Bertram Newman's gun?"

"There was no evidence of a break-in at his house, but the pistol is missing. The puzzling thing is that he kept the pistol unloaded in their bedroom next to a single magazine. The magazine is still there, and we accounted for the rest of the ammunition. It doesn't make sense for a robber to take a firearm without taking the magazine sitting with it. Unless Bertram had ammo his wife wasn't aware of, he appears to have taken an unloaded pistol to work."

"That's odd. Did he stop anywhere on the way to the Annex?"

"We don't think so. Linda knew when he left because he stayed to listen to the end of the Channel 15 weather forecast, and we know what time he came into the building. If he stopped somewhere, it was along his route and didn't take long."

"How did he get to work?"

"He biked, as unlikely as that sounds." Meyer paused at the light at Wilson Street and adjusted the large bag hanging over her right shoulder. A pair of motorcycles stopped near the crosswalk. Both drivers wore Harley-Davidson gear but drove Hondas. "He lives in the Rocky Bluff area, which is about a four-mile trip from here."

"He biked in with an unloaded gun and a laptop. Are you talking bicycle or motorcycle?"

"Bicycle."

"Did the cameras record him as he came into the building that morning?"

Meyer nodded as they walked along the crosswalk. "Bertram used his key card to enter at around seven forty-five. The front entrance camera shows him wearing the backpack. Both his wife and daughter identified it as his backpack. Linda said he would put his laptop into the pack when he biked to the office rather than using a laptop bag."

"When is he seen on that day?"

"As I recall, he had a ten o'clock meeting in his office with two men from the City of Beaver Dam. I don't remember their names, but their stories are consistent and they left together. DOA records show he was reviewing online budget documents and going through email the rest of the morning. He saved a draft contract with the City of Manitowoc at eleven twenty and made a call before noon, checking if Michelle Hendricks, who is the Executive Assistant at the Department of Administration, had returned from a meeting. He didn't call Michelle, but instead a woman who works for her. Do you know what an executive assistant position is within state service?"

"A secretary?" O'Neill said.

"The executive assistant is an agency's third highest ranking officer."

"So this Michelle Hendricks is a big shot? A bigger shot than Bertram."

"Yes. Bertram asked whether Michelle was back from a meeting. This lady said Bertram did not ask to talk to her boss, but just wanted to know if the meeting was over."

"Where was this meeting? And where was this woman's office?"

"In a large conference room in the DOA building next to the Annex." Meyer paused and pointed past the construction, which dominated the block, and toward the Wisconsin Administration Building, which towered above a neighborhood apartment complex. "Michelle's office is also in the DOA building. There is no record of Bertram calling again or sending anyone an email. From there, he disappears, as there is no internet or phone activity and no video evidence of him leaving the Annex. Yet, as you illustrated, someone could exit without being on camera if they left via the loading dock and walked along the building's perimeter."

"But didn't you say the camera from the other DOA building picked me up as I walked along the side of the Annex?"

"Yes, it did. But let's wait until we cross Pinckney Street and I'll try to lay it out for you."

O'Neill nodded, and as they walked, his eyes lined up with her chin. She tilted her head toward him, and he looked away.

"Let's stay on this side of Wilson," she said as they stopped on the corner.

O'Neill looked up at the Wisconsin Administration Building, guessing it was ten stories high. A sign for the sand-colored brick building faced Wilson Street. Beside the building was its neighbor, the four-story Administration Annex.

"The Administration Building obviously has cameras at its front entrance," Meyer said, pointing across the road. "There are also two entrances on the side facing the Annex, and their cameras aim toward the street we are walking along. However, one of the side entry cameras picks up part of the alley between the buildings and the side of the Annex. This camera would pick up someone exiting through the docks and going toward Wilson Street. But someone leaving through the docks and going the opposite direction, away from Wilson Street and toward the back parking lot, would not be picked up on the camera."

"So Bertram could have left the building without being seen."

"Yep." Meyer paused as they arrived across the street from the alley that split the two buildings.

From across the street, O'Neill examined the side entrance to the Administration Building and the awning he had stood under on Tuesday morning. The alley between the buildings was wide enough to fit two directions of traffic, which allowed vehicles to turn and pull into the Annex's dock. Even from across the road, he could see a camera sitting above the dock's gray door. A regular-size door sat beside the larger entrance.

"Who else was in the meeting with this Hendricks woman?" O'Neill asked.

"I'm sure we got the list, but I have not seen it. What are you thinking?"

"Maybe Bertram didn't really care about this Hendricks woman, but was wondering whether someone else that had been in the meeting was free. Maybe he wanted to talk to someone who was at that meeting, yet he didn't want that person to know he was coming."

"It is worth looking into." Meyer pulled out a notepad and pen and, after making a few scribbles, returned them to her bag. "I'll email tonight and get a listing."

"Sounds good. Did you search the building for Bertram's body?"

"Yes, we searched the Annex on Tuesday, and early this morning, we brought a K-9 named Shirley into the building, gave her a whiff of Bertram's dirty socks, and let her go. Shirley found Bertram's office right away, but that didn't help. Her trainer was confident that Bertram was not in the building."

O'Neill wished he had a beer in his hand, but settled for rubbing his hands together. "To me, there are two possibilities. One, Bertram slipped out on his own, avoiding the camera by leaving via that door and walking away from the street, going around back like you said."

"Sure, but why?"

"Assuming we're talking motive for him disappearing," O'Neill said, "odds are lust or money. If it's lust, his wife is having an affair or he's having an affair. If it's money, then it relates to his finances or to this new business he's involved in. This arts business that relates to Shakespeare."

Detective Meyer turned toward him. "How did you hear about that?" she asked, bending down so they were nearly eye-to-eye.

O'Neill was going to answer, but closed his mouth since he was unsure of what he could talk about and what he couldn't.

"Listen," Meyer said, "I'm laying everything out here for you because Garcia says you are legit and, even though you're a vagabond, you have a detective's mind."

"Garcia called me a vagabond?"

"My word, not his." She continued to stare at him. "Are you going to tell me or not? Remember, I'm taking you into the Annex as a courtesy."

"I could get in without you," O'Neill said, knowing he had Tom Hoffman's access card. But he wanted her with him, so he shifted gears. "Okay, sorry. Bertram's daughter mentioned he was involved in a new business that relates to the arts, and she said he recently got into Shakespeare. Also, there was chatter pointing specifically to Shakespeare."

"Chatter?"

"Me making inferences," he said, pleased at the statement, since it was truthful but didn't mention Tom Hoffman's list. "I was checking if you would verify my idea, and you did."

She rolled her eyes and started across Wilson Street, pausing as a blue subcompact drove past.

"What is Bertram's business?" O'Neill said, as he caught up with her.

"As I understand it, Bertram is part owner of a business that purchases and invests in historic books and artifacts relating to William Shakespeare. The business is called Shakespeare's Company."

"Interesting. Is Rob Peacock involved in that business, too?"

"Yes. How do you know about him?"

"Kathy Siler mentioned that Rob was a close friend of Bertram's and was into Shakespeare. She said he used to be Bertram's financial manager before this current guy."

"Mike Gunderson."

"Yeah. Ryder and I talked with Rob and he admitted to being part of Bertram's corporation but wouldn't give us details. He said he couldn't tell us anything until Friday."

"There is some sort of agreement the investors signed which prohibits them from talking about the business with third parties until the business completes some partnership agreement. Shakespeare's Company's lawyer says this prohibition on discussing the company does not apply to law enforcement, so I'm meeting with a few of the investors tomorrow and expect to find out more about the business."

After crossing the road, they paused on the sidewalk in front of the alley. Meyer pointed at the camera above the dock at the Annex and the camera above the entrance to the main DOA building. Then they continued toward the front entrance.

"Getting back to the disappearance," Meyer said, "We talked about Bertram sneaking out of the building as one of two possibilities. What do you think is the other possibility?"

"Someone killed or incapacitated him in his office."

"That's what we initially assumed and was why we were interested in you. There are eighteen people with offices in the building and cameras record thirty-four people entering the building on Tuesday, of which twenty-three were in the building at or after noon if I remember correctly. You were the only one that wasn't identified."

"You put me on Crime Stoppers based on that?"

"The man who saw you in the shower area said you looked suspicious. I think 'shady-looking punk' was his exact description. Kathy Siler was pushing me to put the video out, and she was leaning on my boss to move the case to someone with more experience. I pulled in a favor with a friend of mine to put the footage of you on Crime Stoppers. Poor decision on my part to use up a favor."

Meyer and O'Neill stopped talking as a pair of suit-clad businessmen walked toward them. She then turned onto a short concrete entryway to the Annex, and O'Neill followed. While the building's facade was twenty feet from the sidewalk, the entrance recessed another twenty feet, so the path turned ninety degrees and led to the front door.

"I saw you trying to get inside both buildings on camera," Meyer said. "You looked mad when your access card didn't work on the Administration Building."

"It surprised me. The card related to a separate case, and the guy who had it works in the main DOA building, so I thought it would access that building and not the Annex. It was pouring rain and I wanted inside."

O'Neill looked above the doorway but didn't see a camera. Meyer apparently figured out what he was looking for, so she pointed to a camera in the corner adjacent to a floodlight. The camera was aimed slightly to one side since it didn't need to record the wall on one side of the entrance. O'Neill stepped forward, leaned against the brick wall, and reached.

"I can't touch the camera," O'Neill said. "Can you reach it?"

Meyer's brown eyes flashed, and her lips pushed together tight.

"Sorry, didn't mean anything," O'Neill said. "I'm trying to figure out whether someone could change the camera's direction on their own. I've seen it done to other cameras."

The detective sighed, then reached up. "I can touch it when on my tiptoes, but I can't get a grip to see if it will move."

"Let's try the camel approach," O'Neill said, as he got on all fours below the camera. "Try to keep your feet at or below my belt."

Meyer stepped back and looked at him. "This is the camel approach, huh? This isn't how they teach us to do it at the academy." After taking her shoes off, she put her left foot on his back at his waist, grabbed the side wall, and lifted the other leg. She pulled and twisted the camera. "Doesn't budge," she said, stepping down. "That's what you expect."

"Yeah, but it's not always what you get. Just wanted to make sure someone couldn't move the camera to the side. I was thinking, if you adjusted the angle, you could exit without being on camera. When people fast forward video footage, they might not pick up a change in angle. But you couldn't move it, so that cuts out that possibility, at least with this camera. And the one outside the dock is too high to reach without a ladder or something. How about the other side of the building? There is an exit with a camera there, too, right?"

"The building juts out like this entrance, but there is an awning, so it sits much lower than this one. See for yourself."

O'Neill looked at Meyer and then at the lawn between the walkway and a separate concrete walkway that went from Wilson Street to the side entrance. Beyond the path was another building that was boarded up for remodeling. O'Neill glanced at Meyer once more before jogging across the grass toward the other sidewalk path. He found the side camera, which was set lower. After verifying it wouldn't move, he returned to Meyer, who was looking at a notepad.

"Anything interesting?" she asked.

"Nope. That camera is secure. Did you get any footage from the building on the other side of the Annex? I would think that a building under construction would have cameras running."

"We got footage, but nothing worthwhile. The plywood behind the fence goes up a good twelve feet, so the cameras don't pick up activity outside their property."

"Bummer," O'Neill said. "Getting back to the Annex. Do the windows open?"

"They lock the windows on the first two floors. DOA buildings and grounds staff can open them for cleaning, but that requires a unique key."

"Is there underground access between the buildings?"

"No. The state rents rather than owns the Annex. The buildings don't connect."

O'Neill nodded, and Meyer set an access card against the card reader. The door "thumped" as it unlocked. She pulled the door open, and he followed her inside. The building looked more like a storage facility than an office building. Dim lighting illuminated a six-foot counter in the foyer. Contacts and offices were listed on a whiteboard that stood behind the chair. A single elevator sat on one side of the counter.

"There are no internal cameras." Meyer stopped in front of the elevator. "The only cameras are outside the two pedestrian entryways and coming out at the loading dock. What is it you want to see?"

O'Neill was watching her lips and was not listening.

"What is it you want to see?" she repeated.

"Bertram's office, if that is where you place him last."

Meyer hit the elevator button, and they waited until the bell rang. The doors flipped open, revealing long padded covers on three sides of the elevator. The pads stunk of dirt and sweat. They stepped inside, avoiding touching the pads.

"The Annex is a small office building," Meyer said as they exited on the second floor. "DOA uses it as much for storage as for offices. The first floor doesn't have a single office, except for the lottery operations manager and the mail clerk at the loading dock. Bertram's office is room 209. In case you're wondering, the room showed no signs of a struggle. We already dusted it, which was probably worthless."

They walked down the hallway and past several closed doors. Meyer pointed at room 209 and stuck a metal key into the lock. She pulled the door open with the key inside the lock.

"Small office," O'Neill said, stepping inside. The lights flicked on automatically, and the door to room 209 closed behind them. "What is this, nine-by-twelve?"

She nodded her agreement. "At least he has a private office."

O'Neill peered out the window, which looked out at the Wisconsin Administration Building. "I expected more since he's a big shot. Even the view sucks."

"Bertram is in a lower-level, politically appointed position, and governmental offices are rarely thrilling or exotic."

"Guess I didn't know what to expect." He pointed at the door. "Does the door lock on its own?"

"Yes. The door closes automatically and was locked when we first entered on Tuesday." She touched the doorknob. "I could lock or unlock it from the inside by flipping the turn button. It's a standard office door."

"Bertram locked it when he left the room for the last time?"

"I'm pretty sure we found it locked. I could verify that if it matters. What are you thinking?"

"Bertram's pistol and his computer are missing, but how about his backpack?" O'Neill asked.

"The backpack was here in his office, but is in evidence now."

"What was in the backpack?"

"Mundane stuff, as I recall. There was a calculator, pens, a notebook, cords, a container of white-out, and his cell phone. He didn't make any calls on Tuesday."

"No Dictaphone?"

"We have not found the Dictaphone, so he must have taken it with him. Linda said it connects to his laptop, so it may still be connected."

"Either someone came in here and took Bertram's gun and his laptop, or Bertram left his office to meet someone, taking the gun and the laptop. That is an odd pair, so he couldn't have been going far. He certainly would not take his bike since it would be easy to drop the computer. Either he was going somewhere on foot, or a taxi or someone he knew picked him up."

"I agree, but there are ten thousand people working within walking distance of here. How does that help?"

"It is greed or lust, right?" O'Neill suggested. "Bertram and his wife, Linda, own a condo on West Washington Avenue. Is that within a walking distance of here?"

"Yeah."

"Have you checked it out?"

"A patrol officer checked it yesterday," Meyer said as she sat on the desk. The bag that hung on her shoulder slid onto her leg. "Bertram wasn't hiding out there. Fortunately, the condo has electronic keys for entering the building which, unlike the state office buildings, are identifiable by individual. And neither Bertram nor Linda's keys were used on or since Tuesday. We are working with the management company on reviewing camera activity, but I don't think that's final." She rubbed her eyes. "I should have checked it out myself."

"Wait until tomorrow. How many hours have you worked today?"

She smiled. "I got to work at seven yesterday morning and have been going straight, except for an hour nap. That's like thirty-seven hours. I'm getting batty."

"Holy crap. Going to the condo now won't accomplish anything. Remember, lust is only one possibility. The other thing is greed, which brings me to Shakespeare's Company. The business invests in Shakespeare books and artifacts, right? What else do you know about it?"

"There are half a dozen investors, including Bertram. The corporation was founded a few weeks ago with Bertram as the president and Peter Couturier as vice president. A few of the investors are bureaucrats who work for the state. Couturier is a local art dealer, then Rob Peacock and a few others."

"Is Tom Hoffman one of the bureaucrats?"

"The name rings a bell, but I'm not sure. Perhaps he's an investor I'm interviewing tomorrow. Why are you convinced it relates to this Shakespeare business rather than Bertram's other business or his work with the state?"

"Bertram disappearing just as this company starts is too much of a coincidence. Also, I have a listing of people with code names for people involved in this Shakespeare business. I wish I could access my email so I could show you."

"Code names?"

"Yeah," he replied, deciding there was no longer a reason to hide the list since Tom Hoffman was on the City of Madison Police Department's radar. "This listing shows code names and then initials. One of them is BN, presumably Bertram Newman."

"You could dial in here," she said. "I can hook my laptop into the data line here. Do you want me to hook it up?"

O'Neill contemplated sharing Tom's list with a Madison Police Department detective. Meyer knew the names of most of the investors in Shakespeare's Company. Having her review the initials on the list might clarify the list's purpose. But it was also a risk.

"What do you think?" she asked.

"This might get me fired, but that's life. Go for it."

Chapter 13

Meyer pulled the laptop from her bag and attached a cord. Powered by an apparent adrenaline surge, the detective's eyes no longer looked heavy as she leaned the bag against the wall.

"Sorry about this," O'Neill said. "I was just telling you to go home and sleep, and now I'm asking you to let me use your laptop."

Meyer waved off his concerns and dropped to the floor. She paused, found a flashlight, and returned to the ground.

"What are you doing?" O'Neill said as he watched her backside contort under the desk.

"Finding the data jack. There we go." Her head popped back up.

"You're pretty nimble down there."

Meyer flashed a disapproving look, then set the laptop on Bertram's desk. She was on one knee, and O'Neill stood beside her as the computer booted. Once Windows loaded, Meyer opened Internet Explorer and the City of Madison Police Department's home page came on screen. She turned the display toward O'Neill, who navigated to Yahoo!, and entered his email address and password.

"Your name is your password," she said. "That is lame."

"Yeah, but no one can spell my name."

O'Neill ignored two new emails from Ryder and found the email he sent Mary Hoffman. He opened the message and clicked on the attachment. The photo popped open, and Meyer leaned closer.

"This is what I was referring to," O'Neill said. "I think it's a list of people with code names. 'WS=BN' means that Bertram Newman's code is William Shakespeare. 'Stanley=TH' means that Stanley is Tom Hoffman's alias. DL is Tom's roommate, David Leonard, so he is Marlowe."

"Okay, and PC is Peter Couturier. So you think they are using historical figures involved with Shakespeare to set codes for the investors? Is this something Kathy Siler gave you?"

"The aliases are not just historical figures involved with Shakespeare, they are people who some Shakespearian scholars think may have written Shakespeare's plays and poems."

"Never would have guessed you as a Shakespeare guy," Meyer said, glancing at him. "I have, however, heard the theory about someone else writing Shakespeare's plays. What about the other four names that have questions marks?"

"One is Rob Peacock. Are there three other investors?"

"Let me call up a list of shareholders and, if you're right, we can determine who these people are. But whose list is this and why were they trying to figure out who the investors were?"

"The list came from Tom Hoffman. It looks like he was trying to figure out who all the investors were. I'm not sure why he did that."

Meyer pulled a notepad and a pencil from her bag. "This won't print, so we'll have to write things down. Bertram has a printer, but it connects to his computer, and I don't want to unplug it and get some DOA techie complaining to my boss. Write the names, I'll call up the list of shareholders, and we'll see if we can connect the rest of the code names with individuals."

O'Neill wrote the listing, then Meyer logged him out, returned to the MPD homepage, and logged into her email account. Within a few minutes, she had a listing of the investors and their addresses. O'Neill wrote Bertram Newman and his address and phone number.

"Can you read what you are writing?" Meyer said, looking at O'Neill's handwritten list.

"My penmanship sucks, but I can read it."

"Well, I can't. Give me that." Her shoulders brushed against O'Neill's. "Let me write so we can both read the names." Once done, she made a photocopy using Bertram's copier.

"The numbers add up and having the addresses is helpful," O'Neill said, looking over the list. He leaned toward her, noticing that her hair smelled fresh despite thirty plus hours of work. "Bertram is BN, David Leonard is DL, and Tom Hoffman is TH. I will throw out the guess that Lulu Hanrahan is Elizabeth. That's an assumption since she's the only woman and Elizabeth is the only female code name. Peter Couturier is Oxford. That just leaves Rob Peacock and Steven McCormick. They have to be Raleigh and Bacon."

"Does it matter which is which?"

"Probably not, but having the addresses is key. These are home addresses, right? Work addresses for those who aren't retired might be more important since Bertram disappeared during a workday. I want to find out which of these six people were within walking distance of the DOA Annex on the day Bertram disappeared. Since you're writing, I'll go to the state employee directory and look them up. The art dealer won't be on there, but we can figure out where his office is."

O'Neill navigated to the State of Wisconsin employee directory, entering names one-by-one. They found work addresses for everyone but Steven McCormick, though there were two people named David Leonard. Meyer wrote both the addresses.

"This won't exclude too many people," O'Neill said. "Most work in the main DOA building. One of the David Leonards has an office in the Annex, so that probably is our David. Lulu Hanrahan works at the Department of Transportation. That likely excludes her. And Steven McCormick works for the Department of Natural Resources. And he's in Green Bay."

"I think you have the wrong Steven McCormick," Meyer said. "Steven's a lawyer in private practice who represents the business. His office is on the west side of Madison. I met with him earlier today."

"That means we got seven suspects, unless we find out Lulu Hanrahan was at the meeting that Bertram called about. We have the art dealer, Peter Couturier; Tom Hoffman and David Leonard from DOA; the two finance guys, Rob Peacock and Mike Gunderson; and finally, Linda and Bertram Newman."

"You're excluding Steven McCormick and Lulu Hanrahan because their homes and offices are too far away?"

"Yeah. Though we should verify their alibis. Maybe Lulu was at the DOA Administration Building for the same meeting that Bertram called about. If so, she becomes a suspect."

"Tomorrow, I'll let you know who was at that meeting."

"Thanks," O'Neill said while reviewing the listing. "Hey, I bet you McCormick is Bacon. You said McCormick is a lawyer. Bacon was also a lawyer."

"Fine. Yet, going to your suspects, I would exclude Mike Gunderson. His office is close to here, but he was at a conference in Milwaukee on Tuesday. We verified that."

"Good to know. Then we have six suspects. I'm including Bertram, keeping the possibility he disappeared on purpose. Of these, I've met three: Tom Hoffman, David Leonard, and Rob Peacock. Kathy Siler mentioned Rob, so Ryder and I met with him earlier today. Nice old guy. The other two are roommates. They were kind of coincidentally related to another case."

"Other case?"

"Kind of hard to explain. I used to date Tom's sister, Mary, and I met Tom and his roommate, David Leonard, through her. Hopefully, I'll meet the rest of the crew as well, especially Bertram."

"I have met all six except Tom and Bertram," Meyer said wearily. "I'm going to shut down unless you have something else. It's pushing nine, and I'm tired and starving."

O'Neill watched Meyer's hair slide in front of her eyes, and she knocked it away as she shut down her computer. "I got an idea," he said. "How about going to eat at Luigi's down on the corner of Main and King Street? I was keyed up for Italian food and a glass of wine, but I got stood up. Why not go with me? We could talk about the case if we want to. Or we could forget about the case and just enjoy dinner."

Meyer laughed, almost to herself, and her eyes didn't look as weary. "I should go home and go to bed. As soon as I wake up, I'll shower and go back to the station."

"What will you do at home for food? My guess is you'll heat a frozen pizza or make tomato soup or something, right? Why not eat some quality food and help me out as well? The restaurant is only a few blocks away, and it won't take any more time than eating at home."

"Why not?" Meyer said, almost to herself. She closed her eyes. "Luigi's has an Italian beef sandwich that is fantastic, and I often have leftovers since they also give you bruschetta. They also have a wonderful veggie pizza. That also sounds good." Her eyes opened, and she smiled.

"Sounds delicious."

Meyer pulled her bag over her shoulder. "Just don't get any ideas."

Too late for that, O'Neill thought.

Chapter 14

Meyer closed Bertram Newman's office door, and O'Neill verified it was locked by shaking the handle. Rather than taking the elevator, Meyer started down the stairs and O'Neill followed. The staircase walls were dirty, giving them an off-white appearance.

"Does your key get you into all the rooms in this building, or is it only a key to Bertram's office?"

"The latter," Meyer said. "Why?"

"I was thinking about the Leonard guy with an office in the building. But we can deal with that tomorrow since you are going to interview the investors."

"We already have met with the investors, but we are meeting with them again to verify their whereabouts from noon to three o'clock on Tuesday."

"Ryder is planning to catch Mike Gunderson and Bertram's wife tomorrow."

"I have a meeting with Linda Newman at nine tomorrow morning at her residence, followed by a ten thirty with Mike Gunderson at his office. You or Ryder could join me for Linda's interviews and for the others. There will also be meetings with Peter Couturier, Rob Peacock, the IT guy, and David Leonard, but I don't think the times are firm. Including

Linda, that's five of the six suspects we talked about. Penny is meeting with Lulu Hanrahan and has a second meeting with Steven McCormick."

"What do you know about McCormick?"

"McCormick is the lawyer who filed the paperwork to incorporate Shakespeare's Company LLC, and he's a minor investor. I met with him briefly to get information on the business, but I have follow-up questions, which is why Officer Jefferson is meeting with him. As to the others, Hanrahan is an engineer working for the Department of Transportation, while Leonard and Hoffman are small investors, but also the only compensated employees of Shakespeare's Company. Leonard is also an accountant for the Department of Administration. The lawyer and the accountant are key to getting an understanding of this Shakespeare business, so I want to meet with them regardless of whether they are suspects."

"Makes sense. I'll let Ryder join you for Linda's interview, and he may still want to meet with Mike Gunderson. Can I join you for the meetings with Couturier and Leonard?"

"Sure. When the details are set, I'll pop you an email. You don't want to attend Mike Gunderson's interview?"

"The logistics don't work." O'Neill did not want to wake up early and didn't want to spend all his time in meetings. "Is your boss okay with including us in these meetings?"

"I normally wouldn't suggest it," Meyer said as they exited the building. "But Garcia cleared you as observers, and he's Investigative Services. I shouldn't say this, but we tend to defer to them, so I don't think my captain will give me pushback. But remember, you are an observer and not the interviewer. You don't ask questions."

O'Neill struggled to keep pace as they crossed Wilson Street and cut through an alley leading to King Street. He looked straight ahead as they passed under the Great Dane brew pub sign and noticed a poster for *Shakespeare in Love* on the coming soon window at the Majestic Theater.

"Maybe that is a clue?" O'Neill pointed at the poster.

Meyer laughed and looked up as they walked under the marquee, which said "WORK IN PROGRESS" though several letters had fallen off. The theater had been closed for remodeling, and the fallen letters made its reopening seem doubtful. A couple wearing in-line skates and pulling a toddler in a red wagon cut in front of them, pausing at the intersection. O'Neill and Meyer waited behind them.

"What woman stood you up?" Meyer said, breaking the silence. "Was it business or a date?"

He took a moment to reply. "Business. It was Tom Hoffman's sister, the one I mentioned I used to date."

"That could be uncomfortable. When did you date her?"

"Long time ago. I was eighteen, I think."

The light turned, and they crossed the street. O'Neill stopped at what appeared to be the restaurant's front entrance, but Meyer continued walking. He noticed an arrow on the door's window which directed customers around the corner, so he rushed after her, passing the historical marker on the building's side. He caught up as she entered the restaurant through the side door.

A bar counter was to their left, manned by two bartenders and lined with ten patron-filled stools. The bartenders looked up at Meyer as a Dave Matthews Band song played in the background. O'Neill's eyes were drawn to the building's tin ceiling, and though he had been inside before, he had forgotten the pattern.

Meyer waited by the entrance, so he stayed behind her, glancing at the taps. He considered going to the counter for a beer, but the host arrived, so they followed her into the primary dining area. The tables were close together, allowing the room to fit twenty or twenty-five customers. A mural decorated the doorway, and O'Neill ran his hands along the woodwork outside the bathroom.

"Looks like we don't need reservations," O'Neill said after they sat at the table.

"Not this late." Meyer handed him one of the two menus.

"Makes sense, Detective Meyer. By the way, what is your first name?"

She licked her lips before answering. "Erin."

"I like it. Can I call you Erin?"

"You can, but only when we're here. When I'm working, you can call me Detective or Detective Meyer."

"You can call me Seamus, here or anywhere," he said, glancing at the menu. "Where's the tap listing?"

"I thought you had a taste for wine."

O'Neill smiled. "Yes, I do. Thanks for reminding me. Any wine suggestions?"

"Not really. My mom drinks Chianti or Zinfandel with Italian food, but they don't have either here by the glass, so I'll have a house red, since it's cheap."

"A woman after my heart. Or we could split a bottle."

"I would fall asleep if I split a bottle of wine. One glass of cheap wine is all I want tonight." She yawned, as if the topic reminded her of how tired she was.

A blonde-haired female server arrived with water and a notepad. O'Neill and Meyer ordered glasses of the house red. The server was back within a minute, toting their wine. The pair smelled the drinks, clicked the glasses together, and took a sip.

O'Neill looked upward. "I love buildings with tin ceilings."

"That is a line I have never heard from a guy."

"They built this place in the eighteen hundreds. The sandstone makes me think the original construction is older than eighteen ninety. They have a historical marker outside, but I forget what it says, other than that the building is in the Italianate style." He paused, sensing she was not interested in talking about architecture or tin ceilings. "So, where are you from, Erin Meyer?"

"Illinois. Decatur, to be more precise."

"I played Decatur once, I think. Back in the early nineties."

"In what sport?"

He smiled. "I played *a show* in Decatur once."

"Oh, I forgot. You're a musician."

"How did you get from Decatur, Illinois, to Madison, Wisconsin?"

"After graduating from the University of Illinois, I worked two years as a patrol officer for the University of Illinois Police in Champaign. The job was okay, but I wanted to move away from my home campus, so I applied for a job with the Madison Police Department as a patrol officer in the West District. That was in the summer of '93."

"How long have you been a detective?"

"It will be nine months at the end of May." She took a drink of her wine. "It has been a long nine months."

"You miss being a regular cop?"

"Yes, and no. I miss knowing what's expected of me and being empowered to make decisions. And I miss the immediate feedback I'd get when helping people in a car accident, or when someone had something stolen, or even when there was a fight. The job is about problem solving while keeping an even keel. Being a detective is different. Usually, I'm following up on things for the lead detective in a case, or I'm taking statements or collating files. There's cat herding, question asking, and database wringing. There are growing pains and I sometimes struggle to understand what my boss is looking for from me. Obviously, there is problem solving, but most of it is about people, relationships, and documentation." Wine swirled gently within her glass. "How about you? How did you get to Madison?"

"Born at St. Mary's Hospital here in town. My parents lived in a house in the suburbs, but we moved to an apartment in Madison after my mom died. I was out on my own soon after that, playing music."

The server interrupted them, leaving a plate of bruschetta and asking if they had questions or were ready to order. O'Neill scanned the menu, focusing on the price. Meyer ordered roasted vegetable pizza, and he seconded the order when he saw it was six dollars and fifty-nine cents.

"Sorry about your mom," Meyer said after the server left. "How did you start working for a detective agency?"

"Ryder was at the Regent Street Retreat asking the bartender for contact information on someone. I said I'd get it for him if he bought me a beer. Things progressed from there, I guess."

Meyer chuckled and shook her head slowly. "What other jobs have you had?"

"Never had another job besides playing in a rock band."

"You are kidding me."

"No. I filed taxes this year for the first time."

"How old are you, if you don't mind me asking?"

"Thirty-three" He tried to not look at her lips, which reddened with every sip of wine. "How about yourself?"

"I turned thirty-one earlier this month."

"Well, happy belated." He clicked his wine glass against hers and took a drink. "I take it you're single, correct?"

"Yep, and not looking."

O'Neill took a piece of bruschetta and rubbed it into olive oil. "Ever been married?"

"No, but I was engaged," Meyer said in a quiet voice. "Didn't go through with it and don't want to talk about it."

"Okay, let's talk about the case."

Meyer nodded her approval.

"Do you think Bertram was having an affair, or could Linda be having an affair?" O'Neill asked.

Meyer took a bite of bruschetta before answering. "No. The daughter, Kathy Siler, is quite the prize. She doesn't strike me as the type that would hold back, and she clearly doesn't like her stepmother, yet she doesn't shove her under the bus. She doesn't like me much, either."

"I noticed. Why doesn't she like you?"

"Kathy knows I'm new, and she's convinced someone kidnapped her father because she can't imagine him leaving on his own. She expects the MPD to assign Columbo to her case just because her father is a semi-prominent businessman with political connections. She's pushing my captain to reassign the case to a more senior detective or someone with experience in disappearances, which I don't have. I'm lucky, or perhaps unlucky, that no one is free now, as my captain would assign it to someone else if anyone was available."

"You're doing fine."

"But leading this type of investigation is new for me. I assist another detective on most cases and I want more responsibility, but it is exhausting, especially since I don't have another detective supporting me. Penny helps, of course. Penny is Officer Jefferson. But I don't have the same opportunity to talk about the case that I had when assisting."

"It's good to have a sounding board."

Meyer nodded her agreement.

"It seems this case is about greed and not lust," O'Neill said. "I mean, why did Bertram bring his laptop and the gun to work and then take them to wherever he was going without unplugging the Dictaphone? He wasn't going to bring them to a rendezvous with some woman at his condo or in a hotel. Even if he had pictures or something that he wanted to confront someone with, he could send them via mail, email, or whatever. My guess is he was researching something or he was sneaking out to confront someone with something on the laptop. How far are your people in finding out what Internet activity he had on his personal computer?"

"Bertram was using the laptop for work related to his business, Clean Freak, and his new business, Shakespeare's Company. He approved bank activity on the computer as well."

"I'm assuming his cell phone company and his internet provider have granted you access. Did he use the laptop on the day he disappeared?"

"We got access from Chorus Networks a few hours ago, and that was one of the first things we checked. He logged in on their network using the laptop shortly after twelve on Tuesday, but not since. Our techs are working through his activity. That's one reason I headed out to get shuteye. They want four to six hours to analyze things, and I wouldn't be able to stay awake for another six hours. I should have a better picture of things in the morning. And by morning, I mean no later than five."

"It will be interesting to see what you learn. Unless he's involved in something that we haven't picked up on, his disappearance relates to Shakespeare's Company."

"That is a reasonable assumption," Meyer said. "But, like we were saying, it is nice to talk this stuff through. It helps to firm up the line of inquiry and determine the next steps. I agree everyone involved in Shakespeare's Company is a suspect, especially if their home or office is within walking distance of the annex. If we can figure out a specific motive, we have a tight group of primary suspects. As you said, there is Linda, Bertram, and the four from Shakespeare's Company LLC."

"Rob Peacock mentioned something about competitors. He said that's why the investors can't talk about the business with people like me. Investigating the competitors doesn't seem like fertile territory, but I don't know enough about it. Could a competitor somehow be involved in Bertram's disappearance? A business or individual competing with Shakespeare's Company?"

Meyer smiled and tilted her head to the side. "Anything is possible, but these are just rival art collectors or Shakespeare geeks who want to be involved in a specific purchase. These investors think there is money to be made from owning Shakespeare paraphernalia, but mostly, they are obsessive nuts who want to own something they love. There is nothing to suggest that these rivals are so obsessed that they would kidnap or harm anyone. Bertram and Peter Couturier were worried that one of these competitors would take their spot in the joint venture, but I don't think the stakes are that high."

"And killing someone involves pretty high stakes."

She paused, leaned closer to him, and spoke in a whisper. "You think he's dead?"

O'Neill finished his wine. "If he confronted someone soon after noon, the person he confronted either knocked Bertram out or killed him. This likely occurred at the attacker's office and, other than the art dealer, these are people sitting in government office buildings. The killer couldn't just tie someone up and sneak the body out. If the person killed Bertram, they would need to hide the body. Makes me wonder whether you should have the dog go through the main DOA building as well. Just in case Bertram confronted someone in that building and the killer hid the body in a closet or something."

"I can't believe we're having this discussion, yet you have a point. Rather than getting another K-9, I'll see if we can verify that Bertram did not enter the Administration Building on Tuesday afternoon. The building has cameras and access keys as well, and I would hope there isn't a blind spot on that building."

Pizza arrived and the conversation topics turned mundane. They talked and laughed, and O'Neill ordered a second glass of wine which he finished as the server left the bill on their table. Meyer put her credit card on the table and he slid a twenty-dollar bill to her.

She took the cash and leaned back in her chair. "Once home, I'm going straight to bed and will be out cold before I can even think about this case."

The sun had set as the pair exited the restaurant, pausing outside. Streetlights lit Main Street's sidewalks as customers sat at outdoor tables, finishing their meals and drinks.

"I'm heading east," she said.

"Mine's west. Can I walk you home? It's late."

"No. My apartment is only a few blocks away on Hancock Street. And I can take care of myself."

O'Neill knew she could take care of herself. He just wanted to walk her home.

She stuck out her hand. "I'll send you an email as soon as we finalize times and places for tomorrow's meetings. And Ryder can call me or send me a note tomorrow morning about the meeting with Bertram's financial manager."

O'Neill held her hand an instant longer than he should have. She let go and turned away. He lurched slightly toward her but stopped and glanced at a server cleaning the restaurant's sidewalk tables. Then his gaze settled on Detective Erin Meyer as she walked eastward on Main Street. The bag she carried pulled her dark blue jacket to one side, and he watched as she walked, thinking her hips moved with more of a flourish than they had earlier. Suddenly, her long black hair bounced to her left as she looked over her right shoulder and their eyes locked onto each other. O'Neill lifted his hand to wave, but she turned away.

"Busted," O'Neill said to himself. He watched her for another few steps until a pair of men crossed between them. He smiled as he walked toward King Street, where he turned left. Halfway down the block, he saw the Great Dane Brewing Company, and he knew where he was going.

Chapter 15

O'Neill sat at the Great Dane's first floor bar and estimated the height of every attractive woman he saw. The tallest of the first twenty-two women was six foot one, and the shortest was five foot one. He didn't care. The rush of excitement was undeniable, and he thought about Hancock Street and wondered where exactly Erin Meyer lived. He ordered a second Scotch ale and decided he needed to focus on something besides her, so he convinced a bartender, a blonde man who looked too old to be a student, to let him use their phone, saving thirty-five cents. He tried Ryder's cell first, and he answered after one ring.

"I was hoping you would call," Ryder said. "I'm going to the Big 10 Pub to meet with Mary and Tom Hoffman."

"Really? Mary canceled on me a few hours ago because her daughter had a test or something like that. And it's past ten."

"She called in a panic. She said she was only getting your voicemail, but she had to meet tonight. She wouldn't tell me what's going on, but she said she's bringing her brother along. I'm relieved you called. You can join us."

"Let me guess," O'Neill said. "The police contacted Tom after they got information about this Shakespeare's Company and he's got to go to the station tomorrow morning. He ran to his sister, and now they're worried that the police think he kidnapped Bertram."

"That's a reasonable guess. It's probably an opportunity since we're both working too many hours on Bertram's disappearance. The nice thing about this is you can code some of today's time against her bill rather than against Kathy Siler's. That allows us to avoid that daily maximum charge."

"How do I code hours? You've never had me do anything but give you hours per day."

"Okay, I do the coding. I was just thinking out loud."

"Well, quit it. Why are we going to the Big 10 Pub rather than the office?"

Ryder laughed. "I told her we were closed. I hoped we could meet tomorrow instead. She then suggested meeting at her place. I didn't want to drive to Fitchburg, so I suggested the Big 10 Pub, figuring it would be easiest for me. We agreed on ten thirty, so get your ass there."

"I'll slam this beer and be out the door." O'Neill put the receiver down and picked up his beer.

❧

A bus pulled up to the corner of Main and King Street as O'Neill exited the Great Dane. He stepped on and soon found an abandoned issue of the current *Isthmus*. A pair of women were a few seats in front of him singing, but O'Neill ignored them as he read the entertainment section, which included a listing of area events and concerts. Smoky Joe's Café was listed on Friday with music from Barton Station. O'Neill had never heard of the band, but he assumed they were the band that canceled, leaving the opening for Schumacher's Flour Mill. He read through the band names and realized he knew only about half of them. Just two years ago, he would have known nine out of ten. It was a sign of something, he decided, but he didn't have time to reflect on it since the bus was approaching his stop. One of the women pulled the bell, so O'Neill set the *Isthmus* on his seat and followed the women onto the sidewalk and into the Big 10 Pub.

O'Neill hadn't been to the Big 10 Pub on a Thursday night in years, so he was unsure if students would dominate the place. Fortunately, it was not football, basketball, or hockey season. He ordered a tap of Berghoff, and the bartender filled a glass with one hand while entering the order into the cash register. Two dozen people were in the front room, and the tables were taken. The two women from the bus stayed in the front room, so he walked to the back area, finding an empty table. It was not isolated, but the students milling about the area likely wouldn't bother him.

Ryder arrived as O'Neill took his first sip.

"How did you beat me here?" The detective looked at his watch.

"Caught a bus as I left the brewpub. Took me right here."

"The Hoffmans will be here any minute. How did the building tour go? Did you learn anything?"

"Learned a lot. Turns out that Tom Hoffman invested in a business called Shakespeare's Company LLC, along with Bertram Newman and Rob Peacock." O'Neill pulled out his notepad. "They were three of about seven people involved in the business. The sheet Mary Hoffman found in her brother's closet was a listing of investors with code names related to the Shakespeare authorship controversy."

O'Neill set the printout on the table and added names and descriptions to each alias.

WS=BN=Bertram Newman
Bacon=?=Steven McCormick Lawyer
Oxford=PC?=Peter Couturier Art Dealer
Marlowe=DL=David Leonard Acct
Raleigh=?=Rob Peacock Retired
Elizabeth=1 of 6=Lulu Hanrahan
Stanley=TH=Tom Hoffman IT

O'Neill handed the listing to Ryder.

"We both know who Tom Hoffman, Rob Peacock, and Bertram Newman are. Leonard is Tom's roommate; I met him as well. Besides them, Couturier is a local art dealer. Bertram and Couturier are behind this business which aims to purchase Shakespeare books and artifacts. McCormick is a lawyer who's a partner in a Madison law firm. Hanrahan is an engineer who works for the Department of Transportation. I know nothing else about her. Erin and I are going to meet with Leonard and Couturier tomorrow."

"Erin?"

"Detective Meyer."

"Ooh. What will Mary say about you calling our tall detective by her first name?"

"Can't I call someone by their first name? Get over it. Anyway, I think we're down to four suspects, assuming it relates to Shakespeare's Company. Five if we count Kathy Siler."

"Yeah, you lost me on why that listing is a magical list of suspects." Ryder glanced at his watch again. "What about someone kidnapping him? What about him running away with another woman or going on a bender? And what about his wife killing him because he's a bore?"

"Those are possibilities. I'm just going down what looks to me like the best route."

"You'll be surprised to hear that I met with Linda Newman this evening," Ryder said. "After the meeting, I'm thinking Kathy might be onto something. This could be a kidnapping. You'll ask why we have not yet heard from the kidnappers. My guess is they contacted Linda and told her she couldn't go to the police or to anyone else, so she's working to access cash for the ransom. Linda denies being contacted, but I don't believe her. I think she's worried about her husband."

"Do you think she would pay a ransom for him?"

"She is a sweet lady."

"A *sweet lady*, huh?" O'Neill chuckled.

"Screw you. It was just a comment."

"If you're right and she needs money, she'll be working with her husband's financial manager." O'Neill paused and looked for a name in his notebook.

"His name is Mike Gunderson. I left him a few messages, but have not heard from him."

"Detective Meyer is meeting with him tomorrow morning at ten thirty at Gunderson's office on the square. She invited you to join her, which seems like a good idea."

"Are you going to be there, too?"

"Ten thirty is too early for me, and I don't want to listen to some blow hard talk about stocks and selling short or whatever. Just verify how much Bertram is worth, whether

Linda has leaned on Gunderson to get money for a ransom, and whether Bertram could access the money himself. Meyer told me they verified an alibi for Gunderson, so I'm assuming he's not a suspect. Too bad. I thought he might have been ripping off the Newmans and Bertram confronted him. Detective Meyer said they were requesting access to Bertram's financial records, so hopefully, they'll have that before tomorrow's meeting. I suspect she'll also find out whether Linda has accessed or tried to take money from their accounts to pay the kidnappers."

"You tell me he wasn't kidnapped, and then you tell me all these steps to deal with it as a kidnapping. Do you think kidnapping is a possibility or not?"

"Nah." O'Neill finished his beer. "The kidnapping angle is weak. Think about what happened. Bertram left his office with a laptop and an unloaded pistol. He knew something was going on. What are the odds he got kidnapped when carrying that odd assortment of things? Yet the cops need to cover all the bases. That's why you or Erin need to ask Gunderson about Linda requesting money. I'm assuming Linda has given the MPD approval to access their records. The meeting with Erin and Gunderson will either keep the kidnapping angle open or it will close it off. My money's on the latter."

"Erin again," Ryder said with a smile. "I get the sense that your thoughts have moved on and up in elevation from Mary to Detective Erin?"

"Hello," Mary Hoffman said. Tom Hoffman stood beside her, staring at the floor. "Thanks for meeting so late and on such short notice."

Both O'Neill and Ryder looked up, surprise showing on their reddening faces. The siblings sat without invitation.

"Just so you know, Tom knows about my hiring you," Mary said. "He's upset with me, but we are temporarily moving on."

"I have bigger problems than my sister hiring detectives to investigate me."

"You guys want something to drink?" O'Neill said. "I'm getting a pitcher."

Mary and Tom looked at each other, apparently surprised by the question. Mary finally said she wouldn't mind whiskey and Diet Coke, so O'Neill went to the counter. The bartender poured a pitcher of Leinenkugel's and mixed two ounces of Kessler whiskey with ice and a few ounces of Diet Coke. The bartender replaced O'Neill's twenty-dollar bill with a five-dollar bill and three singles. O'Neill took a sip of the drink and smiled, leaving a three-dollar tip. Walking to the bar's back area, he set the pitcher and plastic glasses in the middle of the table and the whiskey and Diet Coke in front of Mary. She was wearing a white shirt that made her look ridiculously tan. A black braid sat in her sandy blonde hair.

"Holy cow, this is strong," Mary said after trying the drink. She licked her lips, glancing toward her brother. Steve Miller's "Living in the U.S.A." played in the background.

"The police called me this morning," Tom said. "They seem to think I'm involved in Bertram's disappearance. They want to know about a business I work for that Bertram ran. I have a second meeting tomorrow, this one with the detective who is leading the investigation. I am meeting her at the police station and I am scared shitless."

"They clearly view Tommy as a suspect," Mary said, "but he had nothing to do with anything."

"They want information about Shakespeare's Company?" O'Neill said.

"You know about that?" Tom said. "Yeah, the police want to know about the company and my involvement. I already told them most of what I know on the phone, including how I got involved when my roommate approached me about the business back in the fall. David was handling the books and investing in a corporation that was raising money as part of a potential bid for a copy of William Shakespeare's first folio."

"A first folio?" O'Neill set his glass on the table. "Shakespeare's Company was going to buy a first folio?"

"Sorry to sound stupid," Ryder interrupted. "But what's the first folio?"

"No problem, that was my response too," Tom said, chuckling. He sipped at his beer before continuing. "I was not a Shakespeare fan, so I didn't know what the first folio was when I first heard about it, either. Anyway, the first folio is the first printing of *Mr. William Shakespeare's Comedies, Histories, & Tragedies*. Edward Blount and William and Isaac Jaggard published it in 1623, and it is the first time anyone printed all his works together. It may be the most valuable printed book in the world with experts estimating an auction value of over five million dollars."

"For a book?"

"Yes. That's what I thought, too. Either way, David came to me after Bertram asked him to manage the company's books. Bertram and Peter Couturier, an art dealer, started the company and were looking for investors and for someone to manage the business's information technology environment. It was not a full-time position. David suggested me for the job since he knew I wanted to do more than web stuff. David invested a small amount in the business, selling his car to come up with cash. Most investors put in big dollars."

"So you became Shakespeare's Company's IT guy," O'Neill said.

"Exactly. I invested as well, but just twenty thousand, which was all I could come up with. But I am on payroll at a thousand dollars a month for directing Shakespeare's Company's IT. That includes creating and maintaining a secure network environment, managing email, controlling access to systems, and creating and managing a website. Most of it is basic, but Bertram and Peter wanted Shakespeare's Company to look professional and legit. The entire purpose was to attract investors and to ensure that Antiquity Investments LLC viewed us as legit. The website wasn't intended to draw in investors by itself, but we wanted to point potential investors to the site."

"Antiquity Investments is a name I haven't heard."

"We never expected Shakespeare's Company to raise enough cash to bid on a first folio on its own. Also, we don't have the expertise to play that game by ourselves. Peter and Bertram's goal was to raise at least one million dollars. We would be one of three organizations that were part of a joint venture that could access eight million dollars to bid on the first folio. That would include four million in investor money and up to four million in loans. The reality is, we don't know how much money we will need for the first folio. Shakespeare's Company doesn't have the ability to evaluate and price the manuscript. We would be a twenty-five percent partner. Antiquity Investments LLC, which is based in Chicago, would provide the technical and artistic expertise to decide how to approach any auction. They would be the ones making the actual bid and signing the contract on behalf of the joint venture."

"You viewed this as something that would make money for you?" Ryder said.

"Bertram and Peter are awfully convincing," Tom replied. "Peter, Rob, and Lulu are wacko Shakespeare nuts, and they got Bertram drinking the Kool-Aid as well. They want to own part of Shakespeare and what could be better than the first folio? Yet it isn't all bullshit. The data on Shakespeare as an investment is impressive. And Shakespeare is not like something from people's childhood that will fade with a generation. His appeal is timeless, and more and more people with money want to own a piece of the English language's greatest writer. That appeals to me too, but both David and I think we can get a solid return on our money. While I wasn't a literature person, I ended up getting into Shakespeare myself. I found I love his comedies."

"So the company is really just one big investor put into a corporate sheath?" O'Neill suggested.

"That's an interesting but accurate way to put it. We pay a fee to Antiquity for managing legal and technical activities, but they see us as an investor. Yet Bertram and Peter had plans for Shakespeare's Company to make direct investments outside the joint venture, though it would be comparatively small-dollar items. For instance, Peter was looking into the purchase of a quarto of, I think, *Love's Labour's Lost*. A quarto is a pamphlet printing of a play. He was estimating we could buy it for forty-five thousand dollars. Anything related to Shakespeare might interest the business. He was also looking into a different folio as the cost of subsequent editions drops significantly."

"You said Bertram raised a million bucks?" O'Neill said.

"Over a million, including two hundred thousand of his own money. I think Peter put in one hundred thousand. Bertram was hoping to continue to bring in investors. The more money that flows in, the more items we can buy."

"What has the company bought so far?"

"Peter bought a few playbills and other things valued in total at less than ten thousand, and he has the facility to keep the purchases secure. The logic in making these small purchases is to illustrate that we are established, but it is neat to look at and touch something from Shakespeare's time. There are other organizations like Shakespeare's Company and individual investors who want to work with Antiquity, so they have choices on who to bring in. We wanted them to believe we were legit, competent, and low maintenance."

"When is the first folio going to auction?" O'Neill asked.

"We can't be certain. It might go on sale this year or they might delay it several years or another first folio might come up for sale. Yet, Antiquity is convinced there will be an announcement on the auction within a few months. We wanted to finalize the relationship before any announcement. While there are over two hundred first folios, most are in museums or public collections and will never be for sale. There are fewer than a dozen in private collections, so if one goes on the market, it will be a tremendous event."

"I saw a listing you created," O'Neill said, "that showed seven people involved in the Shakespeare authorship controversy. They showed the name with an equal sign and then initials. Are those code words for the investors?"

"Yes," Tom said, glancing at his sister. "I heard you found my notes."

"Tom is not too happy with me." Mary's gaze bounced between the three men.

"The list was something David and I put together a few months ago," Tom said, ignoring his sister. "Bertram promised confidentiality to the investors until we had a formal agreement with Antiquity. But he wanted to talk about and among the investors, so he gave everyone a code name, and I gave us email addresses in the domain that reflected the alias. I was Stanley. Bertram assigned me that name, though he was disappointed he couldn't find a code name that reflected anyone in some sort of specialty that related to data management. He made a game of it, matching a lawyer with a lawyer, a sailor with a sailor, and so forth. Steven McCormick, for instance, was matched with nicknamed Francis Bacon because both were lawyers."

"You got involved, even though you had no interest in Shakespeare or the authorship controversy?"

"At first, I wanted this job because I'm interested in small business and small non-profits, and I want to do more than just web stuff. I want to run IT operations for an organization and this was a splendid opportunity because it was simple, yet it would be a learning opportunity and would provide experience across the entire scope that a business encounters. The job only takes eight to ten hours a week, so it left enough time for me to work for the state, which got me health care and gave me an opportunity to experience organization-wide information technology at a different level. Yet Bertram wanted employees to be investors as well. It reflected his view and values about small business. He believes in entrepreneurship, so he wanted everyone involved in the company to have an ownership interest. The love of Shakespeare has, however, rubbed off on me."

"Tom wasn't doing anything inappropriate." Mary stared at her drink. "I was being nosy, and I jumped to the wrong conclusion. I feel really, really stupid."

"You should feel stupid," Tom said in a low voice.

"Don't be too rough on her," O'Neill said. "A variety of things you did concerned us as well. You explained why you were working for the SWIB, explained the twenty thousand dollar check, and explained the list of code names. Your sister was also worried about the cash and the fake passport and IDs. Ryder and I weren't worried about most of the phony IDs since they were old and expired, and we didn't think there was enough cash to be too suspicious. But what about the fake passport? Why do you have a fake passport?"

Tom pulled the passport out of his pocket and laid it on the table. "Look at the bottom left corner. It says, 'For entertainment purposes only.' It was something David made up for me, basically in Photoshop, as a joke, using my codename instead of my real name. He was Marlowe for a reason."

O'Neill picked up the passport and examined it. His head shook as he read the disclaimer. "You lost me on the Marlowe comment."

"Marlowe was not only a playwright, but a spy. At least David says he was a spy. He thinks making fake documents is something a spy would do. I put things in that shoebox that I want to keep, but I don't want anyone to see. None of it is illegal, but I didn't want anyone to see my IDs because I didn't want people to make assumptions. Yet if someone snoops..."

Mary's gaze dropped to the table.

"We'll want to compare this passport with the photo we have," Ryder said after taking the fake passport from O'Neill. "Maybe that line wasn't visible in our photo."

"Take it with you," Tom said. "Return it when you are done."

"How about the building access codes? Why did you have a half dozen of them?"

"I was supposed to divvy them out to the investors so they could drop in on Bertram if needed. I couldn't do so until I knew who everyone was, so I had kept them at my apartment until we got past our secrecy period."

"Makes sense." O'Neill refilled his beer. "Let's get to Bertram. What do you know about his disappearance?"

"Nothing. The cops, however, think I'm involved."

"The good news," said Mary, "is that Tom took off work on Tuesday to take our mom to Johnson Creek to shop at the outlet mall. I talked to her, and she said Tom picked her up in Waukesha before eight in the morning and brought her home after noon. Tom stayed with her until after dinner. He didn't get to his apartment until after seven at night."

"Is this what you told the Madison Police?" Ryder asked.

"Yes. An officer stopped by my mom's house this afternoon, checking on my alibi. Mom called Mary, who then called me. That's when I found out she hired you two to spy on me."

"They were not spying. I was worried about you and wanted to make sure you weren't doing anything stupid."

"We'll make sure they aren't seriously considering you as a suspect," O'Neill said. "I can't see that being a problem since it sounds like a strong alibi."

"I am worried they won't believe me, since my mom is giving me an alibi."

"The cops will believe a middle-aged woman with no criminal record," Ryder said. "And if she has receipts from your trip, they'll have confirmation. Besides, you don't have a record or anything. I think you should relax and tell the truth."

"I agree," O'Neill said. "And I'm not someone who trusts cops, you know? Yet we still don't know what happened to Bertram. We still have a missing person."

"I wish I could help," Tom said. "I know several of the company's investors, but none of them would kidnap or harm him. I'm at a total loss. You should talk to Rob Peacock or Peter Couturier. Of those involved in Shakespeare's Company, Rob is closest to Bertram, and Peter knows the most about Shakespeare's Company."

"Have you seen anything related to your company's IT that concerns you?" O'Neill asked. "Anyone trying to hack into the system? Anything going on?"

"No. The website gets only ten hits a day. Most of those are from the investors. None of us use company email for anything other than investor relations or contacts with the bank or with Antiquity Investments LLC. There is very little risk, and there hasn't been activity that worries me."

"You don't think Tom should be concerned, which is a relief," Mary said, "but should we hire a lawyer?"

Ryder's head was shaking. "We're pretty sure that whatever happened to Bertram occurred in the early afternoon on Tuesday, and it sounds like Tom's alibi clears him. At this point, we're better off not giving the MPD a reason to think Tom is hiding something. Hiring a lawyer usually makes sense, but in this case, it could be a negative."

"Okay, gotcha," Tom said.

"Thank God." Mary lifted her drink. "Let's do a toast to ending this crazy, crazy nightmare."

Tom filled a glass as O'Neill and Ryder clicked their glasses together. They all drank, and O'Neill refilled his glass.

"Any reason your roommate would be involved in this?" O'Neill asked Tom.

"David? Not that I can think of. He's just a regular joe. Yeah, he's a CPA, but he's normal despite that."

They talked for a few more minutes, and Tom finally looked relaxed.

"Shay, this is totally unrelated, but I have a question." Mary was talking loud and fast. "I was wondering if you could do me a favor? My daughter Lily's twelfth birthday is on the twenty-ninth. Believe it or not, she wants a guitar."

"Twelve is a good age for it."

"Wait a minute," Ryder said, raising a hand between Mary and O'Neill. "My doctor has asked me to leave whenever Seamus talks about musical instruments or his former bands." He stood and poured the last of the beer into Tom's glass. "It's late, and I'm heading home."

"Thanks." Mary reached around her brother and shook Ryder's hand. "I'm sorry I wasted your time. I was such an *idiot*."

"No need to be sorry," he replied as he stepped away from the table. "After all, you'll get a bill. And I got to torch pretend dog poop."

She laughed and turned toward her brother. "I better not drink anything else besides water or Diet Coke. I have to drive home, and it has been hours since I ate."

"Let me grab you a soda," O'Neill said. He went to the front of the bar, catching Ryder as the big detective was leaning on the glass door. "Would you mind giving me a ride home? It has been a long day, and Mary and Tom are heading home. I'm just getting her a Diet Coke before she heads out and I don't want to sponge a ride off her."

"But it's okay to sponge one off me," Ryder said, chuckling. "I'm parked in the lot. I'll wait a minute while you finish. But don't take long. Also, you need to let me see your apartment this time. You say it's a palace compared to your old place on Lake Street, so I want to see it for myself."

"I'll be right out, and I'll give you a tour of the palace."

Chapter 16

Muffled chatter from the Big 10 Pub mixed with chirping crickets as O'Neill walked to Ryder's Chevy S-10, which was parked on Regent Street. O'Neill knocked on the truck's window, and Ryder unlocked the passenger door.

"That went well," Ryder said. The door shut, and he pulled into traffic while O'Neill struggled to find the seatbelt. "Mary is nice. Can't believe she dated you."

"She treats me like... I'm one of her peers, which is cool," O'Neill said, finally getting buckled. "Suppose that's because I was one once—least it seemed like I was one. She's different from most of the crowd I usually deal with. She's normal."

"What about your old girlfriend? What was her name? Sandra? Yeah, Sandra. She seemed normal, and she was hot." Ryder's eyebrows hopped up and down. "And her dad was loaded."

"Yeah, but I was in a band. And she was six or seven years younger than me."

"And the Jane girl? You sulked for six months after she dumped you. I never saw her, but I bet she was hot."

O'Neill didn't reply.

"It's easy to get a little when you're in a band, isn't it?" Ryder laughed, but it sounded more like a squeal.

"Mary doesn't see me *that* way. There may be a spark or two between us, but not enough to make me think there's anything of it. She's good looking, smart, not messed up, and rich. She's probably got a boyfriend, which is fine since I feel out of place around her, kinda small. We don't have anything in common besides ancient history and this case."

"You were interested in her," Ryder said. The truck stopped at a traffic light. "At least until you met our tall detective. You like Detective Meyer, don't ya?"

"Guess I find myself thinking about her."

"Even though she's a cop? Do you think she likes you?"

"Yeah, though I don't think she admits it to herself. The weird thing is that she doesn't think of me as someone in a band. She doesn't even think of me as a musician. I mean, she knows I'm a musician, but she doesn't care about it. She thinks of me as a detective. And as a vagabond."

"How tall are you?" Ryder asked. "Five foot ten?"

"Yeah, though I haven't checked for ten years. How tall are you?"

"Five eleven. Does her height bother you?" Ryder asked. "Not sure I could date someone that much taller than me."

"I focus on what I like about a woman, and there is something I like about how she carries herself. She's also pretty, and I like her shape and the way she moves. When she talks about being a cop, she talks about helping people and problem solving. Hard to not like that."

The truck stopped at a light. O'Neill cracked open the passenger window and the sound of crossing traffic grew louder. The light turned green, and the truck lurched forward as Ryder pushed on the pedal.

"Don't get your hopes up too much, Seamus. She works in the MPD's Central District. Half the patrol cops in that district know who you are. Even if they don't know who you are, they *think* they know who you are and what you are. How do you think the cops view you?"

"I try not to think about cops."

"Then why are we talking about Detective Meyer?"

"Yeah, I get it." He leaned his head against the partially opened window and closed his eyes. The glass was cold and damp on his forehead, and he could smell a coming rain.

"How about our bet? Have you found out how tall she is?"

"Shit, I forgot about that." O'Neill's head shook from side-to-side, but his eyes remained closed. "I don't know how tall she is, but the bet is off. I'll pay you to end it, but don't bring it up again. If someone tells her we had a bet on how tall she was, she'll dust me for sure. I shouldn't have done that." He pulled out his wallet, found a five-dollar bill, and tossed it on the dashboard.

"So you've matured and would never bet on someone's height again?"

"Screw you. In a way, I was trying to defend her because you were acting like she was *too* tall. I was trying to say that she wasn't *too* tall."

"But she wouldn't buy that, would she?"

"Course not."

A motorcycle cut in front of Ryder's Chevy S-10 as the stoplight turned yellow. The motorcycle made the light, but the truck eased to a stop. O'Neill's head leaned against the window again.

"Did I tell you we got another case?" Ryder said as the truck moved forward. "A surveillance job."

O'Neill opened his eyes. "I thought you avoided surveillance. And aren't we too busy for another job?"

"Yes, I hate surveillance, and yes, we're too busy. But we're apparently getting a reputation and this woman will pay full rates and she's cute. I thought I would go with it."

"So you wouldn't have taken it if it was a guy?"

"Not unless he was paying full rates. I'm subbing the surveillance with the ABC Detective Agency, so it won't take any of your time. ABC put this guy named Werlitz on the job. He's got his head up his ass, but they're cheap and I can trust him to show up and stay awake. I don't think it matters much, though, since it shouldn't be hard. He's got a camera set in his van. He'll watch from the back seat. I should call him and check on things."

Ryder let out an enormous sigh before pulling his cell phone from his jacket and dialing a number. "Sammy, John Ryder. How's it going? Uh, huh? Keep with it. Stay with him until two. If he goes home, you can leave at midnight or so. Either way, start up again at eight, okay? You can head home while he's at work." Ryder hung up the phone as they turned onto Main Street. He told O'Neill about the surveillance case, but O'Neill didn't have the energy to pay attention to details about an unrelated case.

Raindrops plopped onto the windshield as Ryder pulled the truck into a spot in front of O'Neill's apartment. Ryder followed up the staircase and O'Neill opened the door and flipped on the light. The room was fifteen-by-nineteen, including a kitchen near the entrance that had a knee-high refrigerator and a conventional oven. The bathroom was to the right of the entrance, and the living area included a large window. Ryder walked in, glancing at the mattress on the floor and the empty beer bottles huddled in one corner.

"I agree that this is a better dump than your last one. At least you got a window this time and the wood floors look decent. It almost looks spacious since you don't have any furniture."

"I got a chair."

"A folding chair doesn't count, nor does a mattress without a bed. And guitars are not furniture."

Seamus turned on his laptop and closed the blinds. "Cheapest place I could find. The place on Lake was getting fixed up, and they were combining my apartment with another one. I guess there were code issues."

"You have an actual oven." Ryder stepped into the kitchen area. "I'm impressed."

"Frozen pizza is my new best friend."

"But you still got a dorm fridge."

"This is all I need since I can squeeze a pizza into the freezer compartment."

"I can't believe you don't have a bed. What do women say when you bring them here?"

"I tell them *that's rock & roll*."

"That works?"

"Guess so."

"At least tours of your places don't take long." Ryder flipped on the bathroom light and peered at the broken shower. "Okay, I'll let you go. Send me an email tomorrow after you have your general itinerary. If you need me to attend a meeting besides the one you mentioned, let me know. God, I wish you had a cell phone. You are such a pain. What other detectives are working with Meyer on the case?"

"There was a woman named Jefferson. She's a regular cop. She's the one I was supposed to meet with for the Annex tour, but she'd gone home, so Erin gave me the tour."

Ryder pulled out a pen and his notepad. "I hope there is only one female Jefferson in the central office. If I can't locate you, I'll call her or Meyer."

O'Neill stumbled as he stood and he accidentally kicked a compact disk case across the room.

"You're getting there, Seamus," Ryder said with a laugh. "I better get out of here. If I stay longer, I might have to listen to your crappy music."

"You go home and watch *The Streets of San Francisco*."

Ryder paused before responding. "Is that on again? The repeats, I mean. They're not making new ones."

"Why ask me? I don't own a TV."

Ryder waved and closed the door. O'Neill turned the deadbolt and sat on his mattress with his laptop. He took off his left sock, pulling out the twenty-dollar bill he hid earlier. Reaching over to a swath of CDs laying at the edge of the mattress, he opened Husker Du's *New Day Rising* and stuck the twenty-dollar bill inside the CD case. He sipped from his flask as he turned to his computer. He navigated to Yahoo!, entering "Erin Meyer" and "University of Illinois" in the search engine.

The first result was from a University of Illinois athletics web page. He clicked on the link and it took him to the 1989 roster for the University of Illinois' women's volleyball team. Erin Meyer was a six foot three freshman. Her position was "MB." He did another search and found out that MB stood for "middle blocker." Then he redid the search, clicking on the next result which was the 1991 roster. It still listed her as a middle blocker, but showed her as six foot four. She was the tallest player on the roster. Then he located the 1992 roster, which also listed her as six foot four. He had already paid Ryder five dollars, but he would not show him the rosters.

Searches uncovered several stories or articles about Meyer's volleyball career, but nothing else. He switched the search to "Detective Erin Meyer" and got multiple hits from recent news stories and from the Madison Police Department's website. One news story from the *Wisconsin State Journal* related to a man who started a fire inside a Johnson Street building. The article included a quote from her, but there were few details and no pictures.

He then checked his email, hoping for an update from The Johnson or Topper on the practice schedule for their upcoming gig. The inbox, however, was empty, and he couldn't remember when they were going to practice.

The wall clock showed it was nearing midnight. O'Neill refilled his flask and walked to the Main Depot, which was a neighborhood bar that was close to his apartment. If O'Neill bought a drink, the bartenders let him use their phone for a local call. He found a spot at the bar counter and ordered a Point Special. The Main Depot had a tin ceiling, but O'Neill thought it was much newer than the building that housed Luigi's. The bartender handed him the phone along with the beer. O'Neill dialed Topper's number, but another man's voice answered.

"Topper?" O'Neill mumbled.

"This is Officer Reynolds of the Madison Police Department. To whom am I speaking?"

O'Neill hung up the phone and only stayed long enough to finish his beer.

Exiting the neighborhood bar, he went east and stopped a block away at the Echo Tap, which was a restaurant and bar that O'Neill had not yet tried, even though it was close to his apartment. A hodgepodge of customers filled the bar, many wearing Wisconsin Badgers hats and shirts. O'Neill ordered a mug of Capital Amber, leaned against a wall, and watched ESPN baseball highlights. After a few sips, he asked about the nearest payphone. The white shirted bartender pointed to a hallway leading to the restrooms. O'Neill stumbled down the corridor and spotted the pay phone on the wall outside the men's room. After dropping in a quarter and a dime, he dialed Ryder's cell phone. He answered after two rings.

"Seamus? What now? It's midnight."

"I just tried to call Topper," O'Neill said, glancing toward the bar, "and a cop answered the phone."

"And what did the cop say?"

"He said that he was Officer Whatever, and I hung up."

"Why did you hang up?"

"I don't want the cops to think I have anything to do with it."

"Anything to do with what?"

"I don't know. That's why I'm calling you. Could you call someone and find out what Topper got busted for? I would call Erin, but she worked like forty-eight straight hours and needs sleep. And Garcia thinks I'm a vagabond."

Ryder let out a breath. "Does Topper have an answering machine?"

"Yeah, why?"

"If Topper got busted for something, they would let the answering machine pick up. I'd guess something happened, like a fire or a robbery or something."

"You sure?" O'Neill ran a hand through his hair.

"No, but it is likely. What are you worried about?"

"My policy is to avoid cops. That way, no one blames me."

"This from the guy with a crush on a police detective. Let me make a call and get back to you. Where you at?"

"A pay phone."

"What number, you idiot?"

His eyes struggled to focus. Then he read the number to his boss.

"Topper lives right above that bong store on State Street, right?" Ryder asked.

"The Piper. I don't remember the address."

"Okay. Wait there a minute. I'll call you back."

O'Neill hung up the phone and walked to the bar. After counting his money, he bought another beer. After two sips, the phone rang. He hurried over and picked it up.

"Is Topper's real name, John McDonnell?"

"Sounds right."

"Looks like your friend got himself shot."

"Shot!"

"Yeah. He's in stable condition at Meriter Hospital, so the injury is not serious. The officer I spoke to said it was an accident. Apparently, some woman picked a handgun up and didn't realize it was a real gun. The woman got brought in for drug possession. You can guess the rest."

"He's got to play tomorrow. Shit."

"Okay, Seamus. Go home and get to bed. Or get *to mattress* or whatever. You sound tired."

"Yeah. Thanks, boss."

O'Neill hung the phone up, finished the beer, and left through the front door. Meriter Hospital was less than a mile away, but he assumed it was past visiting hours. There was nothing he could do, so he turned west and started home. After two blocks, he realized he was going to his *old* apartment. He swore loudly, turned around, and headed toward the *new* apartment where he had lived for nine months.

Chapter 17

O'Neill woke at ten and got presentable. Wearing a plain white t-shirt, jeans, and sunglasses, he started the mile-long walk to Meriter Hospital.

The early June sun sat in the clear sky as a slight breeze cooled the streets below. O'Neill walked slowly at first, but his pace quickened after being passed by a pair of older women. At Meriter Hospital, he waited in line before being told that they had no record of John McDonald being admitted to the hospital. Finally, the receptionist realized they had released a John McDonnell earlier in the morning.

Starting for Topper's, O'Neill walked through the University of Wisconsin's Library Mall, where a half-dozen food carts were ready for the Friday lunch crowd. On State Street, the sun was in front of him and the morning breeze had subsided. He pulled his shirt away from his skin and used it to fan his sweating back.

Rather than ringing the bell to Topper's apartment, he went to The Piper. The shop opened at ten thirty, so he waited outside, leaning against the building's brick wall. At ten thirty-three, the doors unlocked. The salesperson was a college-age woman with blonde hair and a nose ring, and was wearing a midriff-bearing shirt and cut-off shorts.

"How's Topper doing?"

The clerk's expression transformed from disinterested to confused. "Who are you?"

"Seamus O'Neill. I'm a friend of Topper's. Thought I would check to see how he's doing. Is he upstairs?"

"Yeah." She turned around and picked up a telephone. "Just a sec. Hey, Mandy, a guy here wants to see Topper. He said his name is..." she turned to O'Neill.

"Seamus."

"Shaman," she said into the phone. "Oh, okay then. Thanks."

She put the phone down. "You can go up through the back. He's awake. Mandy's with him."

The clerk pulled out a key chain and opened the back door. O'Neill muttered his thanks and entered the back room. The woman locked the door behind him. He paused, glancing at a pair of guitars in the corner before proceeding up the round metal staircase. At the top of the stairs, he knocked before opening the door.

A blonde woman came into the kitchen. Her hair was disheveled, and she was wearing a blue and white robe that went below her knees.

O'Neill looked her over quickly before speaking. "I'm Seamus O'Neill. You must be Mandy."

"Topper is in the bedroom." Mandy opened a cupboard and pulled out a loaf of bread, continuing with her routine despite his presence.

He walked through the living room and into the lone bedroom. Topper was sitting on the bed with a blue blanket on his legs, watching ESPN, and looking even paler than usual.

A white bandage was wrapped around his stomach. He waved O'Neill into the room and turned off the TV.

"How you doing?" O'Neill asked as he kneeled on a cedar chest at the foot of the bed.

"Okay, considering I got shot." Topper picked a cigar off the end table and took a puff. "You know what sucks? The weekend is coming and not only do we have our show tonight, but I have tickets for tomorrow's Clarence Gatemouth Brown concert. Have you ever been shot?"

"Fortunately, no."

"This is my third time."

"You're shitting me."

"No, I'm serious. I got shot once down in Chicago back in, like, '85. I was standing a block off Rush Street and someone took a few shots from a car. Don't think he was aiming at me, but I got hit." He slid the robe off his right shoulder and pointed at a scar on his left bicep. "It was a flesh wound. The emergency room nurse put peroxide on it, bandaged it, and handed me over to the cops. I get shot," he said with a shake of his head, "and the cops charge me because I had two joints in my sock."

"And the second time?"

"Must have been in about '92. I was living here, but I was in Chicago to buy merchandise. Turns out the cops had the deal staked out. The transfer was in a shoe store, believe it or not. I was exchanging a pair of shoes for another—that was how the switch would go. Anyway, this guy I was dealing with, I saw him looking around. Something wasn't right. Then he tells me they don't take returns. Something was wrong, so I headed out. That's when the cops came down on me. There were only two of 'em outside and one didn't look too spry, so once outside I made a run for it. There were gobs of people around, so I threw the shoebox in the air and cash went flying all over the place. One cop dealt with the money and the chunky one stays on the chase. I had this guy beat, so he took a potshot at me, or maybe he was trying to fire a warning shot. There were people around and everything. It was stupid of him. The shot hit me in the ass as I hopped a fence. Worst place for it, you know, though I must have turned slightly since it passed in and out of my left butt cheek. I drove all the way to Madison with my ass bleeding. The pain was terrible. I had to pay this doctor to bandage it up on the sly. The thing still hurts."

"How come I never heard this?" O'Neill asked.

"It's kind of embarrassing, getting shot in the butt. But now that I've been shot three times, it's something to brag about."

"So, what happened last night?"

Topper shook his head before answering. "Mandy had a couple of friends over. One of them took something—not here, but before she got here. Anyway, we were in the living room talking. The *Wild Bunch* was on, so shooting is going on, and I look up and she's holding my pistol."

"Shit. Did the cops bust you for having a gun?"

"The pistol is technically Mandy's. It's legal and everything."

"Okay."

"Normally, we keep it under the bed. She must've gone in there or something. So, anyway, the instant after I see her, she's playing with it and 'Boom!' Mandy and her other friend scream. I fall off the sofa, grabbing my side. When I look up, this girl is standing there, licking at the smoke coming out of the barrel. Mandy's screaming, so I get my ass off the floor, limp over, and take the gun from this dodo. Mandy's standing there yelling, 'You killed him! You killed him!'"

"I'm thinking the cops will be here and they'll find my stash, you know. So here I am, collecting shit to flush down the toilet. By the time the cops come to the door, I collected everything—even the stuff down below. But I'm waiting for the fucking toilet bowl to fill so I can flush again. I close the bathroom door because Mandy is screaming and I don't know what the other two girls are doing. The cops come inside and are banging on the bathroom door, but the toilet's not ready. They bang louder and they're gonna eventually break the door in. I yell, 'Just a minute,' and flush again. Then I unbuckle my pants and open the bathroom door. I was standing there bleeding, and I'm telling them I couldn't wait to take a shit."

"They didn't believe that?" O'Neill said, laughing.

"No, but what else could they do? They searched the place, but I had gotten rid of everything. The only thing they found was a few tabs on this girl. They busted her for that. But she didn't get them from me, thank God. I've been scaling back. I pretty much just keep stuff for friends."

O'Neill glanced toward the door. "So who is this Mandy, anyway?"

"She was hanging around out here this spring. She was doing smack and figured she'd hook up with me so she could score for free. I got her off it. Now she's kind of thankful. I think she likes me."

"What a humanitarian. Doesn't sound like you."

"I don't mess with smack anymore. I learned that from you."

"So I take it your wound isn't too bad?"

Topper shrugged his shoulders again. "The bullet hit my left side and stuck in. This is the first one that stayed in, probably because of the caliber. They had to pull it out, but it didn't really hit anything but muscle and part of the large intestine. That's good, considering. But I'm sore as hell."

"Can you play tonight?"

"I thought you would ask."

"Can you?"

"I don't think I'm up to playing banjo. Could I just play the guitar so I can take it easy? It would be less stressful since I'm used to it."

"Yep," O'Neill said. "You sure you're up to it? We got practice first and the show's tonight."

"We'll see how practice goes, but I haven't played in front of an audience in twelve years, so I don't intend to miss the opportunity. There's one thing, though. Could we practice here or downstairs in the back? I wanna minimize the moving around and stuff."

O'Neill nodded in agreement. "We were going to, anyway, I think. The Johnson said practice is at twelve thirty, but I'm not positive. I'll check my email and see what he says and if that's right."

"What songs are we gonna play?"

"We need to figure that out," O'Neill said. "You got a piece of paper somewhere?"

Topper pointed to an oak desk in the room's corner. O'Neill opened the middle drawer and took out a pad of yellow paper. "I figure we need about eighteen to twenty songs. At least half will be traditional or old-time or whatever you wanna call it. I thought we'd play a couple of *Sun Sessions* songs, maybe 'Blue Moon of Kentucky' and 'I'm Left, You're Right, She's Gone.' The Johnson will know those."

"Do those count as traditional?" Topper asked.

"We'll see."

"Fair enough."

"I'd like to do 'Hello, Mary Lou' for some reason and a few Irish or British Isles songs as well," O'Neill said as he wrote on the notepad. "How about 'They're Moving Father's Grave to Build a Sewer' and 'The Pub With No Beer' since they get laughs?"

"We'll need them."

"Then 'Knockin' on Heaven's Door,' 'Guitars, Cadillacs, Etc.,' 'Shake, Rattle and Roll,' 'Ferny Hill,' and 'Le Marseilles.'"

"The French national anthem? Where'd that come from?"

"France. I always kind of liked it."

"You know the words?"

"Course not. I thought we could do it as an instrumental."

"How about 'Off to Dublin in the Green?'" Topper asked.

"Sure. And I told The Johnson that he could pick a couple of blues songs to sing. And this girl fiddler can pick something. That would make fifteen, counting two from The Johnson and two from The Fiddler. Then, I wanna do 'The Rockford Files.'"

Topper rolled his eyes.

"Oh, come on. I'll do it on the accordion. It will be cool."

"No, it won't."

"Sure it will. Plus, I'm a detective, so it has synergy."

"Okay, that is twelve, excluding The Johnson and The Fiddler's songs."

"Boy, you're good at counting."

"You're assuming I'm right."

"You are. But I have the notepad here. But anyway, how about throwing in 'The Beer Barrel Polka?'"

"People in a coffeehouse don't want to hear a polka—especially that one," Topper said.

"So what?"

"Whatever. So long as you sing."

"And then I was thinking it would be cool to do 'You Can't Always Get What You Want' and finally, 'Nancy Whiskey.'"

"This sounds like a disaster, but most of it is easy enough, and I know all but two. You don't wanna do any of your own songs?"

"Not unless we have time to practice. I'd rather screw up someone else's stuff than my own." O'Neill got to his feet, tore off a sheet from the notebook, and stuck it in his pocket. "I'll bring the set list to practice."

"Good enough."

"I realize you just got shot and stuff, but I was wondering if you minded if I took a quick shower. Mine broke, and it has been a few days. I shower fast, just five minutes, and I only need soap and a washcloth to dry off with."

Topper laughed, pausing as he winced in pain. "Go ahead." He pointed toward the hallway. "Towels are in the bathroom underneath the sink. Use what you need."

O'Neill hurried into the bathroom and was out in less than ten minutes. O'Neill turned off the fan and the bathroom light. "Thanks a ton. Is there anything I can get you before I leave?"

"No, but I was wondering whether you want a TV."

"Course I do. Just don't want to pay for one."

"I got this new Samsung last week, a twenty-seven incher." Topper motioned toward the television set. "That goes along with the thirty-two incher in the living room. But I still got an old nineteen incher on the kitchen counter. No one from the shop wants it even though it's color. None of Mandy's friends want it since there's no remote and it can't connect to a DVD player or a game system. Old TVs are a dime-a-dozen nowadays. If you want it, take it. You should be able to pick up four or five stations on the antenna."

"Yeah, sure. I'll take it. Thanks a lot. See ya at practice, then. I'll get The Johnson to tell you the time."

The television was on the kitchen counter next to a toaster and a George Foreman Grill. O'Neill wrapped the cord around the set and picked it up. Mandy watched but said nothing as he walked out the front door. He strolled down the stairs and started the half-mile walk to his apartment, stopping at Reilly's Wines of the World. He put the television on the floor and pulled out his wallet. He still had thirty-nine dollars in cash, so he decided it would be best to buy another bottle of bourbon and a six-pack. This would prevent him from spending all his cash at the bars.

The woman behind the liquor store counter called him by name and commented on the television. O'Neill nodded and continued to the back, choosing a liter bottle of Old Crow and a six-pack of Berghoff. He set the six-pack on top of the TV and held the Old Crow with two fingers.

"How far do you got to walk with that?" the woman behind the counter asked.

"Quarter mile or so."

"Lucky the bourbon is in a plastic bottle."

"That's why I buy it."

O'Neill dropped the Old Crow as he crossed University Avenue. It bounced on the blacktop and he kicked it gently across one lane of traffic and onto the curb. He set the television on the sidewalk and picked up the bourbon. This time he balanced the Old Crow on top of the six-pack. At the apartment, he put everything on the porch and unlocked the security door. His arms and shoulders ached. He carried the beer and the bourbon up the stairs and into his room, returning for the television.

He placed the TV on top of a milk crate across from his mattress and plugged it into one of the two open sockets on his power strip. There was a small antenna, but it took a few minutes before he picked up a station. He opened a bottle of red ale, sat on his mattress, and found a *Perry Mason* episode as he powered up his computer.

Four emails were in his inbox. He read the message from The Johnson first, which verified a twelve thirty practice session for Schumacher's Flower Mill at Topper's place. The Johnson said he would pick O'Neill up just after noon. O'Neill sent a reply, reminding The Johnson that it was Schumacher's *Flour* Mill and mentioning Topper's accident, but noting he was still up to playing the show. He listed Topper's phone number and encouraged The Johnson to call and verify the details with Topper.

The second email was from Detective Erin Meyer. The note showed times and addresses for three separate meetings, including one with Tom Hoffman at noon. O'Neill replied, letting her know he would miss the noon interview, but would make the other two. He also mentioned that he had met with Tom on the previous night and would update her on it.

The third email was from a generic Madison Police Department email address. The note said that Detective Meyer was summoned to a three o'clock meeting with the Central District's Captain of Detectives and could not attend the interview with David Leonard. Officer Penny Jefferson would conduct the interview in her place. The note said Detective Meyer expected to attend the five o'clock interview with Peter Couturier.

O'Neill was disappointed, but he moved on, reading the email from Ryder that said he would be at the Friday morning meeting with Meyer and would update him later. He wondered whether Meyer had made that meeting.

He closed his eyes and thought about Erin Meyer, saying her name over and over in his head. He decided her name had a lyrical sound, making it an apt title to an instrumental song, one whose waves floated along in the air, sounding smooth but wilting like a breeze. Though his eyes were closed, he thought about pulling out his whistle and finding a melody. But when they opened, it was approaching noon and The Johnson was scheduled to pick him up within a half hour.

Noticing his calendar, he remembered it was Friday, which brought his thoughts to Rob Peacock and Shakespeare's Company. The retired financial manager had told O'Neill that he would talk to them about the new corporation on Friday. And O'Neill had many questions.

Chapter 18

O'Neill locked the door and started down the stairs. His second-floor neighbor, a woman in her forties, waved to him as she stood in front of her door holding keys. He nodded and hurried outside, jogging several blocks before arriving at the Main Depot. A regular saluted him as he sat at the bar. O'Neill didn't recognize the male bartender, so he ordered a tap of Pabst Blue Ribbon and asked if he could use the phone.

"We don't do that," the bartender said. He was wearing a Robin Yount Brewers Jersey but looked more like a football player than a baseball player.

"It's O'Neill," said a regular who was wearing a Mautz painting hat and a blue shirt with a Blatz emblem. "Mark and Betsy let him do it all the time. I've seen it."

The bartender gave O'Neill an inquisitive look. Then he grabbed the phone, setting it in on the counter. "Keep it local."

"Course, and thanks," O'Neill said to the bartender before nodding to the Blatz guy. Ryder picked up after two rings.

"What do you want, Seamus?"

"Have you talked to Rob Peacock yet today? Remember, he said he'd talk about Bertram's new corporation on Friday afternoon? It's almost noon."

"Yeah. Should we stop over and visit him?"

"I got practice and don't have time. Do you want to stop by, or should I call him?"

"Call him. I'm not sure what he'll add beyond what we learned yesterday from Tom Hoffman and Detective Meyer. Yet it's worth doing."

O'Neill didn't think the bartender would be open to a second call. "Okay, fine. If I learn anything, I'll send you an email. Did you meet with Mike Gunderson this morning?"

"Yeah. Linda Newman was there as well. She had Gunderson give us—or rather, the MPD — full access to her and Bertram's financial information. The MPD's financial expert says that nothing unusual appears to be going on beyond the one big payment to the Shakespeare company, which we already knew about. Neither Gunderson nor Linda has transferred or withdrawn significant funds from Bertram's accounts."

"Do you agree that the chance of this being a kidnapping is remote?"

"Yeah. And Meyer says they buy Gunderson's alibi, so I don't see a lot more to gain from him. The MPD will know if anyone tries to access Bertram and Linda's investments or funds, and Gunderson said no payments outside their personal or business checking accounts can happen without both his and Linda's approval. Are you and Meyer still meeting with Tom Hoffman's roommate this afternoon?"

"She has a conflict, so she's sending the Jefferson cop instead. The meeting is at three, I think."

"Meyer has surely got a ton going on."

"Yeah. Either way, I'll tell you if I learn anything important from Peacock."

O'Neill got Peacock's number from Ryder and wrote it in his notepad. He hung up and dialed without looking up.

The bartender put his hand on the phone, hanging up the receiver. Chatter amongst the bar patrons stopped.

"You running a business with our phone or something?" The bartender leaned close enough that O'Neill could smell his breath. "If so, you need to pay for your own phone. I don't mean to be a dick about it, but you're pushing it."

"Come on, Marv," the Blatz guy said. "I want to see if he learns anything about the kidnapping from the Peacock."

The bartender's gaze bounced between O'Neill and the Blatz guy. He muttered something unintelligible and released the phone. O'Neill dialed and Peacock answered after six rings. The Blatz guy moved closer to O'Neill.

O'Neill identified himself.

"Yes, I remember you," Peacock said. "You're the guitar player, right?"

"Yeah, that's me. It's Friday, so I was hoping you could answer a few questions about Shakespeare's Company."

"I'm sorry, but I should have been more precise when I spoke with you earlier. I can't talk about the Shakespeare corporation until the end of business today."

"End of business?"

"Five o'clock central standard time. Sorry to disappoint you. I don't mean to be cagey, but, as I think I mentioned, I signed an agreement on what information I could share and when. That, however, doesn't apply to a police investigation, so I told that tall detective everything I would tell you. Perhaps you can talk to her?"

"Okay, I'll talk to Detective Meyer. But can I ask a few questions that probably don't matter? I'm just curious."

"You can try."

"McCormick's code name was Oxford. I assume that's because he's a lawyer. Why are you, Raleigh?"

Rob Peacock laughed. "Most people think of Raleigh as an adventurer, an explorer, and a military man. I think of him as a sailor. And I was in the United States Navy during the second world war, so it seemed a fit."

"Lulu Hanrahan was Elizabeth because...?"

"There are few options for females in Shakespeare's authorship theory. Elizabeth was the best choice. Bertram liked it, since Lulu enjoys being in charge, not unlike Queen Elizabeth."

"Who came up with the authorship nickname scheme? Was it Bertram?"

"Him, Peter, and I. Peter is a devout Oxfordian, meaning he is sure that Edward de Vere, the Earl of Oxford, was the primary writer of Shakespeare's plays. Bertram and I are agnostic about the controversy, yet we enjoy discussing it. We don't know what's true, but we view it as an intellectual exercise. Peter is the expert, but his viewpoint is quite bent."

"It makes sense that Peter is Oxford. Not only was Oxford a supporter of the arts and a collector, but Peter believed he was the actual Shakespeare. But why is Bertram Shakespeare?"

"Shakespeare?" the Blatz guy said to the bartender.

"As I said, Bertram was agnostic," said Peacock, "but he believed that Shakespeare from Stratford was still the best candidate, and Bertram is a practical man."

"Why was Leonard assigned Marlowe as his code name?" O'Neill asked. "It wasn't like Marlowe was an accountant or treasurer."

"Marlowe was David's idea and not ours. Marlowe was a spy and a counterfeiter and, though David may be a CPA, he liked the idea of being a spy and a counterfeiter."

"What about Tom Hoffman being Stanley?"

"I don't have an answer for that one. Tom was the last one to join the group and, unlike most of us, he's not a Shakespeare aficionado. He probably took whoever Bertram assigned him. Hopefully, we can ask Bertram why he gave him Stanley."

"Last question. I still think Bertram's disappearance relates to Shakespeare's Company. I recognize there is only a million dollars, but to most people, that is a fortune."

"I realize that," Peacock said.

"A million dollars," the Blatz guy whispered, his stare bouncing between O'Neill and the bartender.

"If someone stole from the company, how would you know?" O'Neill asked.

There was a long pause on Peacock's end. "By the end of business today, we will have transferred nearly all of Shakespeare's Company's funds to a separate organization. If the business we are investing in is fake or has cheated us, that's one thing."

"That would be Antiquity Investments?" O'Neill said.

"My, you know most of this already," Peacock said with a chuckle. "Yet Antiquity is legit. I'm one hundred percent certain of that. If someone were to take money from our corporation, it would have to be before we transferred our funds to Antiquity Investments LLC. Now is too late. Yet you have me concerned. I will touch base with Antiquity and verify that there is nothing to worry about. My understanding is that we've already transferred most of the money to them. If there are problems, I will contact you immediately. Or rather, I will contact the police immediately."

"Makes sense. I'm sorry if I'm worrying you for no reason."

"It is best to be one hundred percent sure about investments. Anything else, Mr. O'Neill?"

"No. Though I want to mention one thing unrelated to Bertram. I'm only mentioning it because I'm thinking you share your wife's love of music."

"Yes, I do."

"My band is playing at eight tonight at Smoky Joe's Café on Monroe Street."

"I know where that is."

"We don't play medieval music like I suspect your wife would have played. We play more mid-twentieth century music. A little folk, country, blues, and rock."

"Well, thank you for telling me. It might be too late for me, but I'll see how I feel."

O'Neill thanked him, and the bartender took the receiver and set the phone on the back counter.

"I'm confused," the Blatz guy said. "There's Peacock, Shakespeare, a kidnapping, a million dollars, and a show on Monroe Street. What's it all about?"

"That's what I'm trying to figure out," O'Neill said. "Can I buy you a beer?"

The Blatz guy's expression evolved from one of confusion to one of contentment. "Now that is a question I *can* answer."

The bartender poured a Pabst for the Blatz guy. O'Neill slammed his beer and stuck two dollars and two quarters on the counter and exited the Main Depot.

O'Neill returned to his apartment and was relieved that The Johnson was not waiting outside. He put his black Sweetone tin whistle in one pocket and a flask in another. The security door buzzed, so O'Neill grabbed his accordion and hurried down the stairs.

"I thought you weren't going to play that," The Johnson said, pointing at O'Neill's accordion.

"You get me something better and I'll play it. Where's The Fiddler?"

The Johnson motioned to his green Chevrolet Impala. A girl was sitting on the hood, wearing tennis shoes, shorts, and a red shirt. She had long, straight blonde hair that nearly went to her waist.

"She's thirteen?" O'Neill said. "She looks like she's eight!"

"I thought she was thirteen. Turns out she's ten." The Johnson said.

"She looks like she's eight."

"You already said that."

O'Neill shook his head and walked to the Johnson's Impala. "Don't complain about my accordion," he mumbled to The Johnson, "or I'll complain about you bringing an eight-year-old."

"Mika," The Johnson said. "This is Seamus O'Neill."

"I didn't go to school today," The Fiddler said.

"Me either. I hear you are quite the fiddler." O'Neill said.

She shrugged her shoulders as if she was unsure.

The Johnson walked around the car and got into the driver's seat. The Fiddler called, "Shotgun," and jumped into the passenger seat. O'Neill sat in the back.

Three minutes later, The Johnson's Impala pulled into the Lake Street Ramp. The band carried their instruments down the stairs and along State Street, earning curious gazes from onlookers.

"What kind of store is this?" The Fiddler asked as they entered Topper's store.

"A pipe store," The Johnson replied.

"Oh, hello," a woman at the counter said. "You're here for Topper, right? This way."

They followed her to the back door. She knocked before unlocking it. Topper was inside, wearing sweatpants and a robe and strumming a Gretsch acoustic guitar.

"That woman has an earring in her nose and a skull tattoo on her shoulder," The Fiddler said to The Johnson.

The Johnson shook Topper's hand and introduced The Fiddler. She nodded to Topper, kneeled on the ground, and took out her fiddle.

"How old are you?" Topper asked The Fiddler.

"I turned ten on Wednesday," she said without looking up. "We had a party, and I brought Snickers bars to school for my class. How old are you?"

"Thirty-four," Topper replied with a chuckle. Then he turned to O'Neill. "You want a drink?" He pointed to a small refrigerator in the corner. "You too, Johnson. We have Coke and Sprite in the fridge if she wants one."

"I'll take a Coke," said The Johnson. "You want a pop, Mika?"

The Fiddler nodded, so O'Neill tossed two cans of Coke to the Johnson and grabbed one for himself. He took a gulp, then poured bourbon into the can.

The Johnson pulled three folding chairs off the wall, setting them around Topper. O'Neill sat closest to Topper. The Johnson set the Fiddler between himself and O'Neill.

"What happened to you?" The Fiddler asked Topper.

"He got hurt, but he's going to be fine," The Johnson said. He glanced toward O'Neill. "What are we going to play?"

"Topper and I put together a set list." O'Neill pulled the list from his pocket and handed it to The Johnson. "Since we don't have much rehearsal time, we need songs Topper already knows or that are not too tough to learn. I'm assuming you can figure out everything on the fly. Anything you don't know?"

The Johnson ran a finger down the sheet before answering. "'Le Marseilles,' but I can figure it out." He played the melody on the B and high E strings. "'The Rockford Files?' Are you serious?"

"Sure," O'Neill said. "The accordion will replace the harmonica. Anything else you don't know?"

"Nope. I'm good."

O'Neill turned to The Fiddler. "I'll tell you what key and I will play a few bars, stop and then we'll go into the full song. Drop in and out of songs if you need to. If there are ten or eleven you can play, that's fine. If need be, pluck your fiddle in rhythm or stomp your feet. Anything to bring energy."

"I'm good at energy," The Fiddler said. "Tim said I got to pick two songs."

"Who's Tim?" Topper asked.

"Me, numbskull," The Johnson said.

"Yeah, you can pick two songs, Mika," O'Neill said. "Tim is going to add two songs as well. To start, let's go with something most of us should know. How about 'Blue Moon of Kentucky' in A?"

"I know that." The Fiddler tucked the violin under her chin.

"Let's do it the way Elvis did," O'Neill said. "Johnson, you and Topper strum along. We'll just go with it since everyone knows the song. I won't bring in the accordion until after the introductory part." He turned toward The Fiddler. "Play along as you like. You might think of this as a bluegrass song, which is fine. When we do songs you don't know, just wait for a few bars until you catch the tune and join in when you feel comfortable. Don't feel the need to be fancy. You can always go along with the melody, even if you're just echoing the singer. And if things fall apart, keep going or give us rhythm."

"He means, *when* things fall apart," said The Johnson.

O'Neill put a hand in the air, sang, "Blue Moon," and the guitars started. As they transitioned into the chorus, he added the accordion, and the fiddle joined in. Suddenly, The Fiddler stopped, waving her hands in front of O'Neill. The music stopped.

"What's the problem?" O'Neill asked.

"We're way out of tune. Especially you."

"He's always out of tune," The Johnson said. "That accordion is a piece of junk."

The Fiddler leaned closer to the accordion. "They sell those at Zany Brainy."

"What?" O'Neill said.

"That accordion. They sell that brand at Zany Brainy. Maybe not that accordion, but it looks like the same brand."

"I didn't buy this at Zany Brainy. I got it for free."

"Is that instrument meant for professional musicians?" The Fiddler asked.

"Get me a better one and I'll play it. And we don't tune our instruments. We just play out of tune."

"I thought professional musicians always tuned."

"We let the sound guys do that. And since we don't have sound guys, we don't do it. Okay then, let's go."

They practiced for an hour and a half, with Topper skipping a few songs. The Fiddler knew six songs, including the instrumentals she brought, but she played along on most of the others and displayed rhythm. They mostly worked on the instrumentals since the fiddle and the whistle or accordion worked together. O'Neill even tuned his whistle.

When they finished, The Johnson announced they wouldn't suck terribly and agreed to pick O'Neill and Topper up near the Fluno Center at seven.

"Before we leave, we need a photo," The Johnson said.

"A photo of what?" O'Neill said.

"Of Schumacher's Flour Mill. The manager at Smoky Joe's wants fliers for the windows and doors. She wants them there early this afternoon at the latest." The Johnson pulled out a camera. "I told her I would give her four and would put a dozen up around campus or in the Monroe Street neighborhood. I'll take whatever we come up with to Kinko's and they'll make something up. It won't cost much. I'll take it out of the twenty-five bucks we're getting paid. It will be useful to have a picture in case we play again."

"The show is today. Isn't it too late to put up fliers?"

The Johnson shrugged his immense shoulders. "I'm just doing what the delightful lady who's paying asked me to do."

"Okay. If you're gonna take photos, let's go to the back alley. And we need a photographer, don't we?"

"Let's get Mandy," Topper said in a hoarse voice. "She'll use my digital camera and can make the fliers on the store computer and print them. We do tons of ads for the shop and the bar."

"That would be great," The Johnson said.

"I'll only charge you cost."

"Great." The Johnson's smile disappeared.

Topper sent O'Neill upstairs, where he found Mandy. After a few minutes, she came down, wearing a cut-off Linkin Park t-shirt and gray shorts. She led the band onto State Street. The group walked south, stopping in an alley beside the Lake Street Ramp. Topper, still wearing his blue and white robe, leaned against the ramp and smoked a cigarette while Mandy and The Johnson figured out the ideal spot for the photo. Mandy finally called them together, lining their backs against a sandstone brick wall. O'Neill put his accordion on the ground and sat on i t.

"Hold on to your instruments," Mandy commanded. O'Neill stood and picked up his accordion. "Seamus, stand between The Johnson and the girl."

"Why?" The Johnson asked.

"Because you're too damn big. You make her look like a five-year-old."

The Johnson inched closer to Topper, and The Fiddler moved to the side. O'Neill slid in between them.

"Seamus, sit on the accordion again. And do you really need the sunglasses?"

He took them off.

"Okay," she said after a moment. "Put them back on."

Mandy took a dozen pictures before having the band sit on the ground. O'Neill took out his flask, but The Johnson gave him an elbow before he took a sip. Mandy took another dozen photos as they walked through the alley and a few more as they played "Repeal of the Licensing Laws." A trio of college-aged women walking past the alley stopped and watched.

"Enough," Topper said, looking tired. Mandy took his guitar.

The Johnson and The Fiddler headed to the parking ramp while O'Neill, Mandy, and Topper went back to Topper's pipe store. There was a small crowd of customers and only one employee. Mandy handed Topper's guitar to O'Neill and went to help a customer. Topper winced as he pulled keys from his pocket.

"That wasn't bad," O'Neill said as they entered the back room. "You okay?"

"Yeah, considering I've been shot. Put the guitar on the stand and set the keys on the counter. I got to go upstairs and rest before the show. I'm just glad I got shot on the left side and not the right."

"Are you feeling okay about the band?"

"I don't think it will be a total disaster." Topper passed a wall clock and started up the stairs. "I wish the girl was a little older. I mean, she'll end up being an excellent player, but she's not a prodigy. At least she won't show up stoned."

O'Neill waved goodbye, and he noted the time. He would have to hurry if he was going to *observe* the interview with David Leonard.

Chapter 19

A short police officer with a close-cut afro was pacing on the walkway in front of the Administration Annex building. O'Neill recognized her but did not remember specifics, which he assumed was a positive.

She spotted him as he approached, and it was clear she recognized him as well. "Mr. O'Neill, I'm Officer Jefferson."

They shook hands, and he noticed she was pregnant. At least he thought she was pregnant.

"I was about to go inside without you," Jefferson said. She held the building access card against the card reader. The lock thumped, and she pulled the door open.

"What do we know about this David Leonard guy?" O'Neill asked.

"Thirty-six years old. A financial manager for the Department of Administration where he's worked for six years. Prior to that, he worked in public accounting and, briefly, for a private company as an accountant. He's divorced with no kids." Jefferson paused as they walked through the lobby area and past the elevator. She opened the door to the stairs and waited for him to enter the stairwell. She pulled out her notepad as the door closed. "Leonard graduated from the

UW, no criminal history. He's a Certified Public Accountant and an investor in Bertram Newman's business."

"Yep," O'Neill said as they started up the stairs. The air was stale. "I hear he sold his car to raise money to invest in this Shakespeare's Company business. I thought CPAs raked in the dough."

"Guess not," Jefferson said.

"So what's going on with Detective Meyer meeting with her boss? Is she in trouble?"

Jefferson smiled before responding. "This is a big case for a new detective. Captain Leidel wanted an update. That is what I was told."

"I hope that's all there is to it."

Jefferson opened a door, and they exited the staircase. O'Neill followed her down the third-floor hallway, whose walls were lined with dusty wildlife prints. They turned the corner, stopping in front of a door with a "315" plate. She knocked and a muffled voice replied.

The door swung open, and David Leonard welcomed them into his office. O'Neill hardly recognized Leonard, who looked the part of a successful accountant, wearing a blue sport coat, a pinstriped white shirt, and a bright red tie. O'Neill thought he saw red suspenders beneath the jacket. Jefferson introduced O'Neill as a private detective. He didn't correct her.

"You don't look like any detective I have met," Leonard said, shaking O'Neill's hand. The accountant rounded his desk and sat in his chair. "I didn't think detectives wore jeans and shirts without collars except in the vice squad or the narcotics task force. Don't get me wrong; I think it's great."

The office looked similar in size to Bertram Newman's, but since the window faced the back of the building, it provided a clear view of Lake Monona. O'Neill wondered why an accountant got a plum view while a division administrator's window looked out at another building. The office was clean and decorated with photos, awards, and certifications. Two chairs were in front of Leonard's desk as opposed to the single chair in Bertram's office. O'Neill took a chair, and Jefferson followed.

"We have met before," O'Neill said.

Leonard tilted his head. "I thought you looked familiar. You're Tom Hoffman's sister's friend, right? You were at my apartment when those kids started that fire outside our door. I didn't realize you were a detective."

"I'm a musician, but I do this part time. Bertram Newman's daughter hired the detective agency I work for to investigate his disappearance. My being at your apartment was an odd coincidence."

"Small world." Leonard nodded and gently tapped a ballpoint pen against his hand. "You were wearing an earring, then. One with a cross, I think."

"Excellent memory," O'Neill said.

"We are here to talk about Bertram Newman," Jefferson said. She pulled out her notepad. "Could you tell us about your relationship with Mr. Newman? How long did you know him and in what capacity?"

Leonard nodded and looked at the desk for a moment before responding. "I met Bertram a few years back after I moved to the Annex. We would run into each other in the halls or the elevator, but it wasn't until late last summer when a colleague of mine, Ted Ball, approached me about a business Bertram was starting. Ted was the primary financial contact for Bertram's local government grant division, and Bertram had contacted him looking for someone to run the accounting side of his new business. Ted was more of a governmental accountant and didn't feel it was in his wheelhouse. He thought, however, it was something I might be interested in, so he put us in contact. While I'm not the Shakespeare fan that Bertram is, I enjoy his plays and view him as the English language's greatest writer. We talked and ended up deciding it was a fit, and I signed on as Shakespeare's Company's Vice President of Finance. It may sound like an impressive title but with a small company, it's just a title."

"Did you invest in Shakespeare's Company?" O'Neill asked.

"Only ten thousand dollars. The lowest amount of all the investors. I believe in the company, but unlike most of the other investors, I'm not independently wealthy."

"Are you an employee of Shakespeare's Company?"

"Yes, I earn a thousand dollars a month. It does not sound like much, but it is part-time. The salary is reasonable for the time and level of effort."

It sounded like plenty of money to O'Neill. "How much money did Shakespeare's Company raise?"

"Over one million dollars. Probably closer to one-point-one million."

O'Neill glanced at his notepad. "How much of that money was going toward the joint venture with Antiquity Investments?"

"We paid thirty thousand as a starting fee for the joint venture, and have an annual fee of twenty thousand, which we paid the first year up front. The annual fee only applies if the folio comes up for auction and the joint venture purchases it, so we classify the annual fee as a prepay. One million on top of that goes toward the potential purchase of the folio by Antiquity."

"How does the payment to Antiquity Investments work?" O'Neill said. "Will you cut a check to Antiquity Investments LLC for a million bucks?"

Leonard smiled. "We transfer the funds via wire transfer. We made payment a while back for the starting and annual fees and made four separate payments of two hundred thousand dollars. One last payment is yet to be made."

O'Neill glanced at Jefferson and noticed she was eyeing him, apparently unhappy that he was asking questions. He nodded at her, and she turned toward Leonard.

"I want to talk about Tuesday," Jefferson said. "If you're okay with it, we'll start by detailing what we know."

"Fair enough."

"You had a meeting at the other DOA building that finished shortly before noon. You exited the DOA building at eleven fifty-nine and entered this facility at noon. Records show you logged into your email at five after twelve, and we see consistent activity prior to a meeting you had in the main DOA building at two o'clock. Video has you leaving the Annex a few minutes before two. That meeting apparently ended just before four, and we have you returning through the front entrance at four. You have email and online activity until five twelve. The camera picked you up leaving the office at five twenty-two. Does that sound correct?"

"It sounds correct," Leonard said, tapping the pen on his desk.

"Also, you came back late that night, correct?"

"I came back to the office for five minutes. I forgot to bring a file home I needed for a presentation I had the next morning.

Since I bus in and out of work, it is inconvenient when I forget something." Leonard shook his head and laughed. "It sounds like you know what I did better than I do."

"Yes." Jefferson flipped through her notepad paper. "You came in at eleven ten and left at eleven twenty-two."

"Sounds about right."

"Did you see Bertram that day, even in passing?"

"I don't think so," Leonard replied, saying each word slowly and continuing to tap his fingers against the desk. "I was in meetings for nearly six hours. And this office building doesn't have a lunchroom or anything that encourages us to run into people from other floors."

O'Neill was staring out the window, losing focus. All he could see was the blue sky, but he imagined the lake below.

"Anything else?" Leonard said, his gaze bouncing between O'Neill and Jefferson.

"Did Bertram Newman ever exit the building through the loading dock?" Jefferson asked without looking up from her notepad.

"Not that I recall, but he could have. If he's like me, he uses the front entrance ninety percent of the time. Sometimes I use the side entrance if I am in someone's office on that side of the building. I only use the loading dock exit when stopping at one of the Tourism offices, since theirs are along that side of the building. Neither Bertram nor I have business interactions with tourism staff, but we got to know them a bit and did stuff like basketball tournament pools and so forth. It isn't common for me to leave that way, but it happens."

Jefferson leaned close to O'Neill. "Anything else you want *me* to ask Mr. Leonard?"

O'Neill shook his head, and the three stood at the same time. The accountant took a few long steps and opened the door. O'Neill exited, and Jefferson followed him into the hallway. Leonard muttered a farewell, and the door shut behind them. O'Neill waited for Jefferson to pass so she could lead him to the staircase.

"Keep in mind that you're an observer," Jefferson said without looking toward him. "I should have cut you off."

O'Neill apologized and tried to look contrite as they walked down the stairs.

They exited the staircase and found Detective Meyer sitting in the Annex's lobby. She was wearing a light green pantsuit with a white shirt and an open collar. O'Neill noticed she was also wearing eyeliner and lipstick, which he didn't recall from their previous meetings.

"How did it go?" Meyer asked, putting a notepad in her pocket.

"Uneventful," Jefferson said. "We have his time and activities documented. He didn't remember ever seeing the victim leave via the loading dock exit but noted that he thought most employees would periodically leave via that exit. It would be uncommon, but Bertram was certainly aware of the exit."

Meyer nodded.

"How did your meeting with the captain go?" Jefferson said.

"Short but not sweet," Meyer said, rolling her eyes. "Investigative Services have asked about transferring the case to their unit. The transfer is not a done deal, but it will occur since something clearly happened to Bertram Newman. The writing is on the wall."

"You should expect that. Don't take it personally."

"Also, the captain is not happy," Meyer said, turning to O'Neill, "about how I am working with you, Mr. O'Neill."

"Me? What did I do?"

"Captain Leidel says you may work for a detective agency, but you're not a licensed private detective. He claims I'm leaving the City and the department open to litigation should something go wrong or someone complain. In theory, your involvement could even impact this case, should it go to trial."

Ryder had arranged for O'Neill to sit for the Wisconsin State Licensing private detective exam in June. Ryder was working with the state agency to verify that O'Neill's history did not prevent him from obtaining a license. The Ryder Detective Agency would sponsor his application, and they were working to get a letter of support from Detective Phil Garcia. But those plans wouldn't do him any good today. "Sounds like bullshit."

"Doesn't matter if it is," Meyer said. She stood and looked down at him. "I'm going to the upcoming meeting with Philip Couturier on my own. And Penny, don't deny that Mr. O'Neill attended the interview with David Leonard, but don't bring it up with anyone if you can avoid it. No need pushing me further down the hill." She led the group out of the Annex and onto the concrete walkway.

"What time is it?" O'Neill asked.

"About four o'clock," Jefferson said after looking at her watch.

"Where and when are you meeting Couturier?"

Meyer paused at the edge of the sidewalk. "Couturier's office at five. His gallery is on the Mendota side of the Capitol, which is about a ten-minute walk."

"Can I mention a few points to raise with him?" O'Neill asked. "Figure you have a few spare minutes."

Meyer turned toward Jefferson. "You can head back to the office, Penny. Thanks for helping me out."

Jefferson nodded a reply and headed west toward the Madison Police Department's offices.

"Okay, what questions?" Meyer said to O'Neill. "But to be clear, you are not going to the meeting." She glanced toward the police station, apparently conscious of being seen with him.

"Let's stop somewhere so we can talk. Somewhere nearby."

Meyer eased closer and leered down at him. "Seamus, please don't suggest we stop at the Great Dane and drink beer. I'm heading to Couturier's office. If I'm early, that's fine, as I have files I need to review."

"Right. I'll walk with you for a bit."

Meyer pointed the direction, and the pair walked a block, pausing at a corner intersection. The walk light to cross East Wilson Street turned white and O'Neill followed her across the road.

"How about we stop at the Argus?" O'Neill asked, walking directly behind her.

Once across the road, she stopped and turned toward him. "Seamus, I'm still on probation. Do you know what that means for a detective?"

"No, but it doesn't sound good."

"It means they can fire me without cause. I need to get through my first year before most job protections kick-in. I need to toe the line if I want to keep my job. If my captain tells me to do something, I need to do it."

"That sucks."

"My captain ordered me to stop working with you. He said I could work with Ryder since he's ex-MPD and a licensed private detective, but he doesn't want his detectives bringing street musicians to police interviews."

"I'm not a street musician. I rarely ever busk anymore."

"That's not how he sees it. And we're a few blocks from the station. If anyone sees me with you and tells him... I'm up a creek."

"But it's important."

"What is so important?"

"I know where Bertram's body is," O'Neill said, surprising himself that he said it out loud.

Meyer's jaw dropped. Her lips moved, but nothing came out.

"I'll tell you about it. But I think better with a beer in my hand. Let's stop at the Great Dane. We can hide in the cellar. I've never seen a cop down there."

O'Neill started walking, hoping she would follow. After several steps, he heard the clicking of heels behind him, and a smile crept onto his face.

Chapter 20

The brewpub was busy with the early Friday evening dinner crowd, so O'Neill and Meyer settled in a line behind a group of women. Patrons filled the stools at the first floor bar, mugs sat on most of the barroom tables, and customers milled about. O'Neill saw several open booths near the counter, but each had a 'Reserved' sign. A host led the group away as a second host returned to the stand. O'Neill leaned forward, resting his hand on the wooden host stand.

"Hello, Seamus," the host said, smiling widely. She didn't look old enough to work in a brewpub, but the makeup and a short dress made her age hard to gauge. "I almost didn't recognize you with the buzz cut."

"Hey, I see you're already busy so I don't mean to be a pain, but we're having a beer and an appetizer, and I was hoping we could get a table downstairs, something secluded if possible. Is that doable, or are all the tables downstairs reserved for meal-eating customers?"

"It's still early, so we can get something for you," the host said, looking up at Meyer. The host examined the chart, then crossed out a table with her marker. "Follow me." She led them down a nearby staircase, which descended into the building's cellar.

Built in the 1850s as a hotel, O'Neill preferred to believe that the cellar's jagged rock walls dated from that period. The sandstone walls gave a vibe he liked, and the cellar's darkness seemed appropriate.

There were five booths, and the host sat them at the only vacant one. O'Neill slid to the edge of one side, and Meyer sat opposite him. Couples and a young family were in the booths while two men in business suits took up another table.

"Does this work?" the host asked.

"This is great," O'Neill answered. "Appreciate it."

The host paused near the stairs to talk with a server, pointing at them before rushing up the staircase.

"Seamus, do you or do you not know where Bertram Newman's body is?"

"I think I know."

The server interrupted them. O'Neill ordered a red lager for himself and water for Meyer.

"Did you get an answer to my question from yesterday?" O'Neill asked after the server left. "Were any of our suspects or anyone from Shakespeare's Company in the meeting that ended at noon on the day Bertram disappeared? The one he asked about in his last phone call."

"Yes. Both David Leonard and Lulu Hanrahan were in the meeting. That makes Lulu a potential suspect. But get to your point. Where's the body?"

"The first question we had was whether Bertram left the Annex on his own. Thanks to me, we know he could have snuck out through the loading dock. Yet why would he sneak out?"

"We've been through this," Meyer said. "He may have been running away, or maybe it was about a woman or about money."

"Did that financial advisor guy you and Ryder met with this morning…"

"Mike Gunderson."

"Did Mike Gunderson tell you how much money Bertram invested in Shakespeare's Company and when?"

"Two hundred thousand," Meyer said. She pulled out a notepad, pausing as she read. "According to Gunderson, the money transferred out of his account to Shakespeare's Company about six weeks ago."

"Bertram is worth roughly three million dollars. Did Bertram or anyone access that money recently?"

"No. Linda Newman gave us the ability to view their financial accounts. The only large transaction was the transfer of two hundred thousand dollars to Shakespeare's Company. That happened in April. Both Linda Newman and Mike Gunderson were aware of that transaction. Gunderson says that everything else looks routine. Our techies and financial people agreed."

The server returned with their drinks and O'Neill ordered nachos.

"I can't imagine Bertram running away with a woman without having money," O'Neill said between sips of his beer. "And I can't imagine him stealing from Shakespeare's Company and making a run for it, since there's only a million dollars to be had, of which two hundred thousand was already his."

"You're saying Bertram didn't leave on his own, which has been our thinking."

"I think Bertram was killed on Tuesday. He likely brought an unloaded gun with him to work, implying he was afraid of someone or was going to intimidate someone. If he was afraid, why not bring a loaded gun? I like the possibility of him confronting someone but realizing this person might need to be intimidated. Any confrontation likely relates to Shakespeare's Company. There were five people involved in Shakespeare's Company who lived or worked within walking distance of Bertram's office."

"We agreed last night. There are five suspects," Meyer said, pulling out her notebook. "Couturier, who I'm meeting with in a few minutes; the lawyer, Steven McCormick; the accountant you just met with, David Leonard; the IT guy, Tom Hoffman; and the retired man, Rob Peacock. Six if you count Linda Newman and seven if you count Lulu Hanrahan. How does this lead to a dead body?"

"Why would Bertram sneak out of the Annex and try to avoid being seen on camera? He didn't have bullets, so he wasn't going to shoot anyone. Why sneak out?"

"Maybe he wasn't sneaking out. Maybe he was trying to stay dry as you did that day, and it just looked to us like he snuck out."

"Nah, it stopped raining soon after I left the Annex." O'Neill took a gulp, nearly finishing his beer. "I think he confronted someone in the building, and the only person in the building involved in Shakespeare's Company was their accountant, David Leonard. I'm guessing Leonard was ripping off Shakespeare's Company. Bertram brought the computer to show Leonard what was wrong, hoping Leonard could explain. Bertram was worried enough that he had brought an unloaded gun. I don't know the details, but Bertram was right to be concerned, as Leonard either knocked him out or killed him. He probably kept Bertram's body in his own office on Tuesday. He came back late Tuesday night shortly before midnight. That's when he removed the body from the building."

"Are you thinking he snuck Bertram's body out through the loading dock? He likely didn't since we recorded him leaving on the same DOA camera that recorded you leaving earlier. Our techs checked on that today. He'd have to do what you did, except going the other direction. And would he know about the location of cameras and about the blind spot?"

"Leonard's office is on the third floor. Those offices have windows that open. I'm guessing Leonard opened the window and stuffed Bertram's body out."

Meyer leaned forward. "He threw the body out of a third-story window?"

"Either that or he brought the body to the rooftop and tossed it from there. Both would work, and it would land in the back lot. The lot would have been empty, so the body would land on the pavement. Unless Leonard's an idiot, he put the body into a large bag or a tarp. Bertram would have been dead for nearly twelve hours, but a three-floor drop could leave a mess. The DOA camera doesn't record the back of the Annex, correct?"

"Correct. The camera picks up the driveway from the dock to the road. It didn't pick up anyone pulling a car or truck into the driveway."

"Leonard takes the bus to work. Tom Hoffman said Leonard sold his car to make his investment in Shakespeare's Company. Could be he bought another one, but Tom didn't mention it. So Leonard dropped the body out the back of the

Annex onto the parking lot, but he had no way to move it. All he could do was drag it, limiting how far he could move it. Yet a sewer runs through the back alley. You can access the sewer through a manhole."

"You think he dumped the body down a manhole and into the sewer?" Meyer's eyes dodged between O'Neill and the table. "Would he be able to open the cover?"

"Leonard could see the back lot and the manhole from his office window. My guess is he had seen DOA facilities staff open the manhole. If that's the case, he would have known that they kept a manhole key or maybe a chisel or a crowbar in the loading dock area. If not, he could have gone to the hardware store or to Menards and bought a manhole key, which is basically a crowbar with a hook."

"Is this manhole key thing real, or are you making it up?"

"People use manhole keys everywhere. They are how the city employees get in and out of the sewers. I know about them because you learn stuff hanging around the streets. A hole in the ground is sometimes useful, especially if you got something to hide from the cops or from street people and you know where to get a key. My guess, however, is that the DOA's facility staff has opened that cover at some point since they have a sewer entrance on their property. If Leonard had not seen facilities folks opening the manhole, he could have done an internet search to figure out how to take the cover off."

"If he searched on his work computer or home computer, we'll be able to track it."

The server approached, carrying nachos and two small plates. O'Neill took one plate from her and grabbed a clump of nachos as soon as it hit their table.

They each ordered a beer before the server drifted to the next table.

"It hasn't rained much since Tuesday night," O'Neill said between bites. "The body is lying in the sewer, waiting to be discovered. It rained a few nights ago, but I don't think the body would wash away easily."

Meyer pulled several nachos off the stack and set them on her plate. Then she looked at O'Neill and smiled. "Perhaps I am just overly tired, but it makes sense. But what's his motive? Why does a CPA turn into a killer?"

"CPAs make good money, as I understand. Leonard has a job with the state and he's making a grand a month from Shakespeare's Company. Yet this thirty-six-year-old with no kids who shares an apartment with a coworker had to sell his car to come up with money to invest in Shakespeare's Company? My guess is he has a drug problem, a gambling problem, or both."

"Nothing came up on our background check, but we were only looking at criminal and employment activity and hadn't dug into him further."

"What do we do now?" O'Neill asked. "I'm a little concerned that I may have spooked him today, showing up with Officer Jefferson to interview him. He recognized me from when I visited his apartment. He's got to wonder whether I'm onto him."

"We need to open the manhole and find out if the body is there. Yet we should think this through, since we need to prove that Leonard is the killer. We may find evidence of a confrontation in Leonard's office, but Bertram has been dead for three and a half days. He could argue that Bertram regularly visited his office, so it would have to be blood. If Leonard had Bertram's computer, it would provide evidence as well. Of course, if we can show that Leonard had stolen from Shakespeare's Company, it will illustrate a motive."

"Bertram also had a Dictaphone that connects to his laptop. Bertram may have brought it as a recording device. If Leonard didn't notice it, a recording of the murder might be in Bertram's coat pocket."

"That would be dream evidence. But, even if it was used, the fall could ruin the recording or it could be in water and won't work. Or Leonard could have found the Dictaphone and destroyed it. Ideally, Leonard would run for it or we would capture him trying to move the body or trying to leave the country. Before we do anything, let's put him under surveillance."

Meyer pulled out her phone and called the station. After a discussion and several long waits, she hung up and announced that the City of Madison Police Department would find David Leonard and put him under surveillance.

"It is unlikely that he will come back tonight and move the body," Meyer said. "But we can't take that chance. We need to check if the body is there. If it is, I'll call it in and bring in forensics."

O'Neill nodded as he sipped beer and ate nachos.

"If we find the body," Meyer continued, "we won't be able to keep it out of the news. The local stations will pick up the activity and put it on at ten o'clock news, if not at six o'clock. I would feel better if we had him under surveillance before the story gets on the news."

"How will you know if he's under surveillance?"

"Dispatch will contact me as soon as he's located." She glanced at her watch then took a drink of beer and stared at the table.

"Suppose I walk to the Annex and check out the manhole? If I find the body, I'll come back and tell you. I'll also ask Ryder to put surveillance on the manhole cover. You could wait until after ten before verifying we found Bertram's body and calling forensics. The TV stations would pick it up, but after the ten o'clock news."

Meyer shook her head. "I can't delay calling in a dead body. No way. And once I know about it, we'll send in forensics and we've got a cordoned off site with dozens of police."

"Let me restate things. I'll check out the Annex and its grounds and see if I can find a tool that would allow you to get inside the sewer. If I don't find one, I'll be back. If I find one, I'll also tell you if my theory is worth pursuing. If it is, we'll call Ryder and put the manhole under surveillance. I won't tell you whether I looked into the sewer. But if I still think my theory is good, you can guess. This would give your surveillance time to find our suspect. I would tell you where to find the manhole key, and you and Ryder could check the manhole yourselves at ten."

Meyer shook her head, looking like she was trying to hold back a smile. "This sounds ill-conceived. You think you'll be able to find something to get into the manhole?"

"The manhole is in the alley or driveway between the administration buildings. The Department of Administration might have a key, a crowbar or something in either the Annex or in the main DOA building. Even if they haven't accessed the sewer, they may have a crowbar. It's past four thirty on a Friday, so I'm doubtful anyone is working in the dock area.

If someone's there, I'll come back. If not, I'll search the area near the docks in both the Annex and in the Administration Building. They'll likely either have a key or a crowbar. I think I could open a manhole with a crowbar or even a Halligan bar. If I can't access the manhole, I'll be back and we'll figure out what to do. Okay?"

"Okay, you go for a *walk*. I'll wait for you. Use the building entry on the side opposite the docks. The camera will pick you up as you approach and leave the entrance, but if you don't go toward Wilson Street, it will only see you go onto the next building's driveway. None of the Administration Building's cameras will pick you up. It might be awkward if a camera picked you up leaving the building with a crowbar."

"I see Erin Meyer has a devious side."

"A practical side." Meyer handed him two key cards, one for the Administration Building and one for the Annex. "These better come back to me."

"Course." O'Neill already had a key card to the Annex, but didn't mention it.

"These get you into the building, but inner doors use regular metal keys. If the inside door to the docks is locked, you won't be able to get in."

"I'm pretty sure I can get into the loading dock without one, since code won't allow them to restrict access to a marked exit."

"Before you do anything, check if Leonard is still at the office. The MPD is looking for him and should be checking his office about now. If he is in his office, come back, as he's probably already under surveillance, so we can go together and open the manhole. If not, we'll go with your plan. Knock on Leonard's door and, if he answers, tell him you lost your cell phone and you are checking if you left it in his office. He'll check and won't find it."

"I don't have a cell phone."

"He doesn't know that. Tell him the phone is a Nokia," Meyer said, pulling out a silver phone and laying it next to the nachos. "You can describe this if necessary."

"Nokia. Got it. And if he isn't there, I'll need a flashlight. Do you have one, or should I check with the bartender?"

Meyer handed him a blue flashlight that was the size of a highlighter. O'Neill turned it on and off, then stuck it in his pocket where it clanged against his tin whistle.

"Thanks," O'Neill said. "I'll be back in ten minutes. Don't eat all the nachos."

She rolled her eyes but smiled.

Chapter 21

O'Neill touched Meyer's hand as he slid out of the booth. He walked through the Great Dane Brewing Company's cellar and up the stairs, pausing at the host stand. Dinner traffic was heavy, but O'Neill got the host's attention and told her he would return. The host nodded, and O'Neill slipped past the line and out the door.

O'Neill jogged down King Street, cutting between the Annex and the building under construction that sat next to it. He arrived at the side entrance to the Annex, slid Meyer's key card in front of the reader, and heard the familiar thump. After opening the door, he walked down the hall and realized he was lost. But he knew it was a small building, so he continued and eventually found the lobby. He took the stairs to the third floor, pulling out his notepad and verifying Leonard's room number. At the end of the hall, he knocked on Leonard's door. There was no answer, so he returned to the staircase, exiting to the basement.

O'Neill opened the door between the hallway and the loading docks, wiped the doorknob with his shirt, turned on his flashlight, and stepped into the loading dock. Even with the flashlight, the room was dark. He flipped on the light switch with his elbow. O'Neill figured the Annex's loading dock was the most likely spot for storing a manhole key or a crowbar since it was closest to the sewer. After a brief search, he found a tool chest, but it was locked. A rusty barrel filled with various tools, including hacksaws and pruners, sat beside it. Aiming the flashlight into the barrel, he spotted a sledgehammer, an assortment of saws, and a rusty manhole key.

Adrenaline pumped through O'Neill's veins as he set the manhole key on the counter and searched the area. Noticing a trash barrel lined with a black plastic bag, he emptied the bag's contents into the trash can, then stuffed the manhole key into the trash bag. Finally, he took a pair of work gloves from the side counter and put them on. He picked up the trash bag, opened the door, and flipped off the light. The door swung closed and O'Neill held the key close to his body as he walked the hallways of the Annex. Fortunately, it was a Friday afternoon, so no one was there to see him.

Exiting the building using the same entrance, O'Neill was soon behind the Annex. A lone car with State of Wisconsin license plates was in the back lot. O'Neill surveyed the area, looking upward to where he thought Leonard's office was located. He glanced at the sewer and approached the manhole. The top of the cover included a painted notice: "Keep our lakes clean. NO DUMPING." He slipped the manhole key out of the trash bag, slid the hook inside one of the manhole's three holes, twisted the handle gently, and yanked. The manhole rubbed loudly against the asphalt as O'Neill pulled it along the pavement. He stopped to peer into the hole, set the manhole key on the ground, and pulled out Meyer's flashlight.

The scent of algae and wastewater permeated his senses, and his eyes watered. He aimed the flashlight downward, revealing a black mass on the sewer floor. Yet he could not determine what the mass was or whether it was large enough to be a human body. After pulling the cover fully off the hole, he wiped his forehead, put the flashlight in his pocket, and took several steps down the ladder and into the darkness. He reached for the flashlight, but accidentally pulled out his Sweetone tin whistle. The whistle slipped from his hand and there was a clack as it hit the metal ladder followed by a gentle thump as it landed on the sewer floor.

O'Neill swore and turned the flashlight on, aiming the beam at the ladder. Holding on with one hand, he stepped down three rungs, pausing when he heard movement inside the sewer. He pointed the light at the floor, and it caught eye shine on what he assumed was a raccoon. The animal scurried away, and he focused the beam on the black mass below him. The odor told him it was a body, but he had to be certain. Standing on the bottom step, O'Neill avoided stepping onto the mud-covered floor and leaving a footprint. He tried to get closer, aiming the light at the far end of the object. Holding the ladder with his left hand, he leaned down, but the ladder jolted. For a moment, he thought it might break, but it held.

Keeping the light's beam on the object, O'Neill realized he was looking at a tear in the bag. Inside was a shoe connected to a leg. While unsure if it was Bertram Newman, he was certain it was a body. The light also revealed O'Neill's black tin whistle, lying on the sewer floor only inches from the body. He held both the ladder and the flashlight with his left hand, and leaned downward as his right hand plucked his Sweetone tin whistle from the floor. His stomach lurched as he slid the whistle into his front pocket. He scurried up the ladder, glancing about as he reached street level. Stepping off the ladder, O'Neill ran to the edge of the grass, spitting several times. Then he pulled out

his Sweetone whistle and wiped the mud and gunk on the grass
.

The key was still attached to the cover, so he pulled it toward the hole. Once again, there was noise, and O'Neill looked nervously at the windows of the two state office buildings. Taking large breaths, he pushed the cover closed and put the key and the gloves into the trash bag. He set the bag behind a small row of bushes that lined the building's edge.

Adrenaline aided his jog to the Great Dane. Inside, he rushed past the host stand, slipped down the back stairs, and hurried into the bathroom where he washed his hands, face, and tin whistle. He thought about throwing the whistle in the trash but couldn't do it. After drying off, he smiled at the short-haired man in the mirror and went back into the cellar, sliding into the seat opposite Meyer. She was typing on her laptop.

"Geez, you surprised me," Meyer said as she took her glasses off and closed the laptop. "I thought you would come in the way we came in earlier."

"I had to wash up," O'Neill said as she dropped the glasses into her bag. "I didn't realize you wore glasses."

"Just for reading when my eyes are tired," Meyer said, licking her lips. "How did it go?"

"A manhole key was in the Annex. I put it in a trash bag and set the bag behind the bushes in the back. After looking over the situation, I think my theory is solid." O'Neill picked up a hunk of the remaining nachos. "I see you ordered soup. Chili? Any good?"

"Yes, it was chili, and yes, it was fine. You think your theory is valid? Do you think I should look inside the sewer?"

"Yep. Can I borrow your phone so I can call Ryder?"

Meyer pulled out her phone and handed it to him. He dialed Ryder's office number and, surprisingly, got an answer.

"Ryder, this is Seamus. Can you meet me at the Great Dane? It's important."

"Seamus, I was literally walking out the door when you called. What's so important?"

Meyer leaned forward, presumably trying to hear the conversation. O'Neill tilted closer to her, and strands of her hair touched the spiky hairs on his head.

"I got this theory about where the killer put Bertram's body. I sold Detective Meyer on it. Come down so we can talk it over."

Ryder let out a large breath. "Seamus, I'm tired. Can this wait until tomorrow?"

"No, it can't. Detective Meyer is here with me. Talk to her."

O'Neill handed the phone to Meyer. He leaned further across the table until his forehead rested against hers.

"Hello Mr. Ryder, this is Detective Meyer."

O'Neill couldn't hear Ryder's reply.

"Yes, I understand why you think that, but we would benefit from having you here. It's a long story, and I prefer talking it over in person."

There was a muffled reply.

"One other thing, Mr. Ryder. Mr. O'Neill says you have an employee who does surveillance. Would he be free this evening?"

After further discussion, Meyer handed the phone to O'Neill. She was smiling widely, looking relaxed and comfortable. "Your boss wants to talk to you again."

"What the hell is going on?" Ryder said to O'Neill.

"Come on down and find out. And can you send that guy doing surveillance to the Annex building? I want him to do surveillance on a manhole."

There was a painfully long silence. "I'll be there in fifteen minutes. This better be good and not you just romancing Detective Meyer."

"Cool. We are downstairs in the cellar."

Ryder ended the call without saying goodbye.

O'Neill handed Meyer the phone. "Sometimes, he's so thick. But he'll be here. What were you doing on your computer when I came in?"

Meyer's smile disappeared. She opened the laptop and turned it so the display faced O'Neill. "My captain sent me an email. He's turning the case over to Investigative Services. The official changeover happens in the morning."

"Oh, I thought it was something I wasn't supposed to see," O'Neill said as he read the note. "You know what that means?"

"No, what?"

"That means you looked flustered when I came in because I saw you wearing glasses."

"What do you mean?"

"When I sat down. I could see you were embarrassed. I wasn't sure if it was something on your computer or if it was the glasses."

"I am embarrassed about the case being taken away. Having my first major case taken away pisses me off."

"You already knew that was happening," O'Neill said, waving the server over. He ordered another beer, and the server hurried away.

"That doesn't mean it's not embarrassing."

"Neither is wearing glasses. I should probably wear a pair myself, though it's things far away that I struggle with. What's that, nearsightedness?"

"Yes. Mine is farsightedness."

"Okay. Now that we are past that, we can talk about what you guys are going to do while I'm playing the show."

"The show?"

"Yeah. Didn't I tell you? My band is playing on Monroe Street at Smoky Joe's Café. The show's scheduled for eight. If you're free, you could come down."

"Free?" she said, chuckling. "I'm going to be busy as hell all night."

"Not until ten. The show will finish around nine. There is plenty of time."

"Seamus, assuming you're right, I'm expecting a long night and I already worked a twelve-hour day."

The server interrupted them as she set a beer mug in front of O'Neill.

"Thought Garcia and his friends were taking over?" O'Neill said after the server left.

"Investigative Services may take over, but if your theory is right, everything changes and I will still be heavily involved."

"Bummer."

"No, that's good. But after we set the plan with your boss, I'm going home for a few hours of sleep. Sleep is a priority."

"So you won't be at the show?"

"No. I'll dream about it, okay?"

"Okay, you can dream about me."

Meyer shook her head. "Geez, you are incorrigible."

Chapter 22

Ryder approached the table as the server brought another beer. The burly detective was wearing a sport coat and blue tie which sat loosely around his neck. O'Neill stood, shooing Ryder to his spot, then looked at Meyer. But she didn't move over, so he sat next to Ryder, whose girth pressed against the wall.

"What's going on?" Ryder asked, his eyes darting between Meyer and O'Neill.

"I got this theory," O'Neill said, sipping his beer.

"You got a theory? What a surprise."

"I met with David Leonard and went through details with Detective Meyer and with her one officer."

"Officer Jefferson," Meyer said.

"Yeah. Anyway, I believe Bertram confronted Leonard after Leonard got back from a meeting on Tuesday. Bertram brought his computer and the unloaded gun to Leonard's third story office."

"At the Annex?" Ryder said, glancing around the room.

O'Neill nodded. "I don't know exactly how or why, but Leonard killed Bertram. He couldn't get the body out of the office during the day, so he left it in his office and came back that night."

"We have Leonard coming into the office after eleven that night," Meyer said.

"Leonard can't take the body out of an exit because of the cameras. Maybe he knew about the opportunity to sneak it out via the loading dock, or maybe he didn't. But rather than doing that, he simply opened his window and pushed the body out."

"He pushed a dead body out the window?" Ryder said.

"Yeah. The body landed in the back parking lot, but Leonard doesn't own a car. If he did, a camera from the main Administration Building would record him driving into the alley between the buildings. But it picked nothing up. He couldn't move the body far from where it landed. Yet he knew there was a sewer and a manhole in the back."

"A manhole? You think he stuffed the body down the manhole?" Ryder said, laughing out loud. "That would work in the short-term, but someone would eventually find it or it would wash into the lake grill. The body wouldn't go into the lake since those grills stop large items from entering the lake. But someone would see it leaning against that grill."

"That would take time. Besides, Leonard didn't plan this. Bertram confronted him, forcing his hand. Leonard came up with this on the fly."

"It's possible, sure," Ryder said. "Why don't we go down and you can crawl into the sewer and see what you find?"

"You and I are going to do that later tonight," Meyer said.

"Us? Why not let Seamus?"

"Do you know Captain Leidel?" O'Neill asked.

"Bobby Leidel? Sure," Ryder said.

"The Captain doesn't want Detective Meyer to work with me. He says I'm not a licensed detective and says I'm an insurance risk. And he called me a street musician."

"Okay," Ryder replied. "Then Seamus and I can go by ourselves."

"I got a show. Erin and I talked through this, and both the Ryder Detective Agency and MPD should be involved in any search of the sewer."

"Okay," Ryder said after a break. "But I will be quite pissed if I step into a sewer for no reason."

"I have every reason to be confident in my theory."

"Let's assume you are right. What if Leonard comes back and moves the body?"

"That's where your surveillance guy comes in. Unless you want to do the surveillance yourself."

"You know I hate surveillance. Let's go now and get it done. That way we save paying Werlitz to watch a manhole cover."

"I like Seamus' theory," Meyer said. "But there are a few things I need to follow up on first. I should be ready to go with you to the Annex at ten tonight."

Ryder still looked confused.

"If our theory is correct and you find Bertram," O'Neill said, turning toward his boss, "Detective Meyer will immediately contact the MPD so forensics can find the body and start doing forensic stuff. That is something she's required to do. Local news will pick it up and the suspect might hear about it on the evening news. Erin is putting Leonard under surveillance, but they have yet to locate him. Erin would like it if Leonard was under surveillance before he knew we had found the body. Him making a run for it while under surveillance would be useful, while him running for it before he's under surveillance would create a manhunt."

"Okay. I get it. Sorry. Yeah, Meyer and I will follow-up on this joint MPD-Ryder Detective Agency theory at ten. If this theory is correct, the MPD will move on David Leonard as a suspect, but it won't make the ten o'clock news. That gives the MPD time to locate him and put him under surveillance."

"Boy, we're all aligned," O'Neill said. "I came up with the theory, but I look forward to you two validating it."

The three of them nodded, and Ryder pulled out his phone and called Sammy Werlitz. After a few minutes, there was agreement that Werlitz would stop his current assignment and would meet Ryder outside the Administration Building.

"I'm going to follow up on a few things," Meyer said to Ryder, "but will meet you here at ten. Let's meet upstairs in the bar area. I'll be the one drinking 7-Up. We'll walk from here to the Annex. Also, we've got each other's number in case one of us is late."

"Anything else?" Ryder asked.

O'Neill finished his beer. "The bill."

"I will pay my share," Meyer said. "I had a beer, a bowl of chili, and some of Seamus' nachos. I can claim it."

O'Neill waved down the server, who appeared relieved when he asked for the bill.

"Go meet Werlitz," O'Neill said to Ryder.

"Yeah. Sammy is coming from the Hilldale area, so he'll be there any minute." He pulled out his wallet and handed a ten-dollar bill to O'Neill. "This will catch at least part of your share."

O'Neill took the cash and let Ryder slip past him. The bill came a minute later, and they plopped cash onto the table. Meyer kept the receipt.

"Will you be able to sleep amidst all this excitement?" O'Neill said as they walked up the stairs.

"You bet I'll sleep. I have been so stressed. My body feels like a puppet pulled tight for three days straight. Finally, the strings released at least a little."

"Can I walk you home?" he asked as they stepped past the host.

"You don't need to. I can handle myself. It's not even dark yet."

"I know you can handle yourself," O'Neill replied. "I'm not worried about you. I just want to walk you home."

Meyer exited the Great Dane, and he followed. They stood outside the brewpub, and she looked eastward. There was ample pedestrian traffic and cars were lined up behind a red light.

"Isn't my place out of your way?" Meyer asked.

"I don't mind."

"Okay," Meyer said. "But you are not coming inside. I'm only saying yes because you have not asked me..." her voice faded away. The walk sign turned, and they crossed King Street.

"What didn't I ask you?" he said once they were across the street.

"Every guy I meet asks me whether I played volleyball or basketball in high school or in college. It gets old."

O'Neill hurried along, trying to stay even with her pace. "Guess I should be honest with you. I searched the Internet for you last night and your time playing volleyball for the Fighting Illini was the first result. I figured I wouldn't hold that against you."

"That is big of you."

A group of ten or twelve teenagers approached them, so he dropped behind.

"This might sound like an odd question," Meyer said after the crowd passed. "But why are you flirting with me?"

"Why wouldn't I? I mean, you're beautiful, smart, graceful, and I think you like me. I normally wouldn't think twice about a cop since cops don't usually like me. Oh, and you haven't asked me about my music."

Meyer kept her gaze forward, but she smiled slightly and put a hand to her lips, seeming to wipe the smile away. "You don't want me to ask you about your music?"

"No, I didn't mean it that way. I just meant that most of the women I've dated liked the idea of me being a rock & roller. They like me when they see me as one, but once they don't see me that way, things change. You don't see me as a rock & roll musician, but you still like me."

"What if you're wrong? What if I don't like you?"

"I'll be bummed. You don't have a boyfriend, do you?"

"Me?" She chuckled and turned toward him. "I have not even been on a date since I took this job. I don't have time for it. And it is difficult meeting men when you're a police detective unless you want to date another cop, which I don't. Cops are afraid of me, anyway."

At the corner of South Webster Street and East Main Street, the crosswalk sign turned red. A half-dozen people were within earshot, so neither spoke. The walk sign turned, and they started across the street.

"Why are cops afraid of you?" O'Neill said once they were far enough from the other pedestrians.

"There was an incident back before I was a detective. A sergeant slapped my behind. I turned around and punched him, breaking his jaw."

"Whoa!"

"It was a reaction, but I got disciplined for it."

"*You* got disciplined? What the fuck? He slapped you."

Meyer shrugged her shoulders, implying she had no answer. Then she pointed to the DNR building that was on their right. "You ever shower there?"

O'Neill assumed she wanted to change the subject, so he let her. "Oh, sure. You can get in during work hours without a key card. They're decent showers, too."

They walked silently as traffic drove past.

"Do you date a lot?" Meyer finally said.

"I used to, back when I was in a group. I had girlfriends, but they didn't last more than a year. Not so much lately, though."

"Was this the Theory of Trash band?"

"Theoretically Trashed," O'Neill said, shaking his head. "That was one band I was in. How did you know about them?"

"I did an Internet search myself. There are lots of results about you and your bands. You said you have a new band now, right? Will that bring new girlfriends?"

"It's not a rock & roll band, so I doubt it. And I'm not twenty-one anymore. Either way, that's not why I got the new group together. It's a chance to do what I'm meant to do. I miss being onstage and the camaraderie you have with bandmates and the audience."

They crossed East Main Street, and the spire from St. Patrick's Church peeked over a two-story apartment building.

"I'm up here around the corner, past this apartment complex." Meyer pointed to a three-story building with four white pillars on each floor. "It's a two-bedroom, which is nice. I keep my car on the ramp by the station since there is not an ideal place to park. Otherwise, this is all I need, though the apartment did not impress my parents when they visited. They think I'm in student housing."

Sumner was etched in stone atop the front door.

"Was this originally a house, or was it always an apartment building?" O'Neill asked. "And what's the Sumner mean? There has got to be a story."

Meyer didn't answer as they climbed a handful of steps. She unlocked the outer door and held it open for O'Neill.

"This looks like a layout for an apartment building rather than an old house. I wonder if they built it as an apartment or maybe a hotel. What do you think?"

"You ask the weirdest questions," Meyer said after stopping in the hall. "This is my door. Thanks for walking me home."

O'Neill bit at his lip and looked at the ground. "Would you mind a good luck kiss?"

"Good luck for what?" she said as her bag slid from her shoulder and onto the floor. She leaned against the wall.

"I got my show. And you and Ryder are going to be busy tonight."

"Oh, yeah," she said with a laugh. "I forgot for a moment."

"A goodnight and a good luck kiss?"

Meyer nodded ever so slightly.

O'Neill put his left hand on her waist, and his eyes locked onto her lips. They came closer as she crouched down, and their lips finally met. He thought her lips tasted almost fruity, and his lips parted as his tongue slid into her mouth. She moaned and his hand eased down to her hips, gliding beneath her belt.

Then she pulled away.

He let go, and her eyes lit momentarily with anger.

"Seamus, I was letting you kiss me. I wasn't inviting your hand to visit my bare ass." She paused and looked around, as if recognizing how loudly she was speaking.

"Sorry, I..." O'Neill stammered.

"Seamus, I'm not one of your groupies."

"I know that. I, um. Sorry." He put his hands behind his back. "Can we try once more? I'll keep my hands away."

Meyer didn't answer. Instead, she crouched down and their lips locked once again. He pushed her against the wall, but kept his hands behind his back. They kissed for longer than O'Neill could remember kissing anyone. Then she bit his lip slightly and turned away.

"Goodnight, Seamus."

He could see, feel, and hear her chest pumping.

"Goodnight, Erin."

O'Neill backed away, watching her eyes as he opened the outer door and stepped outside. Through the outer window, he saw the door to her apartment open and close. He walked down the steps and onto the sidewalk and he wondered if she was watching him from the front window, but he didn't look. As he got to the corner of Hancock Street and Main Street, he jumped up and gave the stop sign a high-five.

Chapter 23

An unknown tune played in O'Neill's head as he walked down Main Street. He hummed along for a block until he remembered the show. Panicked, he looked up at the early June sun and guessed it was after six thirty. The walk home would take twenty minutes, fifteen if he pushed hard. A trio of runners passed by and he began jogging, allowing the runners to pull away.

As O'Neill neared the Wisconsin State Capitol, he slowed to a walk and asked what time it was. The first two people he asked ignored him, but the third told him six thirty. Relieved, he nodded his thanks, and continued at a brisk pace, arriving home at six forty. The first thing he did was to look for his Feadog tin whistle. But after rustling through his two closets, two milk crates, and a cardboard box, he gave up and instead re-washed the Sweetone that he'd dropped onto the sewer floor next to a dead body. Playing the whistle was an uncomfortable thought, but the show must go on.

After getting washed up and changed, O'Neill opened his *New Day Rising* CD case, took out the twenty-dollar bill, and slipped it into his wallet. He was spending money far too fast this week.

With the Sweetone whistle in his pocket and his accordion in hand, O'Neill started the fifteen-minute walk to Topper's. One person on Bedford Street commented on the accordion and another said something about Weird Al Yankovic. It was after seven when he arrived at Topper's. The wounded guitar player was inside his shop, sitting on a black stool with a guitar case next to him.

"About time," Topper said.

O'Neill ignored the comment and picked up the guitar. Topper stumbled slightly as he stood. The woman behind the counter walked over, but Topper waved her off.

"Mandy and I will be over as soon as we can," the woman said to Topper. "We shouldn't be long."

The woman held the door open, and the two musicians moved slowly. Pedestrian traffic was heavy, and a dozen people brushed past them before they turned onto Frances Street.

"Just two more blocks," O'Neill said, as much to himself as to Topper.

As they approached the Lake Street Ramp, The Johnson's Impala pulled to the curb. The Fiddler leaned out the passenger window, yelling, "Get in!" The trunk popped open, and The Johnson stepped out of the car. O'Neill stuck the guitar and the accordion in the trunk.

"Thanks for picking us up. I thought we were meeting in the alley behind the Fluno Center."

"I knew which way you would come, and I figured you'd be late. Figured it would be good to save Topper a walk."

Topper leaned against the car door, wheezing with his eyes closed. O'Neill thought the bandage stunk, so he cracked open the window and as The Fiddler pointed at a group of pedestrians, O'Neill pulled out his flask, took a sip, and offered

Topper a drink. Topper shook his head, so he returned the flask to his pocket.

"You look worse," The Johnson said to Topper while looking into the rear-view mirror.

Topper's eyes opened briefly. "You try walking a few blocks after being shot."

The Fiddler peered over the car seat, looking worried.

"He's okay," O'Neill said to her. "He just needs rest."

"Should he really be playing?" she asked.

"Course not."

They arrived at Smoky Joe's Café, walking past two beige fliers for Schumacher's Flour Mill. They had plastered one flier on the door and the other on the window. The flier used a photo that included O'Neill sitting on his accordion, and he decided it looked cool enough. Marlene Schultz waved the band in, shaking each of their hands as they stepped in. She didn't seem concerned about the ten-year-old holding the violin case.

People lounging in the half-full coffee house whispered to each other and stared as Schumacher's Flour Mill opened their instrument cases and set them on the vacant area that was to be the stage. O'Neill ran a hand through his hair.

"Would any of you like something to drink?" Marlene Schultz asked.

Both Topper and The Johnson ordered coffee, while O'Neill, and the Fiddler ordered root beer.

"What's your name?" Marlene asked The Fiddler.

"Mika."

"She's The Fiddler," O'Neill said.

"Welcome," Marlene said. "I can't say we've ever had someone as young as you play. How old are you?"

The Fiddler opened her mouth, but The Johnson answered before she could say anything. "She's ten. She's my brother-in-law's niece."

O'Neill took a sip of the sweet root beer before going into the bathroom. Once inside, he took a gulp of whiskey from his flask. He burped and washed the drink down with a slug of root beer. The door swung open, and Topper stepped in.

"Getting a nip?" Topper said.

"Course."

"I could use one. I'll trade ya if you don't mind." Topper pulled out his own flask. "I brought vodka to keep the smell off my breath. But I got this coffee, which is strong. That'll cover anything, and I thought I might prefer Irish coffee."

"Mine is bourbon."

Topper took the container and poured two or three ounces into his coffee mug. "Kentucky coffee then. Mind if I keep it? You can take the vodka. It's Absolut, which will stay off your breath and will go better with your root beer."

O'Neill took the flask and took a drink from the root beer, clearing room for several ounces of Absolut. As he poured the vodka into the container, the door pushed open. He pulled the flask close to his chest as two men stepped up to the urinals. After adding another ounce of vodka to the bottle, he stuck the container inside his pocket.

"Let's go," Topper said. "I could go for a chair."

O'Neill walked slowly, glancing back at Topper several times. The Johnson and The Fiddler sat in two of the four chairs on the makeshift stage. The chairs were facing the entrance, parallel to the counter and the window. Topper pulled out a cigarette as he walked past the counter.

"We allowed to smoke?" Topper asked.

"Don't think so." O'Neill looked around the café and didn't see a single cigarette. "I wouldn't anyway–not with The Fiddler nearby. No need pissing off The Johnson."

"I'll go outside for a quick one."

Topper stepped out of the café while O'Neill sat on an empty sofa. He pulled a *Wisconsin State Journal* off the table. The front-page article was about Bertram Newman's disappearance and included a picture of him. It was the same photo Meyer had shown him and was the only photo O'Neill had seen of the man he'd found dead in a sewer. He read through the article, which told Bertram's life story and provided a phone number for people to call if they saw Bertram Newman. O'Neill knew it was futile, since he was one of only two people to have seen the man since his disappearance. The only quotes in the news story were from Detective Captain Robert Leidel.

O'Neill finished an article about last night's Milwaukee Brewers loss when Topper returned. Mandy was with him, as were two other women who had more than their fair share of hair and make-up. A table of café patrons whispered to each other and stared.

Topper sat on a chair opposite O'Neill. Mandy sat on the rim of the chair, and the other women settled on the couch. All three pulled out cigarettes simultaneously.

"Can we smoke in here?" one of them asked.

"Don't think so," O'Neill said.

"Shit," said a woman wearing a leather jacket and pink pants. The cigarette returned to its pack.

"Go outside and take a puff. Topper just did it."

A couple came in next with two five- or six-year-old girls. They waved to The Fiddler as they came in.

"Bet those are The Fiddler's folks," O'Neill said to Topper. "The woman looks like The Fiddler."

Another couple came in toting half a dozen ten-year-old girls. The group claimed two tables, which were soon populated with root beer bottles. The Fiddler apparently had more fans than the rest of the band.

Pairs of adults meandered into the café, claiming the few remaining seats, and each sent a representative to the counter for coffee. At eight, Mary Hoffman arrived wearing blue jeans and a white sweatshirt with Wisconsin written across the top in red. Her two daughters followed closely, and the threesome approached the counter, ordering coffee and bottled water. Once they had their drinks, Mary and her girls walked over. O'Neill stood, offering the sofa.

"Glad you made it," O'Neill said. He pointed at his friend. "This is Topper. He's also in the band."

The adults nodded to each other, and both girls stared at O'Neill's earring.

"These are my daughters, Lily and Emmy."

After a brief conversation, Topper pulled himself out of his chair. "We better get to it." He winced as he straightened up.

"Is your brother coming?" O'Neill asked Mary.

"I told him Lily and Emmy were with me, so he'll be here." She turned to her daughters. "Uncle Tom lives upstairs."

"Upstairs from here?" the younger one said. She curled up her lip and shook her head. "The smell would make me barf."

The older one looked the place over but said nothing.

O'Neill started toward the so-called stage before stopping and leaning toward Mary. "Can we talk with you for a minute when we're done? Something about the case."

Mary nodded her agreement as her daughters returned to the sofa.

It was past eight, so the band took their spots. O'Neill and The Fiddler were in the middle, with Topper at O'Neill's side. O'Neill picked up his accordion and ran through the opening bars of "The Rockford Files." The Fiddler shook her head.

"This one's an instrumental our fiddler brought along," O'Neill said to the crowd. A spatter of claps and yells resulted from his reference to The Fiddler. "If you're a Sharon Shannon fan, you might recognize it." He started quietly, easing into the first notes. The Johnson played along, setting the rhythm, and Topper soon followed. The Fiddler waited with her head held down, finally sliding in and playing off the melody on O'Neill's accordion. The music grew louder, and The Fiddler took control.

When they finished, O'Neill took a swig of his spiked root beer. It had not gone as well as he hoped, but it had gone well enough. The ten-year-old girls yelled and clapped. O'Neill glanced at Mary as Mandy and her friends returned from their smoke.

O'Neill announced the second song as "I'm Left, You're Right, She's Gone." He then stood, put one foot on the chair, and rested the accordion on his knee. He played quietly, hoping the strumming guitars drowned out the accordion. The Fiddler plucked the beat along on her fiddle. Topper got to his feet early on, and they sang the refrain loudly and confidently. As they finished the song, they sat, and he glanced toward The Johnson who looked pleased. The Fiddler was also smiling, and she laughed as the applause subsided.

O'Neill counted into "The Mason's Apron," which was another of The Fiddler's songs. It was a song they all knew well. It had been their best number at practice and was better in the show.

As they finished, the crowd applauded and O'Neill was sure the ten-year-old girls were on their side. But as the next song started, he glanced at Topper and noticed that his perennially pale face was sweat covered and his eyes were closed. Topper's guitar slid out of his hands, making a loud, vacant sound as it struck the floor. O'Neill dropped his accordion and grabbed Topper before he fell to the ground. O'Neill and The Johnson lifted him by the shoulders. Mary and her girls evacuated the couch as Mandy and her friends took over, laying Topper down.

"We're going to take a quick break," The Johnson announced to the crowd.

"Sorry about that," Topper said after Mandy put water to his lips.

"Do we need an ambulance?" asked a dark-haired woman wearing a Smoky Joe's apron.

"Maybe you should," O'Neill said to Mandy. "Just in case."

A thin woman in her late thirties squeezed between them. "Move away. I'm a doctor."

"He's been shot," O'Neill said calmly.

"Are you serious?" the doctor said.

"Yeah. Yesterday."

The doctor unbuttoned Topper's shirt, touched the bandage on his left side, and slid her hand to his forehead.

"I'm okay," Topper said. "I just got dizzy."

"He feels warm," Mandy said.

The doctor touched Topper's forehead again. "I don't think it is anything you wouldn't expect from exerting himself. I don't think it is a fever."

"Am I okay, Doc?" Topper said.

"You should be fine, provided you take it easy. When were you injured?"

"Last night."

"What idiot decided you should play?"

Topper, O'Neill, and The Johnson exchanged glances as the doctor put a hand on Topper's forehead again and rolled his shirt up. She ran her hands along Topper's bandage. "Do you have someone to take you home?"

Mandy volunteered as she lit a cigarette.

"Get him water and put him to bed. You should know better," the doctor said to Topper, shaking her head. She turned toward Mandy. "Take his temperature at home and check it periodically. If the temperature increases, call his clinic. And make sure he is taking any prescribed medications. Where are you parked?"

"Down the block." Mandy turned to her friend in the leather jacket and pink pants. "Pull up the van."

"Double park if you have to and put your flashers on," said the doctor.

O'Neill went back to the stage where The Johnson was waiting.

"He shouldn't have played," The Johnson said.

O'Neill nodded as he picked his accordion off the floor. There was a ping as the bellows opened. He played a few notes before setting it back on the floor.

"What's wrong with it?" The Johnson asked.

"Everything," O'Neill said. "I let it fall when Topper dropped his guitar and I think one of the…"

"Can you fix it?"

"No. Might as well toss it." O'Neill picked up his empty root beer bottle.

Marlene Schultz walked over, carrying an empty tray. "Is he going to be okay?"

"Yeah," O'Neill replied. "He's going home to rest. He got shot yesterday, and I guess he pushed too hard."

"Are you kidding?"

"No. It was an accident."

"Do we call off the show?"

O'Neill spotted Topper's guitar. "We can still finish the set. I'll switch to guitar though, since my accordion broke."

"What a shame," said The Johnson.

"You certainly brought in a unique crowd," Marlene finally said. She waved a hand toward a group of girls. "I had to send Jake to Ken Kopp's for a case of root beer. But that's good since we want to bring in new customers. That is one reason we have live bands."

They watched as Mandy and one of her friends helped Topper to his feet. O'Neill walked over.

"Hey, Topper," O'Neill said. "Can I use your Gretsch tonight? My accordion broke when I got up to catch you. We can play most of the set as a threesome."

"Johnson," Topper said after a pause. The Johnson's head turned, and he stepped closer. "I'm leaving my guitar with *you*, not with O'Neill. Understand?"

"Yeah, Topper," The Johnson said. "I'll drop it off tomorrow."

Mandy took Topper's hand. They walked out, followed by Mandy's two friends. The customers watched quietly and two ten-year-old girls held the door open. The door closed, and the crowd turned toward the stage.

"We'll play a few more songs in a minute," O'Neill said.

O'Neill hurried to the counter and asked for a glass of water. He swigged water from the plastic glass as he walked to the restroom. Inside, a college-age man was combing his hair. O'Neill entered the lone stall, closed the door, and drank from Topper's flask. The vodka slid down his throat with hardly a reaction. He licked his lips and took another, then finished the water and re-filled the glass with the remaining vodka.

Once onstage, Seamus set the glass beneath his wooden chair and picked up Topper's guitar. He strummed it once, winced, and tuned it. He looked around the room, finally finding Mary and her daughters leaning against the front window.

"I didn't think we tuned," The Fiddler said as she sat in her chair.

"It got out of whack when it fell."

"Does this mean we don't have to do 'The Rockford Files?'"

"Suppose not," O'Neill replied, pulling the list out of his pocket. The Johnson and The Fiddler waited quietly as he stared into space. "We will also scrub the French national anthem. Johnson, let's do one of your songs. You take the lead."

As O'Neill surveyed the audience, he noticed Rob Peacock in a corner. Tom Hoffman was next to him, leaning against the wall.

Schumacher's Flour Mill played twelve more songs, including one that The Fiddler simply stomped her feet to. But she had rhythm, and the kids enjoyed it as much as her fiddling.

When the last song was done, O'Neill finished his vodka and the audience gave them a round of applause that exceeded the quality of the show. As O'Neill stuck Topper's guitar in its case, The Johnson clasped a hand on his shoulder.

"Here comes Mika's family and my sister's family," The Johnson said. "Try not to act too drunk."

"Course."

"Actually, just don't talk at all."

The Fiddler's father patted The Johnson on the back. "Good playing," he said as he stuck his hands into his Dockers.

"This was a tremendous thrill for Mika," The Johnson's sister announced.

"And for us," The Fiddler's mother added.

"She did great," O'Neill said. "A real natural."

"You think so?" both parents said as the father hugged his daughter.

O'Neill nodded and stepped away. Mary was waiting with her two girls.

"That was nice," Mary said as he sat across from her. "Don't you think so, girls?"

"Yeah," the older one said.

"Let's go," the younger one said.

"Girls, why don't you go to the bathroom before we leave? We'll go as soon as you're ready."

"I don't gotta go," the younger one said, but the older one grabbed her sister's shirt and they meandered toward the bathroom.

Mary and O'Neill watched the girls walk to the back of the café. "There was something you wanted to talk to me about?"

"Yeah," O'Neill said after finally remembering. "There's a break in your case. You should hear about it tomorrow on the news. I can't give you details, but it should be good in that things will close and Tom will be free and clear."

"Thank God."

"I wanted you to hear it from us rather than from the news."

"Thanks, Shay. I really appreciate everything you've done." Mary smiled, and her brown eyes widened. "Maybe someday, after Tom is done being mad at me, the three of us can meet for lunch."

"That would be great."

Mary's daughters poked their heads around the corner. Mary waved them over and turned back to O'Neill. "Tom is over there," she said. "He is acquainted with the old guy next to him. Let him know as well."

O'Neill nodded to Tom and waved to Rob Peacock.

As Mary and her daughters headed out the door, The Johnson walked over holding the accordion. "What should I do with this?"

"Toss it," O'Neill said. "The sucker is broken. It would cost more to fix than it would be to buy a new one."

"To the trash it goes." The Johnson tried to push the instrument into the nearest trash can, but it would not fit. Marlene Schultz opened the lid and dropped the accordion into the can.

"What did you think?" O'Neill asked her.

"A little rough, especially after you lost the one guy. It wasn't quite what we usually have, but it was entertaining. And the crowd was larger than usual and sales were strong." She shrugged her shoulders. "Maybe when I have another opening?"

"Just call me," The Johnson said, pushing his way into the conversation.

O'Neill nodded. Then, despite having played his first show in months, he was not interested in talking about his music. Instead, he looked toward Peacock and Tom and waved them over to a newly emptied table.

Chapter 24

While O'Neill had invited Rob Peacock and Tom Hoffman to the show, he hadn't expected either to attend. The pair approached O'Neill with Tom trailing Peacock who was holding a handkerchief in one hand. As they sat down, Peacock's hands shook and he brushed the handkerchief against his brow.

"Glad you both could make it." O'Neill patted each of them on the shoulder. "What did you think?"

"It was fun," Tom said. "Though I missed the early part of the show."

"We wanted to talk to you," Peacock said.

O'Neill's gaze bounced between the two men. Empty plastic glasses and crunched-up napkins dominated the tabletop. "What's up?"

"I talked to David Leonard earlier tonight," Peacock said. "He wants me to approve the last payment to Antiquity. It is necessary, he said, since Bertram is unavailable to approve the payment."

"How do you approve the payment?"

"I can do it electronically or over the phone, provided I give the proper account numbers and passwords. Bertram,

David, Peter Couturier, and I are corporate officers and can approve payments. Payments of greater than ten thousand dollars require the approval of two officers. David wants me to provide the second approval for this payment since Bertram isn't available. The proposed payment is two hundred thousand dollars. David said this last payment is due at midnight tonight." Peacock pulled out a piece of paper and unfolded it. "This is a printout of the unapproved transaction. David says if we don't make the payment, the entire agreement is at risk. Peter wants me to do it since I understand the finances better than him."

"Does what he's asking Rob to do make sense?" O'Neill asked Tom as he stared at the paper.

"Yes, it does," Tom said. "I don't know if it was the bank that limited wire transfer payments to two hundred thousand dollars or if that was something we put into Shakespeare's Company's bylaws, but that's the limit. They likely were moving funds before Bertram's disappearance. This would be the last payment."

"Is this printout from the bank?" O'Neill asked.

"Yes, from their web portal," Peacock said. "There were four other two hundred thousand dollar payments made within the last seven or eight days, though I didn't print them out. David said he would have processed the last payment earlier this week, but he put it on hold due to Bertram's disappearance."

The printout showed a two hundred thousand dollar payment from Shakespeare's Company LLC to Antiquities Investments LLC. The sheet listed the status as "Awaiting Secondary Approval."

"Did you check with your contact at Antiquities?" O'Neill said to Peacock.

"Yes, but he hasn't gotten back to me. I asked him to verify that they're expecting the last payment to post tonight. He promised to call me back tonight. If he verifies things, I'll approve the transaction. If not, I won't, though it makes me nervous since our friends at Antiquity have been quite particular about timelines."

"Can I keep this printout?"

"Yes. That's why I brought it."

"When and where did you talk to David today?"

"David left a message on my machine this afternoon. I called him back around five."

"Did you see David today?" O'Neill said to Tom.

"I saw him this morning and this afternoon. He borrowed my car to do some shopping. That must have been soon after five."

"He borrowed your car? What kind of car do you have?"

"A red ninety-five Chevy Lumina."

O'Neill looked around the café. He approached the counter, catching Marlene Schultz who gave him a pen. He wrote the color, year, make, and model on the printout then returned to the table.

"Why do you need to know?" Tom asked. "What are you worried about?"

"Hopefully it's nothing, yet I want to play it safe. I'll feel better after Rob's contact verifies that payments really are due tonight."

"What's that got to do with my car?"

"Probably nothing. But if you see David, give my boss, John Ryder, a call." O'Neill pulled out his last two business cards, wrote Ryder's cell phone number on the back, and handed one to Tom and one to Peacock.

"I think I already have one of these," Peacock said. "I'll call Mr. Ryder as soon as I hear from Antiquity. It is, however, getting late, and I need to get home. The folks at Antiquity have my home phone number, so I could already have a message from them."

O'Neill thanked him, and they shook hands. Tom also headed out, saying he expected David to be home soon. O'Neill wasn't sure what to do, so he turned his attention toward The Johnson who had packed the guitars and was talking with three women. The women wore jeans and long-sleeve shirts. None wore shoes. He walked over, pausing at The Johnson's side. He looked over the women and decided they were older than college-age.

"Did the guitar player really get shot?" asked a dark-haired woman with yellow teeth.

"Yeah," O'Neill said. "It was an accident. A friend of his girlfriend's had too much of something. She thought the gun was a toy or something. Wasn't a severe wound, I guess. Just happened yesterday."

"Are you Irish?" said another woman. She was thin with long, black hair and square glasses that clashed with huge hoop earrings. It took O'Neill too long to reply, so she rephrased the question. "Are you of Irish descent, I mean? You play a lot of Irish songs and you play whistle and accordion."

"Four or five Irish songs, I suppose," O'Neill replied. "A few were tunes The Fiddler brought."

"Mika was worried about Topper being able to play her songs," The Johnson said to O'Neill. "I told her that Topper knew most every Irish song there was, so she stuck with Irish songs."

"Why are you wearing sunglasses?" the shortest of the three women asked O'Neill.

O'Neill shrugged his shoulders. "Suppose it makes me feel like I'm hiding out a bit, you know?"

"He's wasted," the woman with the yellow teeth whispered loud enough for O'Neill to hear it.

The Johnson picked up the two guitar cases. "Ready to roll? Mika's parents took her home. I'm heading to The Great Dane to meet some friends. Tooth McGregor's new band is playing tonight. You want to come along?"

"Sure," O'Neill said. "Could I borrow your phone first? I got to call my boss."

The Johnson let out a breath, put the guitars down, and handed O'Neill his phone.

O'Neill tried Ryder's cell but got his voicemail. He hung up, pulled out his notepad, and found Erin Meyer's number. He called but got her voicemail.

"You coming or not?" The Johnson asked.

O'Neill nodded, knowing the Great Dane was near the Annex.

"You got room for us?" the woman with the square glasses asked.

"Sure. It'll be tight, but you can fit," The Johnson said.

The women put on sandals and followed them outside. The crisp night air caught O'Neill by surprise, and a horn blew as the door closed.

The group hurried to The Johnson's Impala, which was less than a block away. The Johnson stuck the two guitars in the passenger seat, relegating the four passengers to the back seat. O'Neill got in first and the woman with glasses got in behind him, crawling onto his lap. He smirked as he remembered what it was like being the singer in a band.

"Do you know 'Whiskey in the Jar?'" the woman with glasses asked.

"Course," O'Neill said.

"He can't pull out his guitar, Angie," said another woman.

"That's me," the woman in the glasses said. "I'm Angie. This is Tracy and LeeAnne."

"Call me Seamus. The Johnson's up there."

"*The* Johnson?"

"Call me Tim," The Johnson said.

"Where's your whistle?" Angie asked. "I know you got one. You played it on the instrumentals."

O'Neill reached into his pocket and pulled out his black Sweetone whistle. A few hours ago, it sat near a dead man in the sewer. "What do you want to hear?"

"'Whiskey in the Jar,'" Angie said.

O'Neill started the tune. As he came to the refrain, she sang along. They clapped at appropriate times, but the song fell apart after the first chorus.

"Play something we all know," the woman with the yellow teeth yelled. "Play 'Danny Boy.'"

"No, not 'Danny Boy,'" The Johnson said.

"Oh, don't listen to him. Play it."

O'Neill played a few notes before Angie started singing. The other two hummed along and though Angie confused some words, she pulled it off.

"What else should we sing?" one woman asked.

"Just don't do 'R-E-S-P-E-C-T,'" The Johnson said from the front seat, "or you'll have to walk the rest of the way."

The women argued for several minutes. By the time they settled on, "Genie in a Bottle," O'Neill's whistle had returned to his pocket and his eyes were closed. The song finished as The Johnson pulled the car into a parking ramp.

"You guys are old enough, aren't you?" The Johnson asked.

"Old enough for what?" Angie asked.

"To drink."

"Sure we are," Angie replied. "I'm twenty-seven, and they're both twenty-five. How old are you guys?"

"Thirty-four," The Johnson said. "O'Neill, thirty-three I think."

"What else do you guys do?" the third woman asked as they stepped out of the car. "Or are you full-time musicians?"

"I'm a manager at Paul's Club — the place on State. Seamus is a computer guy, isn't that the gist of it?"

That was the story O'Neill was using, so he nodded his agreement.

"Oh, really?" the woman with the yellow teeth said. "I'm a programmer for DoIT — which is part of the University. Angie's a programmer too; she works for CUNA. LeeAnne's a paralegal."

They talked about jobs and programming until they got to the Great Dane's entrance, where they waited as the group ahead of them pushed their way in. Angie took O'Neill's hand and pulled him through the entryway and past the crowd. He looked for someone tall, but couldn't find Meyer. The clock on the wall said it was five minutes after ten, so he figured Meyer and Ryder were at the Annex. He settled in front of the bar.

"What you want?" O'Neill asked Angie, who stayed with him.

"Anything." Then she glanced back toward her friends, raising a hand.

O'Neill waved down the bartender and ordered a Scone of Stone Scotch Ale and a Peck's Pilsner. The bartender pumped the beers directly in front of him. He smelled the pilsner before handing it to Angie.

"Where are the others?" O'Neill asked, staring into the mirror behind the bar.

"Not a clue," Angie said as she stood on her tiptoes, trying to see over the crowd. "Either I'm too short or everyone here is too tall. They could be in the billiards area or downstairs. Give them a minute and if they're not back, we'll hunt them down."

O'Neill took a gulp of the beer. He licked the lather from his lips and took his sunglasses off. They talked for a few minutes before deciding to search for the rest of their group. He maneuvered through the crowd, and Angie followed. They took the stairs to the cellar. Out of habit, O'Neill made his way directly to the bar and put his half-empty glass on the counter. He looked about the room, recognizing several faces but not seeing The Johnson or either of the women.

"What's it so busy for?" Angie asked.

"Just a Friday night crowd," O'Neill said. "Why don't we have another beer? If we don't find them, we'll go check in the poolroom area, which is where the band would be. Suppose The Johnson went there."

"I'm okay for now," Angie said, holding up her full pint. "These are enormous glasses."

He finished his drink and lifted the empty glass. The bartender grabbed a fresh glass and filled it to the top. They walked up the back staircase, past the kitchen, and past the front bar. Once inside the poolroom, the volume of the band surprised him. He put his sunglasses on and stepped through, relieved there was no cover charge. As they crossed through an assortment of pool tables, a bearded man wearing a cowboy hat slapped O'Neill's shoulder.

"O'Neill, old boy," the man said as he pulled off O'Neill's' sunglasses. "You're still alive, I see."

"Hey, Hammer," O'Neill said, taking back his glasses.

"Who's the lady?" Hammer asked in a gravelly voice.

"Angie, this is Hammer. He plays with Blue Monday."

"I have heard of them," she said, and they nodded to each other.

Hammer smiled, and his beard lifted higher. "What you doing hanging 'round with this old punk rocker?"

"Better than an old rocker playing the blues," O'Neill said.

Hammer grabbed O'Neill, pretending to put him in a headlock.

"You're spilling my beer," O'Neill muttered. Hammer let him go and pushed him away, laughing the whole time.

"Speaking of old rockers trying to play the blues," O'Neill said, shaking beer off his arm. "We're looking for The Johnson. Seen him around?"

"Look onstage."

The Johnson was onstage, playing the electric guitar.

"Were they short a guy or something? Who are those guys?" O'Neill asked.

"Tooth McGregor's new band. They just started. One of them was sick. He asked me if I wanted to sit in, but Tooth would not pay, so I told him to fuck off. They had an opening band, some group from Fond du Lac called The Delmonicos. One of them was going to sub even though he didn't know any of Tooth's songs. But once The Johnson showed up, they took him."

O'Neill turned toward Angie. "We should find your two friends." He took her hand and pulled her forward. He wanted to find Meyer, but he couldn't leave Angie by herself.

"They're around here somewhere," Angie said.

They circled the room twice, finding Angie's friends leaning on a counter near the bar.

"Where have you been?" Angie asked.

"Here," Tracy replied. "Tim is onstage. He's friends with the guys in the band, and one of them has the flu or something. We waited here since we could see the exit."

O'Neill finished his beer and returned to the counter. "Anyone need one?" he asked, leaning toward the women. They all shook their heads.

"God, you drink a lot," Angie said as he came back with another beer.

"Yeah, I do."

The three women looked at each other.

"Angie, could I borrow your phone quick?" O'Neill asked. "I need to make a local call. You can dial it for me if that makes you feel better."

O'Neill pulled out his notepad and read off Rob Peacock's phone number. Angie hit the call button and handed it to him. Peacock picked up after three rings.

"Rob, this is Seamus O'Neill. Have you heard anything?"

"What was that?" Peacock said. "It sounds like the crowd's gotten bigger."

"Have you heard from your contact at Antiquity?"

"No, but David called. He's coming over. He said he'll help me work through things. I left a message on Mr. Ryder's answering machine."

Angie's hand was out, expecting her phone back. O'Neill's thoughts raced scattershot through his mind. He knew Peacock was in trouble, but couldn't explain why.

"Be careful," O'Neill finally said. "And call Ryder if you hear from your contact."

Peacock agreed and ended the call. O'Neill handed the phone back to Angie.

"Thanks. Suppose I should check on The Johnson," O'Neill said.

"It was nice to meet you," Angie said. "What again is the band's name?"

"Schumacher's Flour Mill."

"I'll just go with the Flour Mill, if you don't mind."

"That works. Everyone messes with band names."

Then it occurred to him.

He pulled the sheet out of his pocket that showed the electronic payment from Shakespeare's Company LLC. It showed the transfer going to Antiquities Investments LLC.

"Shit," he said to himself. He had to talk to Meyer or Ryder.

He pushed his way through the poolroom. The Johnson was still onstage. He hated to do it, but some things were more important than beer. He took one last gulp, set the half-full drink on a table, and hurried outside.

Chapter 25

Sirens blared as O'Neill's walk turned into a run. He paused at the corner of King Street and East Wilson Street and saw two police cruisers in front of the Administration Annex. A third cruiser cut its siren and came to a stop, its blue and red flashers remaining lit. Police tape was being stretched in front of the alley between the two administration buildings. The walk sign came on, and O'Neill hurried across the street.

Two uniformed officers were adjusting poles that were connected by police tape. The poles crossed the entryway to the alley, but one was threatening to pull from the ground. O'Neill ran down the sidewalk, stopping at the edge of the tape. The manhole was approximately a hundred and fifty feet from the sidewalk. Multiple flashlight beams bounced about. O'Neill yelled Ryder's name a few times, but heard no reply. He slipped under the police tape, but two uniformed officers descended on him. One officer lifted the tape, and the other walked him back toward the sidewalk.

"I got to talk to Detective Meyer. My name is Seamus O'Neill. I'm a detective."

"Move it along, detective," one officer said as he put a hand on O'Neill's chest.

"I've got to talk to her. It's important. I'm a detective."

"And I'm the chief of police, so I'm ordering you to move it along. This is a police matter."

"No shit." O'Neill reached for his wallet, intending to pull out a business card.

The other officer, a short man with a crooked nose, swatted O'Neill's hand, relaxing when he saw the wallet.

"Move it along if you don't want trouble."

O'Neill remembered he had given his last business card to Rob Peacock, so he had no business cards to show. Stepping back, he ducked under the tape and onto the sidewalk. He considered returning to the Great Dane and calling Ryder, but he hadn't answered earlier and might not answer this time. The thought of borrowing someone's phone and calling 9-1-1 seemed appealing, but two pedestrians he asked turned away. He even considered running to the City of Madison Police Department's Central District's Office, which was only a tenth of a mile away, but he didn't know whether they were open for foot traffic. And if they were open, he imagined being told to wait in the lobby. There was no time to wait.

O'Neill ambled toward Main Street. The police tape was in front of the Annex and on the side facing the Wisconsin Administration Building, but there was no tape on the other side of the Annex. He walked toward King Street. Once past the police tape and at the edge of the Annex, he walked across the grass, getting to the structure's edge without being noticed.

"This might work," O'Neill said to himself, almost laughing. He went past the Annex's side entrance, waving to the camera and slipping around the back. Police tape at the parking lot's edge forced him to stop. Two police officers stood near the tape, and he thought he saw Meyer amongst a group of five or six people. They were only fifty feet away.

He considered yelling or ducking under the tape and making a run toward the manhole, but after glancing back toward the building, he settled on a different approach.

At the side entrance, O'Neill pulled out the access card that Mary Hoffman had given Ryder several days earlier and placed it against the reader. The door thumped, and he slipped inside, pausing as the door closed. After catching his breath, he decided the police had not seen him enter, so he rushed down the stairs, ran through the hallway, and passed the lobby before arriving at the loading dock.

The dock was dark, except for the exit sign above the door. He walked toward the exit, pushed the door open and stepping onto the walk that led to the alley. The police officers didn't react, so he turned up the alley, walking toward the tallest of six people, most of which held flashlights.

"Hey Erin," O'Neill said as he approached Meyer.

Meyer twisted around. "Seamus," she said, briefly aiming the flashlight in his face. "Are you out of your mind? What are you doing here?"

He couldn't see anything, but he could imagine her expression. "Rob Peacock is in trouble. David Leonard has Tom Hoffman's car and is probably at Peacock's house by now. Leonard wants him to approve a payment to a fake company, and then I'm guessing Leonard will make a run for it."

Ryder's bald head and round frame came into focus.

"Seamus?" Ryder said. "What the hell?"

"Sorry to break in, but I'm worried about Rob Peacock."

"The white-haired guy?" Meyer glanced over her shoulder. "You said Leonard is going to Peacock's house?"

"Yeah. Unlike you two, Peacock was at my show, and he gave me a copy of a two hundred thousand dollar wire transfer that Leonard told him to approve."

O'Neill pulled the sheet from his pocket and Meyer tugged it away, shining her flashlight on it.

"Seems weird that Leonard is still worried about processing a transaction," Ryder said. "Unless he wants more money before making a run for it."

"Look at the name of the business being paid," O'Neill said.

"Antiquities Investments LLC," Meyer said. "Isn't it *Antiquity* Investments LLC that they are involved in?"

"What are you saying?" Ryder asked.

O'Neill's eyes batted open and shut. "Shakespeare's Company LLC is supposed to pay Antiquity Investments LLC one million dollars, but paid Antiquities Investments LLC. My guess is Leonard owns Antiquities Investments LLC. Leonard's company is probably registered out-of-state, which is why we never found it. I'm guessing he intends to get this last payment approved by Peacock. Then he'll make a run for it. I wrote the car make and model on the back of that sheet. It's Tom Hoffman's car."

Meyer turned away from them, yelled, "Jefferson," then pulled out her radio. "Seamus, do you know Peacock's address?" Meyer said, without looking at him.

"He lives in Shorewood Hills. I don't remember exactly."

"I don't know the address either," Ryder said, "but it is off University Bay Drive."

Jefferson rushed to Meyer's side, and another plainclothes officer joined the circle.

"Penny, we believe David Leonard is traveling in a red ninety-five Chevy Lumina registered to Thomas Hoffman.

We also believe he is going to the house of a Rob Peacock in Shorewood Hills. We don't have an address. Get word out on the vehicle and send someone to Peacock's house for a welfare check ASAP."

Jefferson pulled out her radio and stepped away from the group.

"Who the hell are you?" the plainclothes man asked O'Neill. He was tall, but looked short next to Meyer and had salt and pepper hair.

"Captain," Meyer said, "this is Seamus O'Neill. He works for the Ryder Detective Agency."

"I'm the street musician," O'Neill said.

"How did *he* get in here?" the captain asked Meyer.

"I overpowered two cops and hurdled the tape."

Ryder hit O'Neill on the shoulder. "Seamus, shut up."

Meyer stepped away from the group and was listening to a discussion on the radio. She leaned back into the group. "Officer Jefferson is on with Dane County dispatch. She and I are going to Peacock's residence." She turned toward her captain. "The residence is about ten minutes from here, so Shorewood Hills PD will beat us, but we asked them to wait for us barring signs of distress. We'll commandeer a cruiser. Any issue with that approach?"

"No," Captain Leidel said. "I'll manage things here. You two go."

"Seamus and I have been to Peacock's house," Ryder said. "The place is hard to find."

"Shorewood Hills PD will find it no problem," Captain Leidel said.

"We've been inside the house and the backyard," Ryder said to Meyer. "The place has a three-season porch, and a tall wooden fence surrounds the backyard."

"Okay, come along," Meyer said. She took a few steps toward East Wilson Street before going into a run. Jefferson shuffled behind her, and Ryder and O'Neill started after them, not waiting for anyone to tell them to stop.

Meyer got to the police tape first, lifting it high and waiting for Jefferson and O'Neill to pass under. Ryder was several steps behind, so he lifted the tape himself. Meyer took the car keys from an unhappy police officer and hopped into the cruiser. Jefferson sat beside her, and O'Neill and Ryder were relegated to the back seat.

"I can't believe the captain let you guys come along," Meyer said. She flipped on the siren and pulled onto the one-way street.

Jefferson was quickly on the radio, talking to MPD dispatch and then Dane County, which handled the Shorewood Hills PD's dispatch.

"Shorewood Hills has their own police department?" O'Neill whispered to Ryder.

"Yeah," Ryder said. "My guess is we're talking a half dozen full-time officers and a half-dozen part-timers."

"Shorewood Hills PD just arrived at Rob Peacock's house," Jefferson said to Meyer. "The ninety-five red Lumina is in the driveway. They want to know whether they should go ahead with the welfare check or wait for backup."

"Tell them, barring any signs of distress, we suggest they wait for backup. Yet they shouldn't let anyone leave in the Lumina or in any vehicle."

O'Neill closed his eyes as the police cruiser screamed down East Johnson Street.

Chapter 26

A push on the shoulder woke O'Neill. The flashers turned off followed by the cruiser's headlights. The cruiser passed a Shorewood Police car and pulled to the side of the road two houses past Rob Peacock's house. Another Shorewood Police vehicle was parked in front of them. Meyer and Jefferson got out of their vehicle, and Ryder and O'Neill followed.

A lone officer got out of a City of Shorewood police car and two exited the second vehicle. The officer introduced himself to Meyer and Jefferson, and they waited as the other two Shorewood Police Officers jogged toward them.

"What have we got?" the oldest of the Shorewood Hills officers asked Meyer. "I'm Sergeant Brown. I'm in charge."

"The MPD has a warrant for the arrest of David Leonard, a white male, age thirty-six, six foot, two hundred and ten pounds. He is a suspect in the murder of Bertram Newman."

"Murder?" Sergeant Brown said.

"Yes. It relates to Bertram Newman, who has been missing since earlier this week."

The three Shorewood officers nodded.

"We believe Leonard is here to pressure the homeowner, Rob Peacock, to approve a wire transfer of funds," Meyer said. "I'm unclear whether a wire transfer goes through immediately or if we can delay it. So I don't know if our suspect has reason to do anything more than threaten and then incapacitate Mr. Peacock."

"Do you have a description of the homeowner?"

"He's a little white guy with white hair," O'Neill said, yawning.

"Are you all City of Madison Police?" Sergeant Brown asked, looking at O'Neill.

"Just two of us," Meyer said. She pointed at Ryder and O'Neill. "Those two are private detectives. Or rather, Mr. Ryder is a private detective. Mr. O'Neill works for Mr. Ryder."

"Okay, we have five of us." Brown looked back at his officers. "Have either of you been here before?"

They shook their heads.

"The backyard has an eight-foot high wooden fence," Ryder said. "The fence is too high to climb, though there are two gates, one facing the back and one on our left. Both have chain locks. If he makes a run for it out back, he won't get out of the backyard unless he has the key."

"It sounds like we're unsure if the homeowner is in immediate danger," Brown said. "We might be better off seeing if the homeowner can get to the door or seeing if the suspect answers. What do you think?"

"Agreed." Meyer turned toward Ryder. "What do you remember about the entryway and the inside of the house?"

"There's a screen door and a front door with a knocker. No doorbell. The staircase is in the foyer with a room to the right that I did not see and a hallway to the left of the stairs, which goes through the kitchen. A family room is to the left of the kitchen, and I suspect another room to the left going toward the front. I didn't see the entrance to the basement. Beyond the kitchen is a three-season porch which opens to the backyard."

"There are two lutes and a Moorish guitar in the three-season porch," O'Neill added. "Though, technically, all three are lutes."

Brown glanced back at O'Neill, then turned toward Meyer. "Will the suspect recognize you?"

"He'll recognize all of us except Mr. Ryder. Ryder is ex-Madison PD."

Sergeant Brown nodded and turned toward Ryder. "Do you mind knocking?"

"No problem."

"Okay. Open the screen door, then knock and say the guy's first name a few times. Say your first name like he should know it. The four of us will flank around you." He turned to one of the Shorewood Police Officers. "Marcus, you stay in your car in case this guy makes a run in the car somehow. If he does, contact dispatch and tail him. Don't leave your vehicle without contacting dispatch."

The officer nodded.

"If no one answers," Brown said to Ryder, "walk toward the road. Once you are there, we'll knock, announce ourselves, and go in. We'll leave one of us at the entrance." Brown pointed to one of his officers. "You come in after we secure the first floor, but stay at the front door. The rest of us will go in." He turned toward Meyer and Jefferson. "I'll go right, you two flank left. We'll go first, second and basement. I'll make sure the back entrance is locked before we go to the second floor."

There were nods of agreement.

"What do I do?" O'Neill asked.

"Hang out at the car and let the police do their job," Ryder said.

Brown, Meyer, Jefferson, Ryder and one Shorewood Police Officer started up the driveway. The other officer walked toward his vehicle.

O'Neill sat on the MPD cruiser's trunk and sipped bourbon. Then he walked to the edge of Peacock's property and squatted down. Two porch lights were lit, so he had a good view and he watched as Meyer crouched to the left of the door and Brown to its right. Jefferson was beside Meyer, and the other officer was behind Sergeant Brown.

Ryder opened the screen door and knocked. After a short wait, he pounded on the door, calling Peacock's name several times. There was more pounding, then Ryder allowed the screen door to shut. He turned away and walked toward O'Neill. As Ryder neared the road, there was more door pounding.

Brown yelled, "Shorewood Police, open up!"

The Shorewood Police officer pulled the screen door open, then stuck a crowbar into the door. The door soon flung open. Brown shouted, and they were inside.

O'Neill took a few steps onto the grass beside the driveway. It was silent for a few moments. Then the officer standing on the porch stepped inside and closed the door. O'Neill took a few steps up the incline, kneeling on the grass.

Flashlight beams bounced along the window shades and, seconds later, the upstairs lights turned on. O'Neill heard a clinking sound and looked toward the fence as the gate whipped open, slamming into the fence. David Leonard appeared, wearing a white shirt, dark pants, and suspenders. He rushed outside, locking the gate.

"He's outside!" Ryder shouted.

Leonard ran toward the red Lumina. O'Neill ran toward him.

"Seamus, stay back, you idiot!" Ryder hollered.

Leonard pulled the driver-side door open, and O'Neill grabbed him. The accountant turned around, swung his left arm at O'Neill, who blocked the punch with an arm, fell backward and rolled onto the pavement.

O'Neill saw Meyer drop over the fence, almost as if she had jumped. She landed in a forward roll, got on her feet, and launched her body into the open driver-side door, slamming the door into Leonard's shoulder.

Leonard fell backward, bounced off the car, and landed a few feet from O'Neill. Before he could get to his feet, Meyer was on his back. Ryder stopped behind him and the Shorewood Police Officer, who had been waiting by the cruiser, aimed his pistol at Leonard.

"Can't believe you got over that fence," O'Neill said as Meyer snapped handcuffs onto Leonard. "That was impressive."

"Brown gave me a boost," Meyer said. "Though it wasn't *the camel method*." Her eyebrows raised twice, and she smiled at him. Then she got back to being a cop.

Chapter 27

It was a long Friday night. O'Neill waited at the curb while Ryder talked with Meyer and the Shorewood Police officers. After twenty minutes, Ryder joined him. Ryder told him that Sergeant Brown found Rob Peacock tied to a chair in the basement near his computer. Ryder said Peacock told him that David Leonard had arrived a half hour earlier. He tried to trick Peacock into approving the two hundred thousand dollar electronic funds transfer. As they talked, Peacock's contact at Antiquity Investments called. Leonard hung up the phone. After Leonard threatened him, Peacock agreed to authorize the transaction. Once the payment was approved, Leonard tied up Peacock and was preparing to leave when Ryder knocked on the door.

The ambulance exited the driveway, carrying Peacock to the hospital.

More police cars arrived over the next ten minutes. Both O'Neill and Ryder provided statements, and paramedics looked O'Neill over but decided he didn't need treatment. After giving statements, Ryder and O'Neill were driven home by Officer Penny Jefferson. On the ride home, Jefferson told them they needed to come to the station on Saturday for formal interviews.

O'Neill slept until Saturday afternoon. At one o'clock, he logged onto his internet and found a front-page article in the *Wisconsin State Journal* that included a story about Bertram Newman and the arrest of his killer, David Leonard. The article included photographs of Bertram, Leonard, and the City of Madison Police Captain Robert Leidel. The story included quotes from Leidel and from the Shorewood Hills Police Department's chief. The article mentioned Detective Erin Meyer and Sergeant Dale Brown, but did not mention the Ryder Detective Agency.

O'Neill found seven new email messages in his inbox, including one from a *Capital Times* reporter and one from a *Wisconsin State Journal* reporter. O'Neill forwarded both to Ryder without opening them.

The other messages were from the police asking him to stop at their offices on Carroll Street for an interview. They provided a phone number for him to confirm a time. A message from Ryder asked O'Neill to call or email after he met with the City of Madison Police.

O'Neill arrived at the police station and asked for Detective Meyer. The desk officer told him that Meyer was unavailable. Instead, they sat him in a room with two male detectives. They fed him Fritos and a Diet Coke and asked questions about the Ryder Detective Agency's investigation into Bertram's disappearance and murder. He answered everything honestly but omitted finding Bertram's dead body.

Following the meeting, O'Neill called Ryder from the police station and they agreed to meet at the Argus Food & Spirits restaurant. O'Neill walked into the bar just before four. He sat in front of the taps, ordered a Capital 1900, and talked with the bartender and a fellow patron about the building's tin ceiling and about the bar furniture. After Ryder arrived, they ordered a round and sat outside.

It was the beginning of the Saturday dinner rush, but they got a table under an umbrella on the East Main Street sidewalk. A pair of young women wearing shorts walked past, and O'Neill thought of Erin Meyer walking on the same spot after they left Luigi's several nights earlier.

"Who did you meet with when you went to the station for your interview?" Ryder asked.

"Two plainclothes guys."

"You don't remember their names?"

O'Neill tipped his sunglasses down and leaned forward. "No. Two guys. Both were in their thirties, one with light hair and one with dark hair. They were both around six feet tall. Both looked fit. They weighed about one eighty-five or one ninety."

"Martinelli and Gurley. They interviewed me, too. Martinelli is with Central District while Gurley's in Investigative Services. Did anything about the interview concern you?"

"Not really," O'Neill said. "They focused on our interaction with the MPD. You'd think that wouldn't be an issue with the way everything played out. I was straight up."

"What did you tell them about how we found Bertram's body?"

"I told them I decided there wasn't any practical way for Bertram to exit the building or for someone to carry his body out. When I saw the window in Leonard's office facing the lake, I realized the window was the best way to get a body out. Leonard was the only suspect who worked in the building, so it was natural to suspect him. I told them I talked this through with you and Erin and we concluded that, if it was Leonard, he wouldn't be able to transport the body out of the parking lot. Even if he had a car, the camera on the main DOA admin building would have recorded him pulling into the lot. I remembered the manhole because I'd been there one day when it was pouring rain. A sewer is a good short-term place to hide a body if you can open and close the manhole." O'Neill paused as a short, dark-haired server handed each of them a menu and provided glasses of water. "I told them about Erin and me calling you on the phone when we were at the Great Dane."

"Good. Makes sense and our statements are consistent."

"Are you concerned about the cops?" O'Neill asked.

"I'm always concerned. It's hard not to be when I work with you. Yet I expected questions, since they want to be clear about our role."

"Are they coming down on Erin about her involving us?"

"I doubt it since everything ended well. They don't, however, want to give us credit publicly unless they're sure we deserve it."

"I read the article in the *Wisconsin State Journal*. They made it sound like Meyer's boss solved the crime himself."

Ryder squealed and slapped a hand on the table. "They published early this morning and didn't have time to interview anyone other than the talking heads. They'll have a more complete article in the Sunday paper. The *Capital Times* article is better since they publish later. The article has a head shot of your favorite tall female detective and several quotes from her, including her mentioning the Ryder Detective Agency. I talked to both papers, but I haven't seen any articles that quote me."

"Did they give an update on Peacock? Is he okay?"

"Peacock called the office today at about two. The hospital released him and he's home and doing fine. He said the bank stopped the two hundred thousand dollar transfer from going through."

"How about the other eight hundred thousand? Did they get that back?"

"I don't think we'll have an answer on that for a bit. My understanding is Leonard transferred roughly a hundred grand from Antiquities Investments LLC to two separate domestic companies that he has no ties to. Leonard says the payments relate to gambling debts. Leonard transferred seven hundred thousand dollars to three other domestic organizations that he controls. Each of them transferred funds to organizations outside the United States. He is being cagey about the money. My guess is he'll try to use it for leverage."

"What will he get? Will it be second-degree intentional homicide?"

"Yeah. The maximum penalty is twenty years in prison. He's also got fraud charges and assault and kidnapping charges related to Peacock. The funds will give him leverage, but he's got multiple charges. I expect he'll end up with a sentence that adds up to twenty years."

"What did Leonard say about killing Bertram?" O'Neill asked. "I'm guessing Bertram went to Leonard's office demanding an explanation. He probably thought there was an explanation, so he was giving Leonard a chance. Bertram brought the gun because he thought Leonard might threaten or assault him. Why he brought an unloaded gun is tough to understand. Perhaps Bertram thought the gun would intimidate Leonard, but he had no intention of using it. Yet Bertram didn't realize how desperate Leonard was."

"You knew Bertram had a Dictaphone, right?"

"Yeah. Did he actually turn it on?"

"We found it in his pocket. He set the thing to record before going into Leonard's office. Bertram even narrated it, saying the time and where he was going before leaving his office, walking up the stairs, and knocking on Leonard's door. I listened to the first two minutes, and it was consistent with your summary. The only difference is that Leonard begged. He tried to get Bertram to agree that he'd return some of the money. He told Bertram that he was a dead man if he couldn't keep at least some of it. I would have listened to more, but you showed up and told us about Leonard being at Peacock's place."

The server interrupted them. They ordered another round, and Ryder ordered a hamburger basket. O'Neill settled for a grilled chicken sandwich.

"Near as I can figure, David was going to leave the country and live somewhere in the Caribbean. Meyer said they found fake passports and other documents in a hotel room Leonard had booked. They also found authentic documents he received based on fake documents he likely submitted. Leonard was a competent counterfeiter."

"When Bertram confronted him, it forced him to change his plan."

"That sounds about right," Ryder said.

"He hung around for the extra two hundred thousand. That was stupid. If he hadn't, he'd be sitting on some beach."

"Yeah, but that's greed. He wanted the full million, and he needed a second approver for the transaction. It had to be Couturier or Peacock. Couturier knew the people at Antiquities LLC or Antiquity LLC, whatever one it is, so Leonard didn't want to go to him. He thought he could talk Peacock into approving and be done with it. When that didn't work, he forced Peacock to approve the transaction, then he tied the old man up in the basement. He needed a day to leave the country. Leonard at least told Peacock that he'd call in an anonymous tip twenty-four hours later so that someone would find him. Leonard set a bottle of water with a straw for Peacock, so I think that's the truth. That water will keep Leonard from an attempted murder charge on Peacock."

"Wasn't he worried about Antiquity looking for their money?"

"Leonard got the financial contact to agree to a ten-day delay in the money transfer. Antiquity wasn't expecting anything until this coming Monday."

"He almost got away with it."

"If not for the Ryder Detective Agency," Ryder said, laughing. They clicked glasses.

"Have you touched base with our clients yet? I told Mary Hoffman last night at our show that she should expect something to break today."

"Yeah, Meyer and I talked with Kathy Siler within five minutes of finding Bertram's body. We told her we had not yet confirmed it was him, but was likely. She identified the body last night. I talked to her again this morning. She was understandably sad about losing her dad, but I think she knew how it would end. She's worried about getting Bertram's investment back. I saw an interview with her on the local news and she thanked the MPD and the Ryder Detective Agency. I can't ask for a better endorsement. As for Mary, I called her.

She's glad it's over and asked about her brother's investment in Shakespeare's Company. I told her I thought he would get at least a fifth of it back."

"Getting that endorsement from Kathy is cool. She'll probably even pay our bill."

"I would hope so," Ryder said. "One other thing. I got a surprise for you." He pulled a cellular phone out of his jacket pocket. "I got you a cell phone. I activated it this morning."

O'Neill took the phone. "It's a Nokia, the same brand Erin has. Isn't that what you have?"

"This one used to be mine. I got the new one and cascaded this one to you. The charging cord is back at the office. The plan limits you to 300 minutes per month through this calendar year and costs twenty-nine-ninety-five a month. I also got insurance on it, so if you lose it once per year, we can replace it for free. But if you lose it more than once, you have to buy the replacement. They're at least sixty bucks, so don't lose it."

Ryder explained how the phone worked. By the time the food arrived, O'Neill had called Ryder's new phone and received a call from Ryder.

"This will be nice. And it fits into my pocket. I'll just keep it there with my keys. That should work. Should I put Erin's number in my favorites? I mean, it's her work number, and I might need to call her."

Ryder agreed and verified that he had entered the number properly. "You click to get to favorites and click on her name and it will ring through. Why don't you call her? I know you want to. I'll be heading out after the bill comes, so invite her down."

O'Neill took a gulp of his beer and hit her name.

"Detective Meyer," she said, answering after three rings.

"Hey, Erin. It's me, Seamus."

"Hello, you, Seamus."

"I got a phone for work. This is it."

"Great. I have your number now since you called me. How are you? Were you hurt when you fell last night?"

"I'm fine. Falling is one thing I'm good at. So what's up? You at work?"

"No. I got home after four, got something to eat, and now I am relaxing before heading to bed. I'm normally off tomorrow, but I have things to follow-up on, so I'll go in for a few hours."

The server showed up with their food, which was in small plastic red baskets layered with parchment paper. She deftly slid the chicken sandwich basket in front of O'Neill and the hamburger basket in front of Ryder.

"I'm at the Argus with Ryder. We're eating dinner and then he's heading out. You want to come down and have a drink?"

O'Neill heard a tired laugh. "Seamus, I'm not going barhopping with you."

"Okay. Just thought I'd ask."

"If you want to do something, let's go for a walk."

"A walk?"

"Yeah. I would suggest a run since I missed a few days, but I'm tired and you're probably not dressed for running. But a walk would be okay."

"Sure. It's warm out, though. You should wear shorts."

She laughed again. "I'll wear what I want to wear."

"Course. You want me to meet you at your place?"

"No. You know where the path is that cuts in front of Law Park near Machinery Row, kind of across from the Essen Haus?"

"Course."

"I'll be there in fifteen minutes."

"Meet you there. Bye." He looked at Ryder as he hung up the phone. "That's new."

"Going for a walk?" Ryder asked.

"Yeah. It's not something I've done with a woman before."

"You mean, with all these women you've dated over the years, you've never gone for a walk with one?"

"We walk to clubs and to bars and stuff. But I haven't gone for a walk for walking's sake." O'Neill took a bite of his chicken sandwich. It was the first thing he had eaten since Friday night.

"You're not going for walking's sake," Ryder said. "You're going for a walk as an opportunity to spend time with her and to talk. It is a chance to get to know her. If it's an unfamiliar experience, maybe that's not a bad thing. Just be happy she likes you and not the wannabe rock star."

"You think so?"

"Yeah, but you're going to need to straighten up if you're going to have any chance with her. I'm not saying you need to turn over a new leaf, but if you really like her, you're going to need to make some strides."

O'Neill nodded. "Suppose you're right."

Ryder added salt to his salty fries, and they talked for a few minutes as they finished the meal. When the server arrived, Ryder paid, and it occurred to O'Neill that he might somehow finagle a raise out of their recent success.

O'Neill finished his sandwich, but left a helping of fries for Ryder. The sun was high in the sky and a jet airliner flew overhead, leaving a long contrail.

"Seamus, as you head out, think about what we accomplished and the people we helped. It should make you realize that what we do matters," Ryder said.

O'Neill nodded his agreement and headed east on Main Street as Ryder waited for the bill. O'Neill intended to reflect on Bertram Newman and on the impact they had on his family and friends. But he only thought about Erin Meyer. And whether she was wearing shorts and whether he would get a look at those long legs.

Acknowledgments

Thanks to all who supported me in writing this book and in providing help and feedback. Special thanks to my editor, Dannielle Konz, and to Dianna Breen, Matt Breen, Sue Krumenauer, Dan Birrenkott, Kelsey Breen, and Dave Greenwell.

About the Author

Paul Breen plays guitar poorly and spends far too much time on genealogy. A native of Columbus, Ohio, Paul grew up in Madison, Wisconsin, and worked at the University of Wisconsin-Madison. Paul enjoys running, biking, music, sports, history, and visiting brewpubs. He lives with his wife and family in Madison.

www.ingramcontent.com/pod-product-compliance
Lightning Source LLC
Chambersburg PA
CBHW020128310726
48970CB00006B/1771